NOT WHERE I STARTED FROM

KATE WHEELER

NOT WHERE I STARTED FROM

HOUGHTON MIFFLIN COMPANY

BOSTON NEW YORK 1993

For information about permission to reproduce selections
from this book, write to Permissions, Houghton Mifflin Company,
215 Park Avenue South, New York, New York 10003.

Library of Congress Cataloging-in-Publication Data
Wheeler, Kate, date.
Not where I started from / Kate Wheeler.
p.   cm.
ISBN 0-395-66515-9
1. Americans — Foreign countries — Fiction.   2. United States —
    Ethnic relations — Fiction.   I. Title.
PS3573.H4326N68   1993
813'.54 — dc20   93-12456
                          CIP

Printed in the United States of America

AGM 10 9 8 7 6 5 4 3 2 1

Book design by Melodie Wertelet

Some of the stories in this collection have appeared elsewhere, in slightly
different form: "Improving My Average" in *The Missouri Review,* "Snow
Leopard, Night Bird" in *Shankpainter,* "Under the Roof" in *Black War-
rior Review,* "La Victoire" in *The Threepenny Review,* "Judgment" in
Antaeus, and "Ringworm" in *The Gettysburg Review.*

"Stay, if you can.
Go if you must."

—CHARLES BAUDELAIRE

"Things are not as
they seem to be,
yet they are not
otherwise."

—LANKĀVATĀRA SUTRA

ACKNOWLEDGMENTS

I give thanks to Pamela Painter for her generous and relentless encouragement; Sharon Salzberg for suggesting I edit Sayadaw U Pandita's manuscript; Poonja-ji for cutting me loose; Nyoshul Khenpo for indefinable aid; Jeanne Ann for lending her eyes, ear, and heart; Claire for that ending; Dad for not protesting; my writing group for demanding a story a month; my editor, Janet Silver, and my agent, Kim Witherspoon, for making the process fun; and Surya, for lugging my laptop through Karachi Airport at two A.M.

CONTENTS

NOT WHERE I STARTED FROM

IMPROVING
MY
AVERAGE

The prop plane labored up the Andes' blue and white spine at the mercy of blasts and vacuums. My scrambled eggs jittered in their dish, like the coarse yellow foam storms leave on a beach. I had no intention of eating them: I was counting cities on my fingers, dividing in my head. After calculating backward twice, I'd just gotten it straight. Being twelve years old, having lived in eight places, I'd inhabited each location of my childhood for one and four-eighths years, eighteen months, too long.

When I'd arrived where we were now leaving, I was seven and had lived in seven places. I'd been in a state of perfect balance, I now realized, like the Golden Age of Pericles: I couldn't remember having worried about anything. In the yellow desert of the north, I grew old enough for first loves — skinny Mike Grady, who could walk on his knees in lotus pose, and the Pacific Ocean, which almost claimed my life one day in its undertow. Time stretched out so long in Terremotos, I forgot it was dragging me toward this, the day of departure.

Now we were moving to Cartagena, Colombia, on the bathtub-shallow Caribbean. My father's company had promoted him to manage a plant that extruded polyethylene. I'd be able to see Plásticos Revo across the bay from my own balcony, promised my mother, who'd made a househunting trip a month ago and rented the same house my father's predecessor had lived in.

"I hope we leave it soon," I said meanly when she showed me a picture of the house, pink and modern, with a rubber tree over the garage.

"You jackal, I worked so hard," she said, and burst into tears.

"Eat those eggs," she told me now. "A protein breakfast is the best gift you can give your brain."

Before I could hesitate, my father's eye rolled over onto me, and I heard him clear his throat. "Lila."

I stabbed the eggs, wishing I could throw them out the sealed window for condors to eat.

The plane's silver wing hung over the Cordillera Blanca, perfectly static, as if we weren't really moving. If we crashed, I'd touch snow for the first time. I imagined search parties of *cholos* fanning out over a glacier, chewing coca leaves for endurance. By the time they found us, most of the passengers would be frozen, dreaming their way deeper and deeper into total darkness. Not me — I'd read in Jack London how to bury yourself in a drift and remain alive, insulated by snow itself.

Incas' descendants would adopt me; I'd live the rest of my life on the *altiplano,* playing a *quena* among stone ruins.

We landed, and Cartagena clapped itself around us like a boiled towel. The customs official smirked as he ran his hands under my mother's nighties, examined the soles of my U.S.-made saddle shoes for marks of use. He envied us, I knew. Still, I wanted to explain that I'd been born in the jungle in Venezuela and wasn't blood-connected with this mortifying mountain of imported goods. Because our main shipment wasn't due for several months, my mother had packed everything from aspirin to bedspreads in fifteen suitcases.

My father's new driver took charge of us outside customs. His name was Cosme Leña. He was the color of a plum and had no voice, only a kind of hiccup like the catch between sobs. As he gesticulated at the porters, my mother explained that Cosme had had a tracheotomy and so lacked vocal cords. The operation was performed on the *HOPE* ship, a fact Cosme was proud of, my mom said, with a minuscule lifting of her eyebrows. I saw the scar on the pit of his throat, darker purple, thickened skin, like a splash of glaze on ceramic.

Mom and I squeezed in back with five suitcases. Cosme babied the company Fairlane along ruts, through ponds, the thin circle of the wheel stopping, then spinning, in his big hands. Most of the other cars were sturdier, Jeeps or pickups; I'd have preferred one of them, by far, to our fragile U.S. product.

YANQUI GO HOME, all the walls said.

Cosme hiccupped steadily to my father, and bit by bit I deciphered his words of pure breath. He was trying to get his daughter hired as a maid in our house. She was good, clean, hardworking, religious — a Protestant converted by missionaries from the States, Cosme said, as if this were a bond my father must acknowledge. Alas, Señora Leña had just had their eighth baby, and there was no more room in their humble home. So Estrellita, the oldest at seventeen, must leave.

"*Lo pienso, Leña,*" my father said irritably. I'll think about it.

"*Po'a'o,*" Cosme begged. Please.

We rolled past mildewed coral battlements hung with faded wash. Naked boys pranced, an inky cloud hung over the sea, a white goat was staked at the edge of a soccer field. These new sights made me feel I could be happy here.

"There's your school," my father said as we passed a yellow building.

Our house was pinker than its photo. Meters from the bay, its yard was pitted with land crabs' holes. A young woman stood on the front-door porch, a nylon shopping bag at her feet.

"Uh-oh," I said.

"Who's that?" said my mother, who didn't speak enough Spanish to have deciphered Cosme's proposal.

"I think it's our new maid," I whispered.

She came tilting toward the car. Something was wrong with her, too: her right calf was thinner than her left and gave her walk a crooked kind of eagerness, the limp throwing her body forward on every other step. She stopped in the shade of the rubber tree and stood there trying to look eligible. I shrank down as my father cleared his throat, preparing to dispel her.

"Polio," pronounced my mother.

"*E'm'i'a*," Cosme corrected. *Es mi hija,* she's my daughter.

"Oh, hell, Leña," my father said. "What's she doing here?"

Not polio, Cosme was saying, only a problem of the knee.

"She looks nice," I said, meaning beautiful. Estrellita was the color of a bay horse, with an aquiline nose that made her look like she should be riding on a palanquin.

My father surged out of the car, followed by my mother and Cosme. I slid farther down in the seat and ran my fingernail down the vinyl's textured stripes. When their voices stopped I mustered courage to sit up, terrified I'd see Estrellita prostrate and kissing my father's wingtips, or else humping to the bus stop with her sad bag. But all had been resolved; Estrellita Leña was ours. She was following my dad to the front door; he strode ahead, holding the key in front of him like the solution to great problems. Cosme was thanking my mother, clasping his hands and rolling his eyeballs skyward.

My mother nodded sideways for him to start unloading.

"Well, we got a bargain," she said wearily. Inside, she threw herself down on a couch the Martins had left. My mother did not always seem strong enough for her own life.

That night I lay on a buttony, mildewed company mattress between my favorite sheets. They'd been hanging out to dry this morning and still smelled seared by Terremotos' perpetual sun, but I was far from fooled. Outside, blue and orange crabs circled under the porch light, bubbles clicking from their furry, sectioned mouths.

I'd recalculated my life on paper and happily found that my average went down to sixteen months the minute we landed in Cartagena. As I lay in bed it occurred to me that the new maid had acquired an average, too, this very day. After seventeen years in one house, her life was cut in half by moving in with us. Since for myself I did not calculate changes of house in one city, her case allowed me to savor my own magnanimity.

The next morning I peeked into Estrellita's room while she was washing walls upstairs. It was freshly painted chalk yellow, but had a slick cement floor that sloped to a central drain. A pair of pointy white church pumps sat under the bed, deformed to the different widths of Estrellita's feet. She also owned a bottle of perfume, a transistor radio, and a hairbrush. My favorite was the picture tucked into the edge of the mirror. Sinners in a lake of fire. Their mouths were open, screaming for the help of

Jesus, who stood smiling on a blue cloud surrounded by cherubs. The cherubs were bodiless babies' heads with wings, more like moths than angels.

School wouldn't start for weeks. I met a boy my age at a welcoming party, Walter Nugent, but he'd just come down from the States and couldn't speak any Spanish, so I wasn't interested in him. He had one good trick, which was to scrunch his face to show forceps dents he'd gotten in his temples, being pulled from the womb in Pittsburgh.

I tried catching lizards in the yard. They were fast and I got only one; its blue neon tail broke off in my hand while its green trunk scuttled into a crab's hole. "Grow another tail," I said, burying the old one under the gladioli.

My head was pounding from the heat. In Terremotos, Mike Grady and I had had a zoo. We charged half a sol admission to see my iguana, parakeet, and scorpions, plus Mike's dog, Muffin (who we said was a lion), his two dead sea snakes in alcohol, and his father's saltwater aquarium. No one came, but the zoo made us happy, until the iguana opened the cage with its handlike claw and ran away.

I retreated to the shade of my balcony, where a plastic-wicker chair had been left by the previous renters. Staring across the flat, oily bay at the old city, the port, and the pale scientific turrets of my father's chemical plant, I decided all of life was an illusion of the senses. The raw salt smell of the breeze was just molecules hitting my nose. I'd never touch the turrets of my father's plant, even though I could see them perfectly clearly.

In coming days I learned to put myself in a trance by willing my finger to rise and also to disobey me and lie still. Sometimes it stayed paralyzed even when I seriously tried to move it.

I heard the vacuum cleaner stop. A subtle pressure

grew against the back of my head — I was being spied on.

Estrellita.

For two days I pretended not to notice.

The diagonals of her back crisscrossed unevenly as she strolled past me and leaned on the balustrade, lifting her pink heels off her plastic sandals.

"*Bonita la suidá,*" she observed, in coastal patois. Pretty city.

"*Muy,*" I said warmly. Very.

She sniffed deeply and fell back on her heels again. I wondered where her thoughts went as she gazed beyond La Popa, the green promontory that bounded the far end of Cartagena. So I asked her.

She shrugged. "*Monte. Finca. Perro rabioso.*" Bush, farm, rabid dog.

I wasn't very surprised when, the next day, she said, "*Ven.*" Come.

I followed her inside, through my own bedroom, out a door that opened from the second floor onto the roof of the garage. She had no trouble hopping onto the waist-high roof of the servants' quarters. We walked to the edge and looked over into a patio nicer than ours. Striped tiles, potted *adorno* and crotons, bentwood rockers, and a green Amazon parrot.

"*Mírala, que blanca,*" Estrellita said. Look how white she is.

"*Verde,*" I disagreed, thinking she meant the parrot.

She tsk-tsked and pointed. Higher up. "*Blanca, ombé.*"

"*Huy.*" A naked girl was creeping across the floor of the balcony, as pale and bumbling as a white puppy. A bamboo screen hid her from all angles except from where we stood.

This was Isis Román, oldest daughter of the Román family. They owned the factory that made five colors of soft drink, red, black, purple, green, and orange. Estrellita explained that Isis was sixteen but would never marry because of her mental defect. She'd live all her life as a caterpillar on her parents' balcony.

My mother had mentioned that our neighbors were first cousins: the five important families in Cartagena had pure blood from Spain they couldn't bear to dilute. I tried to explain recessive genes to Estrellita, but she already understood them — God sends bad seeds into the womb to punish parents' sins. Especially pride. From the fierce look on Estrellita's face, I could tell that Cosme and Señora Leña had already been cast into her private lake of fire. I wondered whether she saw my face there, too, among the unsaved.

Isis Román swiveled her head, rolled sideways, and, moving as slowly as seaweed underwater, displayed her breasts, black bush, and pale underarm tufts. Her gray eyes slipped over us, hot and unfocused. As her hand crawled down between her legs, a sudden vacuum pulled at my womb, and I had to step back from the edge of the roof.

Estrellita said, "*Pobrecita. Ella no sabe ná.*" Poor little thing, she doesn't know anything.

Back on the balcony, I asked Estrellita if she herself was engaged. Or, I added, remembering her bad leg, did Cosme want to keep her close to him?

No! She had a fiancé, she said proudly, a truck mechanic named Américo Velarde. They'd be married next year.

"Handsome?" I asked respectfully.

"No." She smiled. "I am the only one who loves Américo."

I was filled with joy. It was so romantic, like Beauty and the Beast. "Why don't you marry him now? Then you wouldn't have to work for us."

"It's to marry that I have to work," she said, explaining that Américo's parents had asked for a cash payment because their son was marrying a cripple. Cosme couldn't pay, so Estrellita was earning the money herself. She gave half her wages to her parents, half to Señor and Señora Velarde. She'd be paid up by New Year's.

I was so shocked, my ears rang. "That's not fair," I said. "What about Américo?"

"He is helping."

How could true love accept such a bad bargain? I tried not to think about this, but Estrellita visited my balcony daily and talked about everything, especially love, especially Américo. Américo had called her on the phone while my mother was out shopping. Américo liked green mangoes with salt, and the *cumbia* was his favorite dance. The two of them had already become husband and wife to each other, if I understood what that meant.

I said yes.

She made me taste green mangoes, and brought her transistor up to teach me the *cumbia*. We hardly needed music, for in Cartagena an itching syncopation lived in the air itself. On that big balcony we pursued each other, wriggling our shoulders like lovesick pigeons, burning each other's faces with imaginary candles. The *cumbia* imitates a slaves' courtship in ball and chain, dragging one foot behind the other: it was the perfect dance for Estrellita's lame leg.

"*Soy hombre*," she'd say, grabbing my waist, I'm a man. Looking up at her noble African face, I failed to imagine any future husband. Mike Grady was too far away and had somehow become too young.

I tried to teach her the alphabet, in its Spanish version with extra *ñ* and *ll*, optional *y* and *w*. Copying my letters, she gripped the crayon so tightly she nearly crushed it; her letters came out tall and crooked, mauve and light green beings with an animated aspect, like the living hieroglyphs of a spell. But these lessons made both of us uncomfortable, and after two we dropped them to return to hotter topics, love, the *cumbia,* and the *radionovela* of four o'clock, "Amores Desesperados."

The scion of a rich family falls in love with the housemaid. His parents find out and have her locked in a convent, but he comes in the night and springs her. They elope, and live in a penthouse in Bogotá. The wicked, rich parents try various stratagems to break up their marriage — abduction, the spreading of evil rumors, sending temptresses to the young husband's place of work.

Estrellita listened raptly to this wild plot: I knew she imagined herself in some glittering gown, on a balcony overlooking the winking lights of the capital, and beset by treachery. Alas, I couldn't be the *novia:* I had no poverty, no lover, and no entrapment to be saved from. Instead, I yearned to be the hero. Eighteen and powerful, a rescuer for Estrellita.

Clearly there was no reason why I was I and Estrellita, Estrellita; therefore, no reason for me to be rich and her to be my servant. But, since I found myself in the position of privilege, I was responsible for helping her.

Saving her would not be easy. Having shared their houses with servants for twelve years, my parents never lost sight of their wallets. Our shipment was delayed, too, so there was nothing valuable in the house to steal and sell. Even my piggy bank, with its hoard of Peruvian soles, was out at sea in some container ship.

I lay awake each night, plotting and worrying. In order to sleep, I put my hand between my thighs, imitating Isis Román, the girl who didn't know anything. I loved what I felt, but it was embarrassing to imagine sharing such sensations with another person, especially a man.

First day of school at Teddy Roosevelt. I waited for the bus under a banyan tree with Graciela and Adolfo Román, Isis' sister and brother, and Barbara Murphy, a missionary kid with hard red cheeks and a forehead so shiny it looked like her mother must scrub it every day with Ajax.

Graciela and Barbara were both in my grade, seventh. Graciela was three years too old because she had trouble with English. She wore a tight lavender dress, mourning for a dead uncle, that folded into the three creases of her belly. I could see her body was blocky and abundant, just like Isis'. She right away invited me to her *quinceañera* party, a sort of coming-out; but visions of nakedness, hers and her sister's, discomfited me so much that I said my parents didn't let me go to boy-girl parties. And added, for good measure, that she looked like a boiled grape, *una uva hervida.*

Barbara sat next to me on the bus. "You better wear shorts underneath," she warned. "Adolfo was lifting up your skirt from behind with his Coca-Cola yo-yo. That's what boys at Roosevelt do. Are you saved?"

What a weirdo: I willed her to vanish. "I don't know."

"If you don't know, you're not, and you're going to hell." Lifting her chin, she said, "I'm a half orphan. My real dad was a martyr."

He'd been murdered by members of a jungle tribe he was trying to convert. She told me the story in detail, speaking so fast and smoothly it was as if she'd memorized a script. Drunken men locked her and her mother into the kitchen and then dragged her father into the bush and chopped him up with *machetes.* A bachelor missionary was sent to bring Barbara and her mother down the Magdalena River to safety. This man was now Barbara's stepfather; he was the minister at the Iglesia Bautista Cuadrangular.

I left a silence of respect, then said, "That's my maid's church. Do you know Estrellita Leña?"

"Yup," Barbara said, and I realized she was closer to

Estrellita than I was, less of a *norteamericana* — only because she'd lived all her life in this one country of Colombia, I reminded myself. Still, I felt inferior.

I let her sit by me in class even though it meant I might not make any other friends. She was definitely strange, with that shiny forehead and hard blue eyes glittering with conviction; but a saved half orphan was a powerful being. In the middle of class she got up from her desk, went to the window, looked out, and returned. Mr. Clements frowned but kept writing on the board about capitalization. Inspired, after recess I raised my hand and asked to go to the bathroom even though I didn't need to. Of course, Mr. Clements had to say yes.

Liberation. Walking down the breezeway, I looked into the classrooms at the diligent teachers and distracted students, then outward, past the rattling palms, to where a ball of light hung over the green sea.

I wanted to be Barbara. After school, she invited me to the seawall to look at the black iguanas, and then to ride home together on the public bus. My mother wouldn't mind; in those days Cartagena was as safe as a bathtub.

"Stay away from the edge," Barbara warned. "A barracuda once jumped out and bit off a woman's foot near here."

We admired the iguanas, wet with spray, lying so still and ancient on the reddish coral blocks.

"How do you get saved?" I asked.

"Just ask Christ Jesus into your heart. Knock and it shall be opened."

At home, I lay on my bed with the air conditioner off, so as not to have distracting noise. My heart beat against my ribs, maybe the Lord trying to get in. "Come in," I said, but didn't feel improved. "Give me a sign if I am saved."

Silence pulsed, thick and heavy. Then I heard Estrellita coming upstairs, whistling through her teeth. I'd forgotten about her since this morning. If I'm saved she'll open the door and say hello, I thought, but she passed by.

Maybe, being already saved, she didn't really need me.

I lay there ten minutes before going to find her, down in the patio combing her stiff red-brown hair. She asked me how school was. I said, "Boring. The daughter of Reverend Murphy is in my class."

"*La Bárbara*," Estrellita said, which also means "the Barbarian." I laughed, traitorously.

The next day at school I confessed to Barbara that my conversion hadn't worked.

"You can't throw off sin by your own strength," Barbara explained. "You better come to church."

My mother gave permission easily, saying church would be good for me. "It'll help you think of something larger than yourself." I wanted to tell her I was always thinking about larger things, but I didn't want to sound vain.

I spent Saturday night at Barbara's. The Murphys lived in a converted garage; their biggest possession was an upright piano Eve Murphy pounded out hymns on. No other music was allowed in their home, Barbara told me proudly.

I hated the Reverend Murphy right away. He was a tall, fat, pale, ugly man who made Barbara and me call him sir. He stared at me through Eve's grace, as if trying to force my soul into submission; then between bites of meat loaf he asked if I'd ever been to church.

That night, Barbara started teaching me the books of the Bible. When I memorized them all I could win a New Testament. The books had a rhythm, like the alphabet's, that could underpin your life: that night, I got as far as Habakkuk.

I asked Barbara what God's view of stealing was, if the stealing was for a good cause — for example, to raise money for a Christian wedding — and I described Estrellita's marriage problem. Barbara said I'd be doing my parents a favor. Wealth turned people into camels, too fat to fit through the eye of Heaven's needle.

In the morning we burst out of the bedroom in pajamas and grilled her mother about breakfast food. "Who made this banana? Who made this egg?"

"Why, God, of course. Silly girls." She was wearing a printed smock that tied down the back, like a hospital gown; her eyes were as mournful as a cocker spaniel's, and her secret shone out, plain: she'd loved her first husband, the martyr, but she didn't love the Reverend Murphy.

I heard thunder in the distance as Barbara and I sat down and ate eggs, bananas, and toast.

The Iglesia was in a humble part of town. Plastic shelf lining had been glued to the windowpanes to imitate stained glass; the bright red, green, and yellow light made the room feel even hotter than it was that day, which was still moist, waiting to storm. The whole congregation was black except the Murphys and me; patches of color glinted on their sweaty chins and cheeks and shone around their eyes.

Estrellita and Américo had saved seats in the front row for Barbara and me. Américo was less ugly than I'd imagined. But I was disappointed for my vague ideas of him to be shrunk into any single, unexpected form. He was a pale brown person, shorter than Estrellita, and as solid as a pot. His hand rested on the small of her back as lightly as a dove in its nest; when he and Estrellita caught each other's eyes, a kind of light appeared between them, so that I knew that I was really seeing it — two people in love — for the first time.

Why was I not happy? I couldn't even understand where the light was coming from; they were just two ordinary people.

The sermon was about Jonah and the whale. Barbara's stepfather searched the world's oceans with glittering eyes, he stabbed the air with a forefinger to make his point: God's will is a whale that will swallow us if we resist. His pale, wetted hair straggled like seaweed across his noggin. Outside, thunder was rumbling. God's voice, the voice of the reason for everything.

The congregation was moaning, "*Sí, señor*," as ominously as the sea. In back a woman started speaking loudly in tongues: Ashmada, Yoi, Verrazabal! A jumping lightness attacked my ankles, bounced up my thighs into my chest; I was nearly lifted from the ground.

Barbara said excitedly, "Feel the Spirit?"

Make your heart open to Christ, the Reverend Murphy cried. Humbly say Please, Please, Lord.

I was shaking all over. On both sides, my girlfriends squeezed my arms, wanting me to be one with them in Christ.

"Please, Please, Lord," I cried, really trying to open my heart.

"Come down," the Reverend Murphy said. "Come down." I got up and joined a little file of people who were being converted. The aisle was a tunnel; at the end stood the Reverend Murphy with his arms upraised. When it was my turn, he put his hands on the top of my head and prayed for my new life in Christ. His touch made me cringe.

The rain started outside, a sudden heavy rush that dimmed the light inside the church. Behind me the congregation sang, the collection plate began to go around.

Dear God, I prayed, thank you for saving me. Please help Estrellita and Américo. I couldn't feel anything, or anyone, listening, but I kept on praying anyway.

Some weeks later the principal came to class to announce that the *HOPE* ship was on its way back around the coast

NOT WHERE I STARTED FROM

of South America and would stop again in Cartagena before returning to the United States. Roosevelt students were invited to tour the ship and meet the doctors and nurses.

Desk to desk, Barbara and I made faces at each other. As Christian girls, we were entitled to despise all worldly, adult, pretentious, and American things. We called the principal "Caesar" and the school "Babylon"; we stopped people in the street to ask if they believed God made the universe. Of course, everyone said yes: Colombia is a Catholic country.

At home, I asked my parents if they'd heard about the *HOPE* ship's return. They had but were not excited either. They were having their Scotches in the living room.

My mom said, "JFK is too handsome to be trusted."

My father huffed, "He's offending the Latins with his largesse. They hate to feel we're better than they are."

"I'm going to tour the ship and meet the doctors and nurses," I said.

My mother said quickly, "Congratulations! It's a *good* ship. Saved Cosme from throat cancer. God knows why he still smokes cigars."

"He likes them," my father said.

They let me make them second Scotches.

"Cosme's agitating to get his daughter's leg fixed on the ship," my father reported. "I don't know if he can."

"I thought they tried to stick to life and death," my mother said.

"He wants me to make a recommendation," my father said, "for the surgery list."

"Oh, do it, Daddy. Then she can get married." I explained the uses of Estrellita's salary, the payoff to Américo's parents.

"Now that stinks," my father said. "Cosme makes enough money. Revo's the best employer in town. I ought to fire him. That old rat. That old weasel."

"Firing him would only make it worse," my mother said. "It's no skin off your nose, honey. One phone call."

"I'd better ignore the whole thing," my father muttered. "It's not ethical. The company wouldn't like it."

"That poor child," said my mother.

"Daddy, please," I said, "Ple-e-e-ease."

"Oh, hell," my father said, meaning yes. I kissed him extravagantly; at bedtime I modified my prayers, no longer begging God to find money for Estrellita, but to guarantee all the linked events that would get her into surgery. "Please keep Daddy from changing his mind, please make the ship say yes."

The *HOPE* ship was huge, as white as a sail by day, lit up festively at night, with its name all in capitals written on both sides. Estrellita spotted it sailing into port while I was at school; she compared it to a nurse's hat. She told me the story of Cosme's operation, how he'd been full of tubes and said *barbaridades* coming out of the anesthetic.

She was sitting on a chair in the patio, peeling yucca and putting it into an enamel bowl.

"I'm going to tour the *HOPE* ship," I said, gritting my teeth against Estrellita's disappointment.

"I'm going to tour it, too," she said.

"What?"

She turned her sharp profile to me and shrugged. Her lips curved up slightly, in triumph.

"Come on," I coaxed.

"They're going to cure my knee."

"*¡Qué bien!*" I gushed. "I was praying for you every night."

"Américo was praying, too. I owe it to you two."

Our eyes shone into each other's. No more bad bargains.

"The truth? I'm afraid," she said. She held her two legs

out for comparison, then kicked her right heel against the floor. "It's not that bad. I came out of my mother feet first, that's all. I keep thinking about the scalpel. So sharp." She shuddered. "The blood."

"Don't worry, you'll be asleep when they do it," I said. "Let's go look at Isis."

Today Isis was dressed in a little sunsuit. When her eyes rolled upward, I waved and jumped up and down to catch her attention. Isis saw and was intrigued. She sat up and began shaking her wrists excitedly. Then she began hooting like a chimpanzee. Estrellita and I ran away, giggling, just in time to avoid being seen by the Románs' maid.

The day we toured the *HOPE* ship Cosme drove me to school. He was grateful to John F. Kennedy, who had saved his life and now was going to remove his daughter's defect. He was grateful to the people of the United States, and to my father, a powerful man, as I must know.

I pretended ignorance. "My father helped you?"

Oh yes. It had been difficult because Estrellita had no grave condition, but Cosme worked for the manager of Plásticos Revo and now Estrellita would be perfect for her new husband. "*E'te'de?*" he said, looking at me with complicity and pride. *Entiende,* do you understand?

I said I understood. "Américo Velarde will love her even more, if that is possible."

Cosme's face clouded. Américo, Américo was a little Indian. Cosme knew a young man who worked for a bank downtown, but Estrellita refused to be interested.

"Because she loves Américo," I cried.

Yes, but Estrellita was silly, she didn't know. Now she was afraid of the knife.

His chuckle axed through all warmth, all confidence. Violently I wished I'd never asked God to get Estrellita on the surgery list. Please, God, forget it, get her off it again, I prayed. Then I realized I should make prayers general: God might be angry with me for changing my mind. You never knew what might come along with the satisfaction of a specific request.

Please, God, just make it turn out all right.

"Don't make her get the operation," I pleaded with Cosme. "She's perfect as she is. She works all day, she can dance the *cumbia,* and her children won't be affected."

Silence. Cosme's wide, crumpled baby face was closed up tightly.

The *HOPE* nurses turned our tongues green with Kool-Aid from the States, the captain showed us the seven layers of paint that lay like icing on all surfaces, and Barbara was hilarious, but I hardly noticed. I had an attack of claustrophobia in the operating room, far below the waterline and as inescapable as a tomb. Mr. Clements said seasickness was impossible in port, but still a nurse took me out on deck, where I hung over the railing looking down at the greasy rainbows in Cartagena Bay.

There was no God, really, I thought. Whenever I tried to find Him, there was just a hollow feeling at the base of my skull. How could God let the bay get so polluted? How could He let that poor dog die and be floating, rotting, with its entrails coming out? I'd set evil in motion by pretending to believe in Him. If I'd believed perfectly, my prayers would have been answered perfectly. But I'd prayed selfishly, just to get what I wanted, and I'd lied to Barbara about feeling at home in Christ. So anything bad was going to be my fault.

At home, I couldn't find Estrellita. I searched frantically, upstairs and down, in the kitchen and in her room, out on my balcony, and at the Isis-spying place. The cook didn't know, Cosme smoking a cigar in the garage didn't know, my mother didn't know where she was.

An hour later she came in, beaming. She'd been to the little store to buy milk, and! — her voice dropped to a whisper — she'd had a secret meeting with Américo Velarde to talk about her operation, scheduled for to-morrow.

Américo was happy that her leg would be fixed. He'd convinced his parents to return some of the money, so now he and Estrellita were thinking about a little house. He told her not to be afraid of the scalpel. He would pray for her all through the operation.

"I'm worried," I said. "Why don't you just marry Américo? I can get you money." I was serious now, ready to steal my mother's rings of tourmaline, amethyst, and topaz. I'd sell them in the market. Estrellita and Américo could fly out over the ocean, holding hands, dressed in white baptismal robes.

Estrellita was shocked. "No, no, *señorita*. You are too worried. God and the American doctors will not fail. It is not a complicated operation."

I got up early the next morning to say good-bye and wish her well, but Estrellita was gone. The Fairlane was gone, too: Cosme must have gotten permission to drive his daughter to the ship, and perhaps to visit Señora Leña on the way.

I went into her room and sat on the bed. It was just the same as when I'd first peeked into it, except that there was a sharp smell of her recently sleeping body, and the faces of the sinners in the lake of fire seemed mysteriously fewer. It was the coolest hour of the day; a mist redolent of salt and dead dogs rose from the bay and curled into the courtyard.

I sent out my most powerful wish, for it to be my first day in Cartagena again, without anything having hap-pened yet.

All day at school I wished for the operation's success. Not to God, just to whatever there was. Even if it was just a big nothing, I still couldn't help but wish. I asked Barbara to pray, and she did, in Jesus' name.

"We have to have a talk," my mother said.

Her tone of voice told me all but the location: my average was about to improve. I divided quickly. I was still twelve, so the fractions were easy; next year, I'd have to go into decimals.

One and three-ninths years. A year and four months.

"Your father's been promoted and we're moving to Bogotá after Christmas. He'll be director of marketing for Venezuela, Colombia, and Peru. They haven't named his successor, so don't tell your friends. Isn't it exciting?"

"We'll miss Estrellita's wedding," I said.

"Well," my mother said. She inhaled, hissing through clenched molars, as if she'd just burnt herself; or I had, and she was looking at the wound. Snakes began to crawl inside my chest. Snakes and worms. My mother's eyes shifted. "You'd better talk to your father."

This was how punishments always began. I approached my father's huge knees. He was reading office papers in his Danish chair.

"Dad."

He looked up and when he saw it was me, he took off his reading glasses. Presbyopic is the word: he couldn't see small things near him.

When my father spoke, I knew I'd heard the news before, in a dream or in a previous life. "Honey, there was a problem with the maid's operation." He sounded annoyed.

A Colombian medical student had performed the operation, not the American surgeon. Estrellita's leg had had to be amputated at the knee. "Cosme was arrested this morning trying to get on the boat with a pistol to kill the guy," my father said. "But I'll bail him out. And I'm paying for an artificial leg." My father's voice was loud and hard, as if chiseling in stone these, the last words that would ever be said on the subject.

"Is she still getting married?"

"I don't know."

"Can I go to her house?"

"No, honey, I don't think it's a good idea. We'll have her come back and see us before we leave."

Ashamed, tiny, filthy, and depressed, I went out to see Isis, but there was only a blue bath towel lying on the balcony. Looking carefully, I saw the terry flattened, like grass where a cow has slept.

If only I could be like Isis, nothing to do except lie in the sun touching myself, all my life on that same balcony. Isis had no average; thinking about Isis' average was like dividing by zero, or trying to imagine God. If I fell off the roof in front of her, she probably wouldn't understand enough to care.

Barbara came to pick me up for church. She walked through the living room like Shadrach in the fiery furnace, inspecting the turquoise sculptured carpet and the objects my parents had looted, like conquistadores, from each place we'd lived. These things had just arrived, and soon they would disappear into boxes again. They followed us with touching faithfulness, delayed only because they had no life.

Barbara's stepfather had learned from his congregation that Américo and Estrellita were still engaged. I hadn't told my parents, but after the service at La Iglesia Bautista Cuadrangular, the Murphys and I were going to visit Estrellita at home. I'd packed my stuffed animals to keep her company. Surely she'd one day have a baby and need toys for it, too.

So I told myself. But I was horrified, imagining my Teddy sitting on the flat bedclothes where my friend's foot should have been.

That morning, I believed that I was evil. I realized I'd never wanted to go to the Leñas' house and see how dark it was, how humble and crowded, Señora Leña wringing her hands surrounded by her eight babies. And now, I had nothing to say; I had become a distant stranger. I could not confess the dreams I'd had, of the leg dead and floating in the bay or else merrily toe-heeling down the street in front of our house, the leg in a funeral carriage pulled by eight black horses wearing black plumes between their ears. When, awake, I tried to think what had happened to it, something hit me so hard along the top ridge of my head, I couldn't see.

I didn't want to let Estrellita talk to me, either. She might smile bravely, trying to make it easy for me. She might be glad I came to see her, and then how could I ever leave? How could I bear to know that soon I'd be in Bogotá, maybe even standing on a balcony like the *novia* in the *radionovela*. Standing there, having forgotten enough about Estrellita, and Américo, and all of Cartagena — forgotten enough to enjoy the lights of the capital spread out at my feet?

SNOW LEOPARD, NIGHT BIRD

Looking into Edward Hassan's blue eyes was like looking into the eyes of a snow leopard. You saw something beyond human, as deep and cold as the depths of a crevasse, and you knew he wanted nothing from you. When I saw that, I suddenly wanted to give him everything. It seemed the only natural response. I thought, This man is enlightened and from now on relating to him is my whole life.

The events I'm about to tell you happened two years ago in Mill Valley, before Edward's scene had grown to what it is now. He'd been back from India about a year and was holding sessions every night at The Winterhill School, in a classroom where one of his devotees taught kindergarten. The devotees pushed all the little furniture to one side so they could sit on the floor, while Edward was up front in a green wing chair they dragged in from the teachers' lounge.

The first night I went, I was deliberately late. Edward was talking when I crept in and sat down quickly way at the back, hoping he wouldn't call attention to me. But he interrupted himself; he pounced on me right away.

"Seese!" he sings out. "I'm so glad to see you here."

A normal enough greeting, except that every word was underlined, weighted with meaning. "Folks, this is my old girlfriend C. C. Reynolds," he went on. "We went to the same high school in Houston, Texas. Seese, come on, sit up front."

Everyone stared, of course, and people who were sitting on the floor slid sideways, making a path for me. I forced myself to speak up. "People call me Carol these days. Hi, Edward." I wanted to tell him he looked good with a shaven head, but I didn't want to support being identified as his ex-girlfriend. If I was going to relate to his new status as a spiritual teacher, it didn't seem appropriate to discuss his physical appearance in that way.

He did look good though. With his head shaved, the essence of his face jumped out at you, unclouded. Hawkish features, olive skin, and pale blue Celtic eyes. He was wearing a royal blue silk kimono jacket and black kung fu pants. Someone had spread a blue Guatemalan cloth over the wing chair's seat.

"Well, then, Carol, come on up front." He smiled, as if he knew better than to think of me by my adult name.

As I picked my way forward through the disciples, my head roared and there was a darkness behind my eyes, as if I'd blown a fuse. I passed my friend Angelica, who reached up her thin hand to squeeze mine in congratulation, for coming, and for being noticed.

Six or seven people sat on a tan sculptured carpet remnant right in front of Edward's legs. Obviously these were the special students, the ones who were serious and unafraid. Two men and one woman also had shaven heads. At least they weren't staring at me; they had their eyes shut or were watching Edward. I sank down between a black woman with the sad, noble face of a desert princess and a male grad student–type in pilly blue socks, imagining what secret hurts each one of them had brought into this room. Her exile from her father's palace, his lack of sexual success. Had Edward taken them beyond pain?

"So," Edward said, "where are we?" and everyone laughed. I closed my eyes and asked myself that question. Edward had thrown me off. There on the carpet remnant, I found myself vowing that he couldn't make me go anywhere I didn't want to go, feel anything I didn't want to feel. But it had already happened: Seese, my fifteen-year-old self, had come to furious life inside me.

That was the beginning.

Before the beginning, as the I Ching might put it, Edward Hassan got enlightened. By the time I heard his tale, it had been retold so many times that it had flattened into myth, the verbal equivalent of a mural on an Egyptian tomb. Images stopped in time because they're moving at the speed of light.

Frowns, and arms at angles: Edward fighting with his girlfriend while they were traveling in India in 1987. Solitary figure under temple domes: Edward going off in a huff by himself to Rishikesh. A little blue god: meeting a holy man who was an emanation of Shiva.

Squiggly rays go from holy man to Edward.

They say Edward got enlightened in less than one week; and then he and his master wandered around India for a year, visiting holy places where Edward developed insights and powers. When it came time for the master to vanish back into the icy Himalayan potentialities he'd come from, he gave Edward a final zap and sent him back to the West to teach. Edward was now a peer of the Buddha, Christ, and the ancient Himalayan rishis.

You do get tired of all the great teachers being little brown men in diapers, or else long dead. This was part of Edward's appeal, the idea that it could be happening again, among us. Edward might have been strange, but he was neither foreign nor ancient. He liked Godzilla, and he often wore two Bic Accountant pens stuck in his front pocket: points his disciples adored to mention, as if human quirks threw his divinity into relief. I'd have preferred the new savior to be a woman for a change, but you can't have everything.

Edward had promised his master never to advertise, arrange for his own housing, or buy any major possessions. These vows didn't slow him down. He held a small session in a friend's loft in New York, where people got so high they begged him to keep doing it. Dialogue cut down their illusory thoughts, yogic transmission built up their minds-beyond-mind. People started quitting jobs and ending marriages to follow Edward Hassan. A few shaved their heads spontaneously. They all moved up to Boston, until Edward declared that New England's bedrock had a fixating effect and that they should go to the Bay Area. In a week, his devotees got him an apartment and a teaching space, plus housing and menial jobs for themselves. They slept three and four to a room, lying to landlords about occupancy.

When they came, I was living in Sausalito with two roommates, one of them my friend Angelica. I owned five hundred dollars' worth of Tupperware in which I delivered meals like Pad Thai and shiitake mushroom pesto to the harried New Age yuppies of Marin. It was a decent living, and I met a lot of nice people doing it. Around March of 1989, a few clients and friends started mentioning this new guru. The first night Angelica went, she came home and called her father to tell him that she loved him, but she was going to live her own life no matter what. Then she went into the kitchen and rearranged things so her dishes were all on their own shelf. I laughed at her and said that if this was the same Edward

Hassan I knew from high school in Houston, I'd started him off in spiritual practice by showing him my Tibetan art calendar.

"Yes," Angelica replied, "Edward did grow up in Houston."

Her tone said it was a different Edward, even if the same.

I put off going until I was the last one who hadn't met him.

"Go on, Mary Alice," Edward said. He was dialoguing with a woman two-thirds of the way back, using her first name with the same unspeakable condescension as he'd used mine, like an unpleasant forefinger pointing at her heart. Or at her ego, to be precise and fair.

"I was saying," Mary Alice said. Her voice was high and brittle. "I was saying, I feel like I've stopped making progress, and is there anything you can do to open me up to the energy again?"

Mary Alice was the type of middle-aged woman who tries a little too hard to make other people comfortable. I'd noticed her on my walk up the room, happily overweight, wearing shiny support stockings under a hot pink muumuu. I'd judged her for a member of one of the martyred female professions: legal secretary, librarian, junior college department head. My advice would have been to get rid of the support stockings and do some upside-down bicycles, but after living four years in a yoga ashram, my advice tends toward the physical.

Edward sneered. "This is just the kind of question that really turns me off. Aren't you here to get off that selfish point of view? If you'd shut up and listen to what's going on around you, maybe you'd learn something."

No one stood up for Mary Alice, not even I. Of course, my mind was full of rationalizations. Maybe being yelled at was just what she needed. Or maybe it was like the good Germans and the Jews — I still wondered whether shocking methods might break the grip of ego. For example, the Indian *siddha* Tilopa enlightened his pupil Naropa by hitting him across the face with a sandal, which in Asia is a mortal insult. He also broke Naropa's legs. If this was all right hundreds of years ago, why not now?

Edward said, "Okay, it's nine o'clock. Enough talk. Let's sit together in silence."

I closed my eyes. My first sensations were pretty ordinary — aching feet; the greasy, sated feeling I get from cooking all day — but then something else was creeping up on me, enveloping me slowly, like the smell of something burning, or something getting done.

His *shakti* was amazing. I simply felt the boundaries of my mind dissolve. When I recognized this event, the recognition was a tiny concrete object, a speck floating in a vast and silent mystery. Then the recognition disappeared and I was sucked into the mystery itself — beyond body, beyond mind, beyond everything except the presence of Edward Hassan. He was with me in a way I'd never been with anyone before; I understood that all human love was an attempt to reach this state. I heard Edward say wordlessly, soundlessly, "This is just the riverbank," and I knew the next thing was to jump in.

But I stopped, and suddenly wanted him out of me. Do you know how, in cities at night, sometimes they illuminate trees from beneath, for decoration? I've never liked it: I feel as if the trees' privacy is being violated, as if the lights were being shone up their skirts, and I wonder what distorted photosynthesis they're being forced to do when they need to be sleeping, or exhaling, or doing whatever trees do at night. My mind wrestled against Edward's, but he was far stronger. He kept battering against me, his voice in my head saying, "Do it, go on, let me!"

Shocked, I opened my eyes. Edward was looking right at me.

He said, softly, "No one's ever come to you before."

"No," I said, feeling ashamed. Did everyone else on earth enjoy that kind of union?

"Let me," he said. "It's okay."

People were blinking, looking to see who Edward was talking to, but he distracted them by saying loudly, "Okay, folks, wake up. Ha, ha. Wake *up*," as if he'd been kept waiting for a long time.

Whenever I see a girl like I was at fifteen, I imagine her inner life as something quite depraved. Carol Cecilia, C.C., Seese. I never invited anyone home. Sometimes I'd loiter on the way home from school so that my mother could imagine that I was a happy child, with friends, but she never once asked me where I'd been. All her energy went to my sister, Lola, who was retarded, from eating mothballs.

I was a year ahead of myself in school, too smart to distinguish plaids from stripes. At fifteen, I was over-weight, with glasses and dandruff; my body was like a contagion I carried everywhere. I wrote a history paper on Catholic saints who fasted and whipped themselves at night; I studied the Kāmā Sutra, making dawn-cloud love bites on my inner forearms which I hoped my classmates would notice. I devoured the Book of the Dead and tried to carry out Tibetan visualizations. The Adept sees his body walking in the sky; the Adept becomes a red monster, angry enough to devour the world. These last only worked if I was stoned, which I was, about three-quarters of the time, buying pot with money stolen from my mother's purse.

Edward swam into my ken one day when he refused to take off his sunglasses in Latin class and Mrs. Donatio sent him to the office. Later I overheard that his older brother had given him two black eyes. That night I dreamed that Mrs. Donatio had made Edward and me take off all our clothes and leave them in the classroom closet. It seemed quite natural to be naked until we left the class, but then I noticed that Edward and I were the only naked people in the school.

Edward wasn't popular either, partly because of his father's being Iranian. Our part of Houston wasn't that progressive. I started following him everywhere, waiting at his locker in the morning, sitting at his table at lunch. We never spoke, nor did I expect him to notice me. In fantasies, though, he squeezed my fat self against his knobby chest.

One day he said, "So. You want a date?" My body flooded with glittering, delicious terror. On the agreed Friday night, I met him on the corner near my house, two joints in my purse to ensure against rejection. We drove to Memorial Park, where Edward parked his brother's car and we smoked one. I gave Edward the roach. He ate it, then pulled one knee up onto the seat and turned to me. His face approached me swiftly.

I'd touched tongues with Lola, once, as an experiment, just the tips. Neither that nor medieval Hindu sex tracts had prepared me for Edward's tongue, its twisting, muscular slipperiness. My efforts to push it out excited him, I could tell. So this was kissing. So this was being a good kisser.

Eventually he started the car and drove in the opposite direction from the movie theater we'd planned on. I lay back and watched the live oaks slip past, their crowns like lung shadows on the X-ray sky. Edward stopped the car and said, "Okay, keep low." I giggled as we snuck past lighted windows into Edward's back yard, where his brother kept a pup tent.

Yellow canvas, fug of mildew, menthol, and boy sweat.

We smoked the other joint and then Edward introduced me to Pertussin cough spray. He sprayed it into a T-shirt that he pressed over my nose and mouth until the world slowed down and started going WOW WOW WOW. Somewhere within that pounding, Edward fucked me in the ass, using some 3-in-One Oil his brother kept in the tent. Afterward, he put his Jockey shorts back on and fell asleep with his head hanging out the tent door.

My mind awoke while I wasn't sleeping, an interesting sensation. Edward's body was blocking my exit, his face turned up toward the freedom of the stars. My anus throbbed redly, a torn-open passageway, and I remembered how forbidden parts of me had been made accessible.

I had a vision of my being, spherical, and layered like the earth. Its white outer shell was smoking cold, under threat from the inner layers, which were semimolten and glowed red like the coils of a car's cigarette lighter. My core was a small graphite sphere that was neither hot nor cold. It consisted of all bad things.

I should not have come into the tent; I should have remembered to bring the rubbers I shoplifted last week, so that Edward could have screwed me normally. I shouldn't have wanted him. The black core was responsible for these omissions and commissions. There seemed to be a word trapped in it, or words, but I didn't know what they were. If I screamed, I might find out, but at this hour of the night screaming was out of the question.

I held the palm of my hand over Edward's thigh, close enough to feel the electricity between us. Now that we had done It, or some version, we must be boyfriend and girlfriend; all barriers should be broken down.

"I made my sister eat those mothballs," I confessed.

It wasn't true, but it was the shortest explanation for how I felt. We used to play that I was the princess and Lola was my white Persian cat. Spoiled, tyrannical, and vain, the cat was the dominant figure; all our games revolved around her whims, her illnesses and beauty treatments. One day the cat decided she'd eat nothing but frozen milk-snow, and I watched in awe as Lola swallowed seven balls of naphthalene. She took them like pills, with milk, a skill she'd recently learned.

"Don't," I said, foreseeing trouble. "You'll get sick."

"Nope." Daring me to stop her, Lola looked me in the eye as she swallowed the next mothball, and the next. "Don't tell," she commanded, and I didn't, almost believing that her will could override the poison.

Seizures, permanent brain damage.

Afterward, everything pointed to my weakness, a torn muscle deep inside. How could I have let a five-year-old convince me of something I knew was wrong? My parents asked me this every day, until the counselor told them not to.

"Do you love me?" I asked Edward, not too loudly. No response. I lowered my palm onto his thigh: his flesh was so alive, smooth there above the knee where the jeans rubbed.

Now I thought I heard him go, "Mf." His hand came down, brushing at mine in sleepy annoyance, but when he touched me his fingers curled around my wrist, and held.

I lay forward carefully, bending one arm under my breasts, leaving the other arm positioned so my hand could stay in Edward's grasp. When dawn overcame the porch lamp, Edward drove me home. My neck had cricked so badly that I couldn't turn my head.

Monday I hid, but creased June from my Tibetan calendar into Edward's locker vents. Wrathful deities made love; the male had a horse's head, the female a sow's. "Us," I wrote in tiny ballpoint letters, then scratched it out thoroughly, so he could never read my hopes.

Senior year, I watched Edward date real girls while he

and I had periodic sessions in the tent. Regular sex, it usually was, and I enjoyed it; but I never dared ask when I'd see him next. He'd catch me in the hall or pull up in his car as I stood at a corner, and just say, "Wanna go?"

When we talked, it was mostly about spiritual and philosophical topics. There was a way in which the voidness of our relationship was, for me, ecstatic.

Edward stood up and went out a side door without stopping to speak to anyone. The man next to me, Bob with the shaven head, hopped up and began folding Edward's Guatemalan sitting cloth. I half expected him to fold it into triangles, like we were taught in school to do to the American flag.

My body still buzzed with the volts of Edward's *shakti*.

All over the room, people stood up and stretched, looking around to see who they could talk to. Angelica came up to me first. "You never told me you used to be his girlfriend."

"Way back," I said, "when we were both teenaged werewolves. It wasn't much of a relationship."

"He was really, really focused on you tonight," Angelica said.

People I knew started coming up to hug me and say hi, isn't he wonderful? Angelica stood beside me, like a bodyguard, or a booking agent.

"Is he always like that?" I asked. "It's intense."

"Every night it's different, but, oh, God, every night it's amazing. You saw how he took out his sword with Mary Alice. He's miles ahead of any therapist."

Mary Alice, too, was the nucleus of an admiring group. She was waving her hands in the air, happily describing. So what was I worried about? We all walked out through the dark brown halls. Proudly taped above the wainscoting, each bright watercolor by Jason, Emily, and Ti-Kwana stabbed at my heart. Though she was nearly thirty, my sister would never draw an apple tree, nor a house with wrongly angled chimney smoke, much less visualize a planet turning yellow from no recycling.

Lola frustrated: throwing herself on the floor, arching her back and spitting. She was still someone, I reminded myself. She had a personality as real and fundamental as anyone else's. All that was left was its directness, which I could still connect with on the level I'd just experienced Edward. That much was suddenly clear tonight, a gift. In fact, when I'd said no one had come to me before, I'd forgotten Lola, who always had. It was her main form of communication.

We were milling about on the sidewalk out front, trying to decide where to go and who would drive, when Edward rolled slowly up to us at the wheel of a silver Nissan. "Hey, Carol."

"Yeah?" In that moment, I was feeling exactly as I should have felt in high school. Bright, happy, protected by a herd.

"I feel like something was unfinished with you tonight. You opened your eyes while we were working."

"I chickened out," I said lightly.

"Go on," he said.

"Go on, what?"

"Tell me why you, as you say it, 'chickened out.'"

"I don't know," I said, beginning to falter. "It was my first night, I guess."

"Reality is . . ." Edward snapped his fingers. "Instantaneous. You're only ready for freedom if you're ready now." He snapped his fingers again, jauntily. "Hey, what do you say, kids, is Carol committed? Will she go all the way?"

"Yes," said Angelica stoutly.

"Wrong! Trick question," Edward said. "Carol can only answer for herself. So, Carol. Do you want freedom?"

I was tongue-tied. Then "Yes!" exploded out of me.

"She's hot," Edward declared. "You know what? She was my first guru. I really owe Carol my enlightenment."

"Oh, wow," my friends said.

"No, you don't owe me that," I said. "You can't."

"You're right, I owe you nothing," Edward said. "So let me repay you. Paradox is the essence of liberation. There's nowhere to go, so let's go somewhere. Come on, I'll drive you."

I still had fifteen portions of hot and sour soup to cook for tomorrow. "It's the middle of the night," I protested.

"Night? Day?" Edward took a slow and elaborate look at his watch. It was ten-thirty. "Are we awake? *That* is the question."

"Oh, Carol," my friends said.

"I'll bring her car home," Angelica said, speaking to Edward, not me. This struck me as odd, though it didn't register too deeply. I was walking around to the passenger side of Edward's car, telling myself that hot and sour soup was an easy recipe.

We went to different colleges. Edward to Columbia; I dropped out of Radcliffe after moving into a yoga household in Cambridgeport. We wore all white and fasted so much, I couldn't think. The yoga people were kind and soft, or at least they tried to be, and they gave me a good name: Usha, Dawn. I got involved with a male teacher of the Mukti Yoga system, which was based on a spontaneous flow of movements. When the head of Mukti moved him to California, I followed along, but we both got infatuated with other people and soon ended our relationship.

My mother died the first summer I was in San Francisco; my dad put Lola in the state school and married a widow from his church's grief group. I went into therapy.

I quit yoga, started Zen, and took back my Christian name. When I sat on my black cushion in the mornings, my mind reverberated like a gong struck in an empty room.

Once, visiting New York, I ran into Edward at a Krishnamurti lecture. He still had a ponytail and black scientific glasses and buttoned his shirt to the top, but this nerdy look had become avant-garde. He looked like someone who did videos or performance art.

He was with a woman, a redhead, maybe the girlfriend before the one he went to India with. She wore green boots and looked capable of meanness. After spending zillions of dollars on therapy, I congratulated myself that I could notice my jealousy and still walk up to them.

"You've totally changed," Edward observed; I did a pirouette, to be admired. While my back was turned, he said, "What's the matter, didn't you like yourself before?"

"No," I said. "No, in fact, I didn't like myself before, but I do like myself now."

His girlfriend looked me up and down with distaste.

"Meet Akasa," Edward said. "Akasa is a painter. She paints Greek friezes on car windshields."

"Oh, 'Ether,'" I said. "Who gave you that name?" I hadn't intended to be as sarcastic as my tone came out. "I used to be Usha," I added, too late.

Edward laughed. "Same old Seesee." He pressed my biceps with his forefinger. It was summer, I remember: his fingertip clung to my damp skin like an electrode, sending a message shuddering around my heart.

We sat far apart. This was in Madison Square Garden. Krishnamurti came out on stage and sat in a folding chair. Dignified and desiccated, he reminded me of a praying mantis. "Think . . . together. Think . . . together . . ." he urged us, over and over. I knew that what he meant went far beyond thinking, and far, far, far beyond the words.

"Nice, huh?" Edward said as I strapped myself into the car's softly chiming interior; I understood the Nissan was a donation. As it began to roll, a female voice said sternly, "Door is open. Door is open." Edward reached across me, opened the passenger door and slammed it again. The back of his hand brushed my breasts, perhaps by accident. We were just going around a curve.

"Where are we going?"

"Nowhere. Anywhere. Where would you like to go, Carol?"

"I don't know," I said, shrugging. "I still have to make fifteen hot and sour soups."

"Right," he said, laughing. "You're grounded, I see that. You've got a spiritual practice and probably everything else you need in your life. Tell me about yourself. I really want to reconnect with you. Forget enlightenment. It's all a game anyway."

"Is it?"

"Yes. No. Let's talk about you."

"I have a meal delivery service," I said, feeling hopelessly prosaic. "I can't say I feel so complete in my life. Not that I need you to be the one to fix it." This came out a little too defiant.

"Ah," said Edward. "So what is missing?"

We rode along in silence while I chewed on this question and its various possible or appropriate answers, finally discarding all of them. My tongue felt thick at the back of my throat.

Edward looked at me keenly, and I could feel him tuning into my energy. I asked, "What is the energy you put out? I've felt it with gurus before, but none of them was my high school, uh, friend, that I could ask about it."

Edward smiled to himself. "You're cute, C.C. The energy is supposed to help you shift out of the conscious mind."

"I was almost at something."

"Yes, you sure were."

"Was it enlightenment?"

"You tell me."

More silence. "No." I hoped this was right.

"Right," Edward said. "It's not the fireworks, it's the reintegration."

"Are you enlightened?"

He pulled the car off the road and turned to me. "I never know what that question means. You want to be enlightened, don't you? What's important is what it is to you."

I felt frustrated with him for not giving me a simple answer. Rolling down the window, I listened to the soothing rattle of the eucalyptus and prayed to the tree goddesses to protect and heal me. We were right near Green Gulch, on the road that winds up over the hill.

"More than life," I finally admitted.

"From my sense of you," he said, "it'll take a little while. But not too long."

"Okay," I said brightly. "I'll do whatever."

"Good." Edward turned the car around. As we crossed the red bridge, I understood that I couldn't possibly be home before three A.M. Then I wondered whether I'd go back at all. Even if we turned around right now, it would be extremely late to be asking a guru to drive me home.

Edward had a second-floor apartment near Castro Street, with a large terrace. Angelica had given up her yellow rattan armchair, which I'd always admired, to decorate it. When she took it out of the house I'd felt ripped off, as if she should have given it to me. Angelica's decorating skill was something I could never emulate.

My own bad taste had left my body proper but still cluttered around me in the form of mismatched *tzotzkes*.

It was curious to see Edward pushing his key into the scratched aluminum doorknob, like an ordinary working man coming home. Inside, a TV barked and roared. I thought it might be the shaven-headed man's, the one who acted so much like Edward's personal attendant. Yet no guru I'd ever known condoned television watching; they called it psychic poison, to a man.

But Edward was different, American. I thought I heard his voice inside my head, saying freedom meant getting rid of all prejudices and barriers. I looked at him sharply, but he appeared oblivious.

Walking into the living room, Edward called out, "Hey!" and a young Indian woman walked out of the darkness. Young, very: she was sixteen, seventeen at most. She had on Western clothes, a bright red top, white jeans.

"Mira, this is Usha," he said, indicating me with his palm. When had I mentioned my Indian name?

"Usha, *namaste.*" The Indian greeting: I salute the light within you.

"*Namaste.*"

"Tea," said Edward, Indian, lordly. Mira disappeared into the kitchen. Clanks, the faucet's hiss, rapid clicking from the gas stove.

"Mira's my wife, in case you were wondering."

"She must be the only thing I haven't heard about you."

Edward smiled. "My wife is not that relevant."

I sat down on Angelica's chair, admiring again its yellow fabric printed with cockatoos and palm trees. She'd done a good job decorating: the room was spare and yet luxurious; its objects well chosen but not intimidating. Berber carpet. A small Thai Buddha's hand making the "fear not" gesture. Most of the light came from a rice paper cylinder that hung in one corner, from ceiling to floor. Clearly, not a single touch was Mira's.

The coffee table was crowded with photographs, exactly like family portraits, except they were all of Edward, Edward's Master, and Edward and Master together. I picked up the one of Master in his youth. It was out of focus, but he'd been beautiful, with big eyes and long, black hair like a woman's.

"See any resemblance?"

"To who? No."

"Mira!"

Unmistakable now, the heart-shaped face with its pretty, pointed chin.

"She's his daughter, and she's enlightened, of course. She wanted to come here to go to school. I married her as a kind of gift to him."

A strange notion whizzed across my mind. Maybe it was appropriate etiquette for a recently minted guru, lacking social peers, to ask his ex–high school lover to befriend his Indian wife?

But Mira looked quite self-sufficient, coming out with a tray. "I watch a video about computers," she announced. "Oh, nice," I chirped. She set down the tray, poured three cups of tea, and went away again, taking hers into the bedroom. As she opened and shut the door, a man's voice ballooned out. "They require a special language of their own."

"No one comes here," Edward said. "You're the first."

I felt certain that Angelica had visited regularly, but it must have been while she was decorating, before Edward and Mira had actually moved in.

"Milk? Honey?"

"Milk? In peppermint tea? Weird."

"It's tasty."

"Okay, milk and honey." I drank the greenish ichor, dragon's milk, and liked it. Lola might like it too, cool and warm at once.

"So." Edward settled himself back against the cushions. "You asked about the power. It's his, or I should even say, it's him." He bowed his head toward the photos. "Before we start, I should tell you that you may find my behavior inconsistent. Freedom is free. And it does not meet the demands of conscious thought. If you make any claims or statements based on our relationship, I won't acknowledge them. You understand my position, I hope."

Inside my body, anticipation's orchestra tuned up: deep thrills on cellos, reedy squeaks. Who would I be when this was done? "I mean. Look, it's 1989. We're in San Francisco. Is our, um, past sexual practice, all you're talking about?"

"The past is dead," said Edward. His tone was so chilling that I looked into his eyes and saw that he was free in such a way that you couldn't quite call him human anymore. They were blue, blue eyes, fringed with thick black lashes, their pupils as deep as wells. Everything and everyone else in the universe disappeared from my consciousness. No speck, nor trace, of impurity or pain anywhere on the universe's shining drum.

My ears heard my voice speaking. Not to Edward, but to his eyes, and to the thing, or being, or quality, I saw in them. "Who are you?"

"You."

I recognized the riverbank place where I'd stopped earlier this night — I'd jumped. Where was shame, where was hesitation?

Nothing mattered.

"Come," Edward said, taking my hand.

In the morning, he drove me home. Moving fast, against the clotted rush-hour traffic, made me feel triumphant over the delusions of the world. What we'd done the previous night broke limits: all was one, beyond pleasure and pain, man and woman. I was with Lola, too — we'd shattered prohibitions and distinctions. Where we lived mere consciousness was bliss, sufficient.

Who could be sad? For Lola, or for anyone? Everything was exactly as it was.

My house looked small and alien; for an instant I was almost afraid to go in, lest it shrink my mental state. I reminded myself that I could not be touched by anything in form. "Thank you," I said, kissing Edward's cheek. "I feel so free!"

"Stake your claim," he said.

I delivered my fifteen meals late, each with a note promising a free lunch next Monday; but within a week, I'd quit doing any food whatsoever. I had a little money saved up, and Edward thought it would be good for me to let go of obligations for a while in order to go deeper spiritually. He said I should move into a group house, to save money and to remain in the atmosphere of enlightenment. There was a scene with Angelica the day I left; she accused me of not having paid my share of the electric bill. I just wrote out another check. Inwardly, I was traveling boundless realms of light. My new house's tatty shag might as well have been blue lotus flowers. I wondered whether I needed to go to session at all, or if I should just meet Edward afterward.

I decided to go, and when I got there I was glad. Being one with Edward granted me an X-ray vision; it was utterly clear how people got stuck in problems. Suffering was where the mind grasped onto appearances rather than unconditioned reality. For one second, I even saw the magic sword in Edward's right hand as he attacked someone's delusions; it flamed with bluish, pearly light.

He was working with Angelica. "I thought I was so special," she said. "Now I feel like I'm totally abandoned and alone."

"Christ said the same at one point. Where do you think he went? Seek the deeper meaning of abandonment!"

"There is nothing. I just want to die."

"Christ died on his cross, apparently. I'm saying it's that time for you. The time of total letting go."

Angelica fell forward on the floor, her arms flung up over her head. "Let it happen, Angelica," Edward said. She sobbed and sobbed, and we all ignored her until the end of session, when a few devotees picked her up and half carried her outside.

Everyone said how radical the session was, but that it wasn't the only time it had been so deep.

Later on, I described to Edward my profound understanding and detachment. "I'd be feeling so guilty about Angelica," I said. "It's been like my whole life, to be the destroyer. To feel responsible for someone else's pain." In a way I was still fishing to see if he'd heard my confession, that night so long ago.

"But you are," Edward told me. "Can't you see? You're a goddess, you're Kali herself. You're responsible for Angelica, and for the slaughter in Cambodia, and the landing on the moon. Burn away your personal mind, and the whole universe is you. But it's all perfect, so, the good news is, no guilt."

"Holy shit," I said.

"It's no big deal." He shrugged. "You just accept it."

The next night at session, he started pushing me away. He sent me to the back of the room, to "cook," he said, among the devotees. When I called him later, there was no answer.

Like when God withdraws His Presence from the Catholic saints, I was sleepless, wild. I drove around the city in my car until three A.M., when I finally went into a phone booth and called him up again. "Where are you?" he asked sleepily. "Sure, okay, come. I was late getting home. Somebody was freaking out."

"Who? Angelica?"

"None of your beeswax."

Mira let me in and I raced down the hallway past her,

not even answering her *"Namaste."* Maybe her mouth looked smaller than usual: I didn't care, didn't see. I curled myself against Edward's back and, in the morning, poured out my devotion. I kissed his feet, actually sucked his toes.

He said he'd felt the same way about Master, and that according to tradition, I should now experience self-sufficient union. When I protested, he said the signs were coming from every direction. Two of my housemates had come to him saying I wasn't participating in communal life. It was true: my suitcase was still half packed, my clothes in piles on the bed.

"Don't worry," he told me. "I'll be with you, even if we seem to be apart."

"Do you love me?"

"We're one. It's more than love. You're the only one who really knows me."

I resolved not to let myself feel any distance from him. Surely our nights together would resume when and if I passed this test.

So I became an ordinary devotee, undistinguished as a fish in a school. Every night we went to session; every day we sat around talking about how far people had gone, who was ready and not ready, who was courageous and who wasn't letting go. Edward's energy filled everyone, continuing the ruthless work he did with us at night.

My housemates didn't spare me. I learned to clean the sink drain and to contribute honestly to a discussion. There was something reassuring in hearing exactly what people thought of me. My personality, my habits, weren't so awful as I'd tended to assume. For the first time in my life, I slipped into fearless harmony with others. These people knew everything about me except that I was Edward's woman, and even that began to seem less important, as I immersed myself in being a devotee. Edward

Edward Edward: this mantra unified us all, a love affair from which no one was excluded.

He was so tuned in to me. "Carol's gone. She doesn't need me anymore," he joked one night when I'd been feeling especially merged.

"But I do," I said, quite unashamed. "My life is all you. We've all gone into you."

"Phew, yuck! Don't we find Carol a little slow? A little . . . unindividuated?"

I'd thought I'd grown accustomed to the sword; but these words cut me up inside. If Edward and I still had our private understanding, I wasn't sure what it was.

Meanwhile, Angelica was still coming to session, but she seemed too quiet, pale and held in. Every night she and I sat in the last row, in the folding chairs against the wall, among those who had back trouble or weren't spiritually committed.

Every few days Edward would just ask her, "Are you done?" and she'd shake her head no. My housemates and I couldn't decipher her case. We couldn't tell whether she was holding back, or working on something particular.

"She's not sharing with anyone," I observed.

"Neither are you," said my housemate Patrick. He and his wife, Morgaine, took the role of den parents; they were the ones who'd gone to Edward about me earlier. "Edward started you the other night," Morgaine echoed, "and you haven't finished your dialogue."

"I'm just in his presence." I made kitten eyes at Morgaine, who was one of the biggest bliss freaks. Every night, she sat right at Edward's feet, rocking to and fro with her eyes shut. Sometimes he let her put her face against his knees.

She said firmly, "He pointed straight at your obscuration!"

I wanted to tell her that Edward had enlightened me

privately, a memory I was trying hard to hold. What if she was right, and I needed a further breakthrough? On the other hand, why should I listen to bliss freak Morgaine?

Doubt is the greatest enemy of enlightenment, as Edward always said. As other devotees had catharses and moved forward in the room, I began to feel internal pressure to speak, but all that I had to release were the things I'd done with Edward.

When the words climbed into my throat, I strangled them.

He'd said there would be inconsistencies that didn't fit with the conscious mind.

Night after night, I burned in silence. I kept the faith. Refusal made me strong. See through everything, I told myself, vaporize concrete.

Angelica came to me in a dream, floating down a dark stream on a striped mattress. Passing me, she sat up and began baaing, making noises like Lola used to. Her tongue was dried out, which was why she couldn't speak in words. It looked horrifying, like some animal run over on the road.

The next night she sat next to me at session. I couldn't tell if this was deliberate on her part: she came late, and there weren't many seats left to choose from, but whatever the reason, I felt the cosmic net tighten around us. I reached for her hand, to offer reassurance, but Angelica pulled away.

It was one of Edward's brimstone nights. "You're all walking in a graveyard," he cried out. "The past is dead! Am I the only living human in this room? I'm sick of waiting for you. I really ought to quit." He slumped down in his chair. "What do you have to say to me?"

Angelica turned toward me and made a fish's mouth, a word: no. She closed her eyes, smirking like a little kid who's just licked ice cream. Then she snapped into life, crossed her skinny, freckled arms across her chest, and said loudly, "You have no real love. You're not capable. In fact, you are a damaged individual." There was something comical about her diction, and I stifled a giggle.

"Angelica!" Edward sat up. "At last!" He opened his arms and fell back in his chair. "Your hostility's been silent much too long!"

"This is real," Angelica said. "I'm not kidding. I'm talking, this is not a one-way street. Look out, there's a car coming at you."

"Yeah, we all *really* have to kill the authority figure. I did it, too, with Master."

Angelica said, "So now you're the great power. I hope you get AIDS. No, wait. You'd give it to someone." She stood up from her chair and spoke to all the devotees. "How many of us has he slept with? Any of you know his wife, Mira? She's Master's daughter. She told me a lot. Master trusted Edward at first. But now the whole thing —"

Edward said, "Bob?" He crooked his finger, and the shaven-headed guy went up to the throne, where Edward spoke into his ear. Little, thin Angelica suddenly ran out of the room, which made Edward start laughing.

Bob followed her.

From the parking lot, we could all hear Angelica's wailing, three liquid notes over and over. Oh, ah, oh. Oh, ah, oh. She sounded insane, like a peacock I heard once in Mexico. Then her car started and tore out with a screech, laying rubber.

Edward cleared his throat. "Hysteria speaks for herself," he said. "Anyone want to add anything?"

The shaven-headed guy came back in and sat down. I looked around the room: people's eyes were too bright, like dogs staring at raw lungs, but no one said anything.

"So let's sit and quietly let go of her," Edward said. His energy was not as strong as usual.

I defended Angelica to my housemates later. "If she was with Edward," I said, "we can't judge her. You don't go back to square one after that."

"She's mentally unstable. What do you see, Carol?"

That she and I were like one person. "I don't know, it's upsetting. I can't believe she would attack him like that." There was fear in me. Morgaine had not come home, and, late that night, Patrick went out.

The next morning they were back. I announced that I was going to the supermarket; I shopped at the speed of light, so I could drive home past the place I used to share with Angelica without anyone's getting suspicious. It was a low, yellow house built in the 1920s, with a veranda no one ever sat on but which was pleasant, nonetheless, to imagine sitting on. Angelica's dusty red Toyota was not in the driveway.

I let myself in with my old key.

My room was closed; I had no interest in it. Some guy had moved in who worked in the space industry. Just as I'd suspected, Angelica's room was empty except for an empty reel of packing tape and a few tarnished pennies and wax drippings in a saucer. The carpet had been freshly vacuumed, so she must have prepared her own departure. No one else was so meticulous.

Thank God, thank God, my sinister imaginings were wrong. I shut my eyes and tried to tune in to any message that the room might have for me. Alone was what I felt, alone and hollow. There was something missing in me, something as solid as a lug nut that would have permitted me to hate Edward: but Edward had removed it. Through the hole that was left, I could see the heart of light, all the people who were disappearing into it.

Then, all at once, my skin began to crawl, and I really didn't want to be there anymore.

Leaving, I saw why. She'd burned her photograph of him on a saucer on the mantelpiece. All of us had the

same picture of Edward taken shortly after his enlightenment, looking pure and fresh in a long, white Indian
shirt. The burnt emulsion had held together so that he
looked dark and distorted, a ghost of black flame. I
pressed that image with my finger until it fell apart.

UNDER
THE
ROOF

$\mathcal{O}$

Moist, lead-lemon Bang-
kok dawn — Miss Bi Chin's Chinese alarm clock goes
off, a harsh metallic sound, like tiny villagers beating
pans to frighten the dragon of sleep. She opens her eyes
and sees a big fire ant crawling up her yellow mosquito
net; feels how the black earth's chill has penetrated her
hipbones. At first she does not know where she is.

Tuk-tuks, taxis, and motorbikes already roar behind
the high garden wall, but the air is still sweet, yesterday's
fumes brought down by the dew. She has slept outside,
behind her house, under the sal tree. All around her lie
pink fleshy blossoms fallen during the night.

She lies still on her side, allowing last night's trip to
Don Muang Airport to bloom in her mind, seeing the
American monk stalk from the barrier, his brown robe
formally wrapped to form a collar and tight scroll down
his right arm. Straight out of Burma. It delights her to
remember his keen, uncertain look as he scanned the
crowd for her unfamiliar face. Then she waved and he

smiled. On the way home the taxi driver charged them only half price.

She heaves up to sitting; the monk, who is standing now at her screened upstairs window, sees her hips' awkward sideways roll, her hands pressing the small of her back. Both of them have the same thought: the body is a heap of sufferings! The monk steps back quickly, lest Miss Bi Chin catch him gazing out the window, worrying what will become of him out here in the world. As he moves into the shadow he realizes that worry itself is the world's first invasion. Again he is struck with gratitude for his robes. Having to be an example for others protects me, he thinks. It works from the outside in, the way forcing yourself to smile can make you feel happy.

Miss Bi Chin rolls up her straw sleeping mat and hurries into the house with it under her arm. Her bones ache, but she takes joy in that. Why should she rent a hotel room when she can sleep for free in her own back yard? It's not the rainy season. She will earn great merit for helping the monk to sleep as the rules require, under a roof where there is no woman. By now he must have completed his morning meditation.

In her mind she sees the Thai monks going for alms food right now all over the city, hundreds of them in bright orange robes, bare feet stepping over broken glass and black street garbage. They shave their heads only on a full-moon day, they have TVs, and they seduce American tourists. They don't care if the tourists are women or men. Thai people crave too much for sense pleasures. Miss Bi Chin would not donate so much as an orange to Thai monks; she saves her generosity for the good clean monks trained in Burma.

As she lights the gas under the huge aluminum teakettle, the old man comes shuffling into the dark kitchen. He pulls the light cord, searing the room with jerks of blue fluorescence. "Why do you cook in the dark, Chinese sow," he says in Malay. He is her mother's second husband's brother, who lived off the family for years in Penang. Now he has come here to torture her and make her life miserable.

"Shh," she says, motioning with her head. The American monk sits cross-legged at a low table in the next room. His eyes are downcast and a small smile curves his lips. Beautifully white, he resembles the marble Buddhas they sell in Rangoon.

"So what? He doesn't understand me," the old man says. "Why don't you bring in a real man for a change? You'd be a lot less religious if you were satisfied." And I'd be happier living here, he thinks, if she were a normal woman, not lost in pious dreams.

His words roll off her mind like dew from the petals of a white lotus. "You will go to all the hells," she predicts. "First the hot and then the cold."

The old man laughs. "I am Muslim. Will I go to the same hell as you and your rag-wrapped *farang*? I am waiting for my breakfast." He walks in and shows all his teeth to the American monk. "Goo' mornin', sah!"

"Hey," the monk says. "Thanks for the bed, I slept great."

The old man can only nod. He doesn't understand English. Miss Bi Chin bites her tongue, deciding it is better for the monk's peace of mind not to know it was her bed that he slept in. Of course, she moved it into the sewing room.

This American monk is the favorite of the Rangoon abbot, Miss Bi Chin has heard. He's been in intensive meditation for three years, completing two levels of insight practice and the concentrations on the four heavenly abodes. But the monastery's friend in the Department of Religious Affairs lost his position in November and the monk's last visa renewal application was rejected. He has come to Thailand to apply for reentry into

Burma. Approval will take at least three months, if it comes at all. Conditions in Burma are unstable. The government has had to be very strict to maintain order and it does not want too many foreign witnesses to its methods. Recently it changed the country's name to Myanmar, as if this would solve its problems.

If the monk cannot return, the abbot may send him back to America to found a monastery. The monk has not been told. The streams of defilements are strong in the West. All of the American monks that the abbot has known disrobe soon after they go home, so they can enjoy sense pleasures. Ideally, the monk should stay in Burma a few more years, but the abbot hasn't worn robes all his life to forget that the world is not ideal. This monk is addicted to pondering, a common Western vice, but he has a devoted heart, and his practice has been good. Pork should fry in its own fat. The American devotees cry out for a monastery. This monk may be the perfect candidate.

The abbot sees no reason to make a decision yet. He's asked Miss Bi Chin, the monastery's great supporter, to report on the monk's behavior, on whether living unsupervised in capitalist Bangkok becomes his downfall.

Seeing him wait for his food, so still, Miss Bi Chin has no worries. She's studied his face, too, according to Chinese physiognomy. A broad forehead means calm, the deep lines at each side of the mouth mean kindness.

"Breakfast for you." She kneels at the monk's side, offering the dishes from a cubit's distance, as the Buddha prescribed. The monk touches each plate, and she sets it on the table. Wheaties, instant Nescafé with condensed milk, sliced mango, lemon cookies from England, and a bowl of instant ramen noodles.

He hasn't seen such food in three years. He smiles in gratitude at Miss Bi Chin and begins eating.

Miss Bi Chin sits on one side with her feet tucked

behind her and her hands in the respectful position. Rapture arises in her mind. She has helped Western monks before, and she knows they do not do well on the diet in Rangoon. Too much oil and hot pepper. This monk is bony, his skin rough. She will buy chicken extract, milk powder, and vitamins for him; she will take early lunch hours to come home and cook his lunch. Monks eat no solid food between noon and dawn.

She stops her ears against the sound of the old man, slurping in the kitchen like a hungry ghost.

The monk wipes his mouth. He has finished everything except the noodles, which remind him too much of Burmese food. Miss Bi Chin notices. She'll reheat them for herself with fish paste; the monk's future breakfasts will be entirely Western.

Because the monk is American, he sometimes feels unworthy of being bowed to and living on donations, guilty about the extent to which he has learned to enjoy such treatment. Miss Bi Chin, for example, is not rich. She works as a secretary at American Express and says she refused promotion twice so that she can feel free to neglect her job when monks need help. He'd like to thank her for the food, for everything she is going to do for him, but this is not allowed.

If he were still a carpenter he'd build her a kitchen countertop. As a monk, example and guidance are the only returns he can offer. They're what she expects, he reminds himself, slipping again into the Asian part of his mind. Her donations bring her merit. She supports what I represent, the possibility of enlightenment, and not me specifically.

He clears his throat. "Where did you learn such good English?"

"Oh! My mother sent me to a British school in Penang."

"And you speak Burmese, Thai, and what else?"

"Malay, Cantonese, a little Mandarin."

The monk shakes his head. "Amazing. You're one smart lady."

Miss Bi Chin laughs in embarrassment. "I am Chinese, but my family moved to Malaysia, and we had to learn all the languages on the way. If you had my same *kamma*, you would know them too."

"Listen." The monk laughs. "The abbot did his best to teach me Burmese." It's hard for him to imagine that this woman is also a foreigner here.

"Better for you," Miss Bi Chin says promptly. "For a monk it is most important to maintain virtue and concentration. Learning languages is only worldly knowledge. The Burmese won't let you alone if they know you can speak. When I go to meditate at Pingyan Monastery, I have to hide in my room." She laughs.

The monk smiles, charmed. Faith makes Miss Bi Chin glow like a smooth golden cat, yet her black eyes sparkle wickedly. He will have to be careful to see her as his older sister, or even as a future corpse.

He'd be surprised to know that Miss Bi Chin thinks of herself as ugly. As a child, her mother would tweak her arm hairs and say, "No one will marry you, Black Dog. Better learn English so you can feed yourself." True, no Asian men want Miss Bi Chin, but the reason may not be her skin — there are plenty of married women as dark. No, she is too well educated, too sharp-tongued, and most of all too religious. From her own side, the only Asian men she is interested in are celibate, monks. She had a long relationship with an American, Douglas, the heir to a toy fortune who does business in Bangkok and Singapore. He smokes Dunhills in a holder and sponsors the publication of Buddhist texts. Younger than she, he left her a year ago for a glamorous twenty-year-old Thai. She still sees him sometimes at Buddhist meetings, drawling his reactionary opinions. How she ever was involved with him is a mystery to her.

Now she cries, "What is there in this world worth talking about? Everything is only blah, blah, blah. I must go to work now and type meaningless reports so that I can sustain my life and yours. I will come back to cook your lunch. Please use my house as you wish. I have many Buddhist books in English. The old man will not bother you."

She shuffles toward the monk on her knees to remove the plates. Not to introduce the old man as her uncle is one of her secret acts of revenge.

How terrible my life would be without monks, she thinks.

The monk paces slowly up and down Miss Bi Chin's unfurnished living room. His body feels soft and chaotic among the sharp corners, the too shiny parquet, the plastic flowers under a tinted portrait of his abbot, the most famous teacher in Burma. This photograph shows the abbot's terrifying side, when his eyes, hard and sharp, pierce into each person's heart to lay bare its secret flaws. The monk prefers the abbot's tenderness, eyes so soft you want to fall over sideways.

This is the first day in three years the monk has not been surrounded by other monks, living the life called "pure and clean as a polished shell," its ten precepts, 227 rules, daily alms round, chanting at dusk. The monastery wall was a mirror facing inward; beyond it was another barrier, the national boundary of Burma. He often used to speculate on what disasters could be happening in the outside world without his knowing. Meanwhile, cocooned within the walls, the discipline of the robes, and the fierce certainties of his teacher, the monk's mind grew dextrous. It plunged into nothingness too subtle to remember, which left him only with a yearning to return to them. Now ordinary happiness feels harsh and coarse.

Outside, traffic roars like storm surf. What a city! He was a different man when he passed through on the way to Rangoon, drank a Singha beer at the airport bar, defiantly toasting his future as a renunciate. Even then he'd been shocked by Bangkok, where everything was for sale: plastic buckets, counterfeit Rolexes, bootleg software, and of course the women, dressed as primly as third-grade teachers, hoping a client will choose to marry them.

Burma may attack your health, he thinks, but Bangkok will suck you to your doom.

What if his visa is denied?

Will he disrobe? His civilian clothes are even now in a suitcase in the monastery's strong room. They must have been eaten up by mildew. He's not ready to go back home as a bald, toga-wearing freak. No way would the abbot let him stay and practice under a Thai, not down here where they've got monks running around claiming to be reincarnations of Sariputra the Arhat. There's a Burmese center in Penang which Miss Bi Chin supported before she moved up to Bangkok. But she said last night it's near a huge highway and so is unsuitable for the absorption practices. Plus, she added confidentially, the head monk in Penang hates Westerners. She ought to know: he's her cousin. If I get sent to Penang, the monk thinks, I'll be able to practice patience for about two weeks and then I'll be out of the robes. I was never a lifer, anyway. Or was I?

I know this is only a form.

He isn't ready just yet to lose the peace, the certainty of being a monk, nor to be separated from the abbot, his teacher, the only man on earth, he's often told himself, he truly, deeply respects.

He catches himself planning to sneak across the border at Chiang Rai and run up to Rangoon through the forest with help from Karen insurgents. Bowing three times at the abbot's feet. Here I am. In his mind the abbot laughs at him and says, Peace is not in Burma or in

Bangkok. Peace comes from dropping one's preferences. That is why we beg for our food, we take what is given.

The monk stops in front of the abbot's portrait and makes the gesture of respect, palms together.

He feels the world stretching out around him. I'm here, he thinks; suddenly he's in his body again, feeling its heaviness and insubstantiality. He can even feel the strengthening effect of the milk in the Wheaties he just ate. Conditions in Thailand are good for healing the old bod; he can make it a project. In the States he ran and did yoga fairly regularly; in Burma he never exercised. He was never alone, and people would gossip if they saw him in an undignified posture.

Carefully he spreads his sitting cloth, a maroon-and-orange patchwork square, on the straw mat where he ate breakfast; now he lies flat on it, easing the bunched muscles of his shoulders. Slowly he raises his legs to vertical, letting the small of his back flatten against the cool straw. His sacrum releases with a loud pop.

He tucks the skirt of his robe between his knees and raises his buttocks off the ground until he is in full shoulder stand, the queen of poses, the great redistributor of psychic energy.

His mind flies, faster than light, to Vermont.

He's lived as if he'll never go back to where people know him as Tom Perkins, a carpenter and the more or less unreliable lover of Mary Rose Cassidy, who still lives in Brattleboro, where she's a partner in a cooperative restaurant. She's known he would ordain ever since they came East together in seventy-three. They were both moved by the calm faces of monks they saw; but only Tom had that realization at the great dome of Borobudur in Java. Tapped it, and said, "Empty. That's it! There's nothing inside." Mary Rose saw something in his face and said, "You're going to have to follow this one through." After coming home, they learned to meditate together at a center in western Mass. She kept saying the tradition was sexist and stifled your *joie de vivre;* Tom wondered if she meditated only to keep close to him.

Mary Rose didn't expect him to be gone this long. He's written her four letters saying: my practice is getting deep, it's fascinating, I want to renew my visa.

He should've broken up with her. A year ago he knew, but it seemed cruel to cut her off by mail, and more appropriate as a monk to be vaguely affectionate, vaguely disconnected, than to delve into his past and make a big mess. He halfway hoped she'd lose patience and break up with him herself, but she stays faithful. She claims she's had no other lover since he left, and she sends a hundred dollars every other month to the monastery treasurer for his support. It's more than enough.

She would have stopped sending money; he would've had to be supported entirely by the Burmese. God knows they have little enough to spare. Think what his plane ticket to Bangkok would have cost in kyat. Four months' salary for the average worker, even at the official rate. At the black market rate, the real value of Burmese money, probably about three years' salary.

He lowers his legs as slowly as he can, feeling unfamiliar pulls in his belly and chest.

He turns to look out the large front window — the old man is staring in at him. He's been sweeping dead leaves off the cement courtyard. He wears ancient blue rubber thongs and a checked sarong; his fine-skinned purplish breasts sag over his ribs. His gaze is clouded and fierce, an old man's rage. The monk has assumed that he is some sort of servant, a trusted retainer of Miss Bi Chin's. He didn't quite take the old man into consideration. Now, this stare rips away all barriers between them.

Lying on the floor, his robes in disarray, he's Tom again, for the first time since he ordained.

With as much dignity as he can muster, he gets to his feet and goes out the back door into the tiny walled garden, where Miss Bi Chin slept. The old man has swept the pink sal flowers into a pile. The fresh ones look like parts of Mary Rose; the decaying ones, black and slimy, remind him of things the abbot says about sensuous desire. He watches one blossom fall, faster than he'd expect. It's heavy, the petals as thick as blotting paper. He picks it up, rubs one petal into bruised transparency.

I should call Mary Rose while I've got the Thai phone system, he thinks. I need to tell the truth.

Now he wishes he'd studied the rules, for he doesn't know if using the phone would break the precept against taking what is not given. It's a subtle thing, but how impeccable does he have to be? Miss Bi Chin offered her house, but then steered him into her library. She surely expects to do all his telephoning for him. Surprising Mary Rose with an overseas collect charge isn't too monkly, except that she still considers him her lover.

The irony of this is not lost on him.

Well, it's ten P.M. in Brattleboro. If he waits until Miss Bi Chin comes home it'll be too late, and what's more, she'll overhear everything. The phone is in the kitchen, where she'll be cooking lunch. He walks around the corner of the house and asks the old man's permission to use the phone.

The old man waggles his head as if his neck had lost its bones. He says in Malay, "I don't understand you, and you don't understand me!"

The monk decides that this weird movement contains some element of affirmation. In any case, his mind is made up.

As he watches his hand travel toward the phone, he remembers the abbot talking about the gradations of defilement. Desire shakes the mind. Then the body moves, touches the object, touches it causing the object to move. When he touches the receiver, he picks it up quickly and dials.

"Tom?" The satellite transmission is so clear, Mary

Rose sounds like she's in the next room. "Oh, it's fantastic to hear your voice!"

When he hangs up, an hour later, he feels sick. She was right: he has wasted her time. And what a bill she's going to get. Yet he has to admit, he's intensely alive, too, as if he'd stuck his fingers in a socket, as if someone had handed him a sword.

He thinks, maybe this divestiture will create a vacuum that my visa will rush into.

He goes up to Miss Bi Chin's sewing room and closes the door. Cross-legged on his sitting cloth, he tries to cut off all thoughts of Mary Rose so he can send loving-kindness to the abbot, his benefactor. At first tears come, his body feels bludgeoned by emotion. But then his loving feeling strengthens, the abbot's presence solidifies. Suddenly he and the abbot are welded together. The monk's lips curve up. Here there is no grief.

Miss Bi Chin and the old man are eating dinner, chicken and Chinese cabbage in ginger sauce; the monk is upstairs reading a list of the Twenty-Four Mental States Called Beautiful.

"Your monk talked on the phone for two hours," the old man says slyly. "He put his feet above his head and then pointed them at the portrait of Pingyan Sayadaw."

It is not true that the monk pointed his feet at the portrait, but as soon as the old man says so, he begins to believe himself. He's tired of having monks in the house, tired of the prissy, superior way his stepniece behaves when these eunuchs are about. What good do they do? They live off other people, beg for their food, they raise no children. The old man has no children either, but he can call himself a man. He was a narcotics agent for six years in Malaysia, until a bullet lodged near his spine.

Miss Bi Chin pretends he does not exist, but he pinches her biceps, hard.

"Ow!" she cries, and jerks her arm away. "I *told* him

he could use the house as he pleased." Too late, she realizes she shouldn't have descended to arguing: it causes the old man to continue.

"Well, he did that. He only waited for you to leave before changing his behavior. I think he's a very loose monk. He wandered up the stairs, down the stairs, examining this and that. Out into the garden to stare at the sky and pick up flowers. Then he got on the phone. He'll be poking in the refrigerator tomorrow, getting his own food."

"You just hate monks."

"Wait and see," the old man says lightly. "Have you noticed his lower lip? Full of lust and weakness."

Miss Bi Chin lowers her face until all she can see is her bowl of soupy cabbage. The old man is her curse for some evil deed in the past. How he abuses her, how he tries to poison her mind! She tells herself that the old man's evil speech is a sign of his own suffering, yet he seems to cause her more pain than he feels himself. Sometimes she enjoys doing battle with him — and she has developed great strength by learning to seal off her mental state so that he cannot infiltrate. This strength she uses on different occasions, say on a crowded bus when an open sore is thrust beneath her nose, or when her boss at American Express overloads her with work. At other times the old man defeats her, causes her defilements to arise. Hatred. Fear. A strange sadness, like homesickness, when she thinks of him helpless in the grip of his obsessions.

She could never kick him out. Crippled, too old to learn Thai or get a job, how would he survive in Bangkok? And he does make himself useful, he tends the garden and cleans the floors and bathrooms. Even more important, without him as witness, she and her monks would not be allowed to be in the same house together. The Buddha knew human nature very well when he made those rules, she thinks.

Washing up, she hears the old man has turned on his TV and is watching his favorite talk show, whose host gained fame after a jealous wife cut off his penis and he had it sewn on again.

"Why do you have to watch that!" she scolds at his fat, unresponsive back.

She goes up to the sewing room in a fury, which dissipates into shame as soon as she sees the monk reading. The light from the window lies flat and weak on the side of his shaven head. His pallor makes him look as if he has just been peeled. Her ex-lover Douglas had a similar look, and it gives her a shiver. She turns on the yellow electric lamp so he will not ruin his eyes and leaves the door wide open, as is necessary when a monk and a woman are together in a room.

"Hello, sister," he says. The edges of his eyelids feel burnt by tears. Miss Bi Chin notices redness, but thinks it is from ill health.

She begins to speak even before she has finished her three bows. "Please instruct me, sir. I am so hateful. I should practice meditation for many years, like you, so I can attain the *anagami* stage, where anger is uprooted forever. But I am tied to my six sense doors, I cannot become a nun, I must live in this world full of low people. I think also, if I quit my job, who will support you monks when you come to Bangkok?"

As she speaks he takes the formal posture and unconsciously sets his mouth in the same line as the abbot's in the portrait downstairs. Usually when someone bows to him, the beauty of the ancient hierarchy springs up like cool water inside him. Today he'd like to run from this woman, bunched up on the floor, getting ready to spill out her hot, messy life.

But he has to serve her, or else why give up Mary Rose?

"I'm not *anagami*. I'm just an American monk."

"You are so humble!" she says, looking up at him with eyes as tormented and devoted as a dog's.

Oh God, he thinks. He forces himself to go on. "I understand you wish to renounce the world. Look at me, I left behind a very good woman to do this. I don't regret it," he adds quickly.

She thinks, he should not be talking about his woman. And then: who was she? He must have loved her, to look so regretful even after three years.

"Of course not. Monks enjoy a higher happiness," she says.

"But you don't need to be a nun to purify your mind. Greed, hatred, and delusion are the same whether you are in robes or not. Don't be hard on yourself. We all get angry."

"I am hard because hatred is hard." She says something in Pali, the scriptural language. But he can tell she's relieved, she's heard something that has helped her. She goes on more softly, "Sometimes I want to strike out against one person."

Miss Bi Chin feels a great relief as she confesses this, as if a rusty pin had been removed from her flesh.

"You'll also hurt yourself." The monk regrets his occasional cruelties to Mary Rose. Once, feeling perverse, he called her a cow, only because he knew she was sensitive about her big breasts. The word, the moment, the look on her face, have come back to his mind hundreds of times. And today she said he was a coward and that he insulted her by not speaking sooner.

"I know! I know!" Miss Bi Chin falls silent.

The monk tries for a better topic. "Who's the old man you have living with you? He gave me quite a look through the window."

He has the psychic powers, Miss Bi Chin thinks. "You've guessed my enemy. My stepuncle. My mother sent him to me. I cannot get rid of him." She picks like a schoolgirl at the hem of her dress, hearing the old man's mocking voice: "If you don't have the guts to throw me out, you deserve whatever you get."

The monk sees her face go deep red. That horrible old man! He sees him staring in the window again, his rheumy, cruel eyes. I'd better be careful, though. Maybe they've slept together. You never know, when two people live in the same house.

"Every personal relationship brings suffering," he says, cautiously.

"Better to live alone if one wants to free the mind," Miss Bi Chin quotes from the admonitions of the abbot. "Should I ask Uncle to leave?"

"Um, any reason why you can't?"

"Why not!" She giggles. She is not so much planning to kick out the old man as letting herself fall just a little in love with this monk. He is so breezy and American, like a hero in the movies, yet he has much wisdom. "Well, he has to stay here until you get your visa, because you and I would not be able to be in the house alone."

The monk smiles uncertainly. "I may not get a visa."

"Of course you will, you have good *kamma* from practice."

"Yet we never know when our *kamma* will ripen, do we. Good or bad."

They both nod slowly, looking into each other's eyes.

"What will you do if you can't go back?" She really wants to know; and it gives her a thrill to talk about this, knowing that the monk is ignorant of the abbot's intentions. Perhaps she'll report the answer to Rangoon.

"I'll try to remain in equanimity."

That's a good answer for the abbot, she thinks, but it's not enough for me. She extends herself. "Would you like to go back to your country and begin a monastery?"

"No way," he says lightly.

"Why?"

"I have no interest in making others follow rules. I'm not a cop, basically."

"Don't you miss your home?"

"Yes, but —"

"I should have offered you to use the phone. Maybe you want to call your parents."

"I've already used it. I hope that's all right."

A shock runs down Miss Bi Chin's back. So it's true what the old man says. "You used the phone?"

"It was sort of urgent, I had to make a call. I did it collect. There'll be no charge to you. Maybe I should call Penang and confess?"

"Oh, no, no, no," she says. "I offered you to use my house as you wished. Who did you talk to?"

"Well, my old girlfriend from the States," and he finds himself describing the whole situation to Miss Bi Chin, confessing. Recklessly, he even says he might have postponed breaking up because he was afraid to lose a supporter. Because Miss Bi Chin is a stranger — and because she knows so much more about being a monk than he does — he feels compelled to expose his worst motivations. If forgiving words come out of these quietly smiling lips, he'll be exonerated. If her face turns from gold to brass and she casts him out, that will be right also.

As he speaks, Miss Bi Chin feels she is walking through a huge house where rooms open up unexpectedly one after another. When she was in the British school, she had to read a poem about the East being East and the West being West, and never the twain shall meet. This is not true: she knows she can follow this monk far into his labyrinth, and maybe get lost. For him it is the simplest thing to say: the old man is bad, ask him to leave. But for himself, life is so complicated. In one room of his mind he is a monk, and using the phone was an error; in another room, calling was the right thing to do. First he is too strict with himself, then he lets go of the rules altogether.

Should she tell the abbot? What would there be to tell? That the monk used the telephone after she had already given permission? That he was impatient to perform a wholesome act?

Miss Bi Chin's water heart flows in uncontrollable sympathy toward the monk. She knows he was afraid to be forgotten when he went so far from home. That is the true reason he did not cut off this girlfriend. But he is a man and cannot admit such kind of fears.

She interrupts. "If I were Mary Rose," she tells him, "if Mary Rose were Burmese, or even Thai, as soon as you ordained, her reason for sending money would change. She would donate to earn merit for herself. You would then feel grateful but not indebted. You would feel to strive hard in meditation, to make her sacrifice worthwhile. And I think that your mind is very pure and you are trying to perform your discipline perfectly, but because you were in intensive practice you do not know in precise way what monks should do and not do when they are in ordinary life. Therefore I think you should spend your time here studying the texts in my library and learning what you did not learn."

At the end of this speech she is breathless, shocked to hear herself admonishing a monk.

"Thank you," he says. "That's great." His face is broken up by emotion. He looks as if he might weep.

Now, she thinks, should I tell the abbot that his monk is falling apart?

Not yet. It's only his first day back in capitalism.

Within a week it is obvious to the old man that Miss Bi Chin and the monk are in love.

"I should call Rangoon," he teases Miss Bi Chin. They both know he will never do so, if only because he will not know how to introduce the topic to a person he has never met. But the threat gives him power over her. Miss Bi Chin now ignores it when he fails to sweep, or clean the bathrooms. The monk sometimes sweeps away the blossoms under the sal tree; the old man stands at the window of the sewing room, enjoying this spectacle. Miss Bi Chin made loud remarks about the toilet, but ended up cleaning it herself. She also serves the old man his meals before going in and prattling with the monk. The old man has never felt so satisfied since he moved in here two years ago.

Miss Bi Chin, too, is happy. These days she feels a strange new kind of freedom. She and the monk are so often in the same room — he sits in the kitchen while she cooks, and otherwise they go to the sewing room and study or meditate — that the old man has fewer opportunities to pinch or slap. In the past she even feared that the old man might kill her, but even he seems calmed by the monk's purity of mind.

The monk actually wants to know what she thinks about this and that. When she comes home from work, he asks respectfully how her day was, and they discuss her problems. He sees so clearly people's motivation! Then they go to the texts and try to look behind the surface to see what is the effect on the mind of each instruction, always asking, what did the Buddha intend? When they disagree they don't let each other off the hook. Their arguments are fierce, exciting.

"Why do Burmese and Thais call each other lax?" he asks one night. "The Thais accuse the Burmese because Burmese monks will take an object straight out of a woman's hand. Then the Burmese turn around and say Thais drink milk after noon. Can't they see it's all relative?"

"You don't know Thai monks," she replies hotly. "Won't take a pencil from a woman's hand, but you don't know what they take from her other parts."

"Yeah, but not all Thai monks are bad. What about those old Ajahns up north? They live under trees. They eat leaves. They must think Pingyan Sayadaw is corrupt for keeping that closetful of food." Too late he remembers that most of that food was sent by Miss Bi Chin.

"Insects also live under trees! Burmese get good results in their meditation, in the city or in the forest. You better listen to your own teacher to know what is right. No one reaches enlightenment by saying 'it is all relative.' "

His lips go tight, but then he nods. "You're right. Pingyan Sayadaw says Western skepticism makes people sour inside. You stay at the crossroads and never go anywhere. 'I don't believe this path, I don't believe that path.' Look at the power of mind he has."

"Such a strong monk," she says joyously. "Incredible," the monk replies, his pale eyes shining.

No man has ever yielded to her thinking; it fills her heart with cold, delicious fire.

Then they meditate together, her mind becomes so fresh. She feels she is living in the time of the Buddha with this monk. When the old man accuses her of being in love, she retorts that she's always been in love with the truth.

The monk is getting healthy, eating Wheaties and doing yoga every day. Miss Bi Chin often asks if there's anything he needs, so he can say "A bottle of vitamin C" or "A new pair of rubber thongs" without feeling strange. He feels pleasantly glutted with conversation. In Burma, he never sifted through his thoughts. The idea was simply to take in as much as he could. At Miss Bi Chin's, he can sort, digest, refine. She helps direct his studies, she's almost as good as a monk. He knows he's helping her in turn, to deal with daily life.

A perfect marriage would be like this, he thinks, except sex would screw it up with expectations. At times his feelings for Miss Bi Chin do grow warm, and he tosses on her bed at night, but there's no question in his mind about these feelings. They'll go away at the third stage of enlightenment. Having left Mary Rose, he feels more like a monk than ever. It's good exercise for him to see Miss Bi Chin's loveliness with detachment, as if she were a flower or a painting in a museum. When she exclaims that she's ugly and dark, he corrects her, saying, "All self-judgment reinforces the ego."

He writes the abbot every week. "Living in the world is not as difficult as I feared, but maybe this is because Miss Bi Chin's house is like a monastery. I am studying in her library. Her support is generous and her behavior is impeccable. She sleeps outside, under a tree. One night it rained and she went straight out to a hotel."

The monk has only two fears during this period. One is that the embassy of Myanmar will not approve his visa. The other is that it will. When he thinks of Pingyan Monastery, he remembers its discomforts. Diarrhea during the rains, in April prickly heat.

I have my head in the sand, he thinks; I sleep between my mother's breasts.

Miss Bi Chin is showing the monk a large bruise on her upper arm. It is the blue-black of an eggplant and has ugly spider's legs spreading in all directions around it. If he were not a monk, he'd touch it gently with his finger.

"I can't believe he does this to you," he says. "Don't you want him to leave? I'll be there when you say it. I'll stand over him while he packs."

"If he left, you'd have to go also. Where? He'd come back the next day. He was in the narcotics squad in Malaysia. I don't know what he would do. I think something. He has his old gun in a sack. It is broken, but he could fix it."

Hearing about the gun makes the monk's stomach light with horror. Human beings, what they'll do to each other. Imagine a rapist's mind, a murderer's. Delusion, darkness, separation. How has Miss Bi Chin let this evil being stay in the house? How has she been able to live under the roof with fear?

"He's got to go. If I'm still here he'd be less likely to

bother you," the monk says. "I'm an American, after all. He'd get into big trouble if he pulled anything. Now that I can use the phone" — he laughs a little — "I can get on the horn to the embassy."

"But he is my stepuncle," Miss Bi Chin says weakly. She doesn't really want the monk to be proposing this. He sounds not like a monk, but like any other American boasting about his country's power.

"Look," the monk says. "I'll sleep outside. I'll eat outside. I'll stay outside all day. We can leave the gate open so people in the street can see us. I think this thing with the old man is more serious than you think. We can work out the monk part. The Patimokkha only talks about sleeping under the same roof and sharing a secluded seat, and in the second case a woman follower has to accuse me of seducing you."

"I'll get you a tent," Miss Bi Chin says.

"No way. You didn't have one," the monk retorts. "Why don't you find him a job instead?"

The old man knows something is wrong: when he comes back from the soda shop at six, the two of them are sitting in the patio chairs side by side, facing the gate, like judges.

"You must leave this house tomorrow," Miss Bi Chin says. The monk's face bears a look the old man knows is dangerous: determination mixed with terror, the look of a young boy about to pull a trigger. In a flash he calculates his chances. The monk is not healthy and probably knows no dirty fighting tricks but is thirty years younger and much larger. He must have been a laborer once. His arms and chest show signs of former strength, and he's been exercising every day.

The old man makes his hands into claws. "Heugh!" he cries and fakes a pounce, only six inches forward. Of course the monk leaps to his feet. The old man laughs. This kind of thing brings vigor in old age.

"So you lovebirds want privacy?" he says. "Watch out

I don't take the kitchen knife to you tonight. I'm old but I'm still a man."

"I got you a job guarding the Chinese market," Miss Bi Chin says. "They'll give you a room in back." She was surprised how easy this solution was once the monk opened her mind to it. Now she owes the monk her happiness. Her house suddenly seems vast. Her nostrils fill with the sweet scent of sal flowers. It is as if the old man were a fire emitting sharp smoke which had been put out.

The next morning she calls a taxi. All of the old man's clothes fit into a vinyl sports bag, but his TV is too big to carry on the bus.

Watching him go, old and crooked, out the gate, Miss Bi Chin feels bad. Her mother will not understand. Loyalty is important in a family. She's been living in this house with the American monk who tells her about the youth revolution when everyone decided their parents were wrong. This was the beginning of meditation in America. Even the monk got interested in spiritual things at first because of drugs.

Now the monk meets her in the garden. He's smiling softly. "Remember the test of loving-kindness?" he asks her. "You're sitting under a tree with a neutral person, a friend, and an enemy, and a robber comes and says you have to choose who he'll kill?"

"I remember," she says dully. "I refuse the decision."

The abbot's letter has taken a month to arrive. He writes through an interpreter: "My son in robes: I hope you get a visa soon. I am glad you keep good morality. Miss Bi Chin says you are suitable to be a teacher and your speeches are refined. I praise her for sleeping outside, but I can agree that it is your turn. Be careful of desire and do not ponder."

Miss Bi Chin has sent glowing reports by aerogram. Now she is full of doubt. She hates sleeping in the bed;

she feels she has lost her power in some obscure way. She and the monk are trying hard to keep the rules. They avoid being in the house together, but there are too many robbers in Bangkok to leave the street gate open so they rely on the fact that they're always visible from the second floor of the elementary school across the street. They joke about their debt to one small, distracted boy who's always staring out the window. But this is almost like a lovers' joke. Miss Bi Chin feels disturbed by the monk's presence now. When he looks at her with soft eyes, she feels nothing but fear. Perhaps he loves her. Perhaps he thinks of her at night. She dreads his quick buzz of the doorbell, announcing he's coming in to use the bathroom.

One morning at work she types an aerogram to the abbot. It makes her happy to see the clarity of the Selectric type on the thin, blue paper. "I worry about the American monk. We're alone together in my compound. He made my uncle to leave my house. We keep his precepts, but I want your opinion. There was a woman in love with him at home. He said the precepts are relative."

She tosses this in her Out box and watches the office boy take it away with her boss's letters to America. For some reason, she thinks of the gun lying in the bottom of the old man's sports bag as he walked off down the street.

"Don't you want to go home and teach your own people?" Miss Bi Chin asks again.

She's brought up this subject many times, and the monk always says no. But today his answer surprises both of them. With the old man gone, things have fallen into place. He likes sleeping under the sal tree, the same kind of tree under which the Buddha was born and died. Monks in ancient times dwelt at the roots of trees. He loves its glossy green leaves and pink flowers. He imagines it is the tradition, and at night his roots go down with its roots, deep into the black soil. "Maybe I'm in a special position," he says. "Americans are hungry for truth. Our society is so materialistic."

"You don't want to be an abbot though," Miss Bi Chin says. "It is too tiring."

"I don't know," he says. "If my teacher asked me to, I guess I'd have to go."

"Well, an abbot wouldn't be staying here alone with me, I can tell you that much," Miss Bi Chin bursts out.

That night he lies awake under the sal tree. Why didn't she tell him sooner if it wasn't proper for him to stay? Is she in love with him? Or is she teaching him harder and harder lessons, step by step?

He remembers the rules he's studied. Miss Bi Chin could be the woman follower who accuses him of seduction. They haven't shared a seat, but if she brings a charge against him, there'd be no power in his denial. They've been secluded together and that is enough.

He understands something new. A monk's life has to be absolutely clear-cut. Ambiguous situations mean murky feelings. He can thank Miss Bi Chin for showing him that it is time to go to Penang and live with other monks and prepare for the responsibilities of the future. If the Penang abbot hates Westerners, it's probably because he's never met one who appreciates the robes. If it's difficult to be there, it will develop his mental strength.

He imagines himself a monk in old age. The stubble on his head will grow out white; he'll laugh at the world as his teacher does. Old Burmese monks are so alive, he thinks. Their bodies are light, their skin emits a glow. If you can feel free amid restrictions, you truly are free.

In the morning he is quiet as Miss Bi Chin serves his breakfast on the front patio.

He is red now, not white. He keeps his eyes down as she hands him the plates. Wheaties, mango, cookies, Nescafé. Talk to me, she cries inside herself. She stares at his mouth, seeing its weakness and lust. It shows the part of him she loves, the human part.

She hasn't slept all night, and her mind is as wild as an untamed elephant. Maybe the abbot will get her aerogram and make the monk disrobe. He'll stay in her house and live a lay life; they can make love after having their conversations. I could call the embassy and withdraw his visa application, she thinks. What is the worst that could happen? That I am reborn as a nun who'll be seduced by a foreigner?

At last she understands the old man, who said once he didn't care if *kamma* punished him in a future life, as long as he got to do what he wanted to in this life. How can we know who we'll be, or who we were? We can only try to be happy.

Frightened by her thoughts, she watches the monk bite a U shape out of his toast. He's being careful, moving as stiffly as a wooden puppet, and he must have shaved his head this morning. It is shiny, hairless. There is a small bloody nick over his ear.

She knows she won't be able to cancel his visa application and that her aerogram will result, not in the monk's disrobing, but in his being sent to Penang and forbidden to stay with her again. She hasn't accused him of downfall, nor of disgusting offenses. So he'll go on with his practice and become an abbot, or a fully liberated arhat. At least I was full of wholesome moral dread when I wrote that aerogram, she thinks. When the benefits come, I can enjoy them without guilt. Such as they'll be. Someone will give me a new Buddha image; I'll be offered another promotion and refuse it. She laughs under her breath. Is this what I was looking for when, as a young girl, I began running from temple to temple and lost all my friends?

"What are you laughing about," the monk says.

"I was thinking of something."

"I have to go to Penang," he says. His voice is low and hollow, so neither of them is sure he's actually spoken.

"I am sorry my house is unsuitable for you to stay."

"No, it's been wonderful to be here. But I need to be around other monks. I feel like we've been playing with the rules a little bit, we're in a gray area."

He smiles at her coaxingly, but she refuses the bait. "I'll buy you a ticket to Penang this afternoon."

How can she be so cold suddenly? She's pulling him out, compelling him to make the contact. "I'll miss you. Don't tell the abbot, okay?"

"If there is no lust, a monk can say he will miss."

"I want this to stay between us," he says. "You've been like my sister. And my teacher."

"Every personal relationship brings suffering," she says, but she's smiling at him, finally, a tiny complicated smile he'd never believe could appear on her golden face. Suddenly he sees her eyes are full of tears and he knows he'll be lonely in Penang, not only for Miss Bi Chin but for Mary Rose, who also fixed things so he could ask for whatever he wanted.

Nothing changes, the old man thinks. There they are, sitting in the front courtyard, talking about nothing. He's standing at the window of the third-grade classroom, during the children's first morning recess. He knew this was the time. Bi Chin doesn't go to work until nine-thirty.

He woke up in a rage that drove him to the bus stop, still not knowing what he would do — something. He has his pistol in the sports bag. He has fixed it, and late at night has practiced shooting bottles that float in the *khlong* past the Chinese market. His aim isn't what it was. The pistol is heavier than he remembered. His eyes are bad. His arm shakes.

He knew an idea would come when he was actually standing at the window, and it has. He sees one thing he can succeed at. He can hit that plate glass window, shatter it behind their heads. He sees it clearly, bursting, a shower of light. They will run inside and slam the door. Miss Bi Chin in her terror will grab the monk. Ha! They will find themselves embracing. Nature will take its course. That'll be a good one, if the old man does not miss and blow one of their heads off.

Happy with this solution, the old man begins to hum as he unzips the sports bag. The gun's cold oil smell reaches his nostrils, making him sharp and powerful. He's always wanted to break that window, he doesn't know why. Just to see it smash. I'm an evil old man, he thinks. Good thing I became a cop.

MR.
PEANUT

$\curvearrowleft$

A week into our affair, Severo Marquez told me he had shot his own dog. He'd already told me about his crazy female cousin who locked herself into the bathroom every Sunday and pounded nails into her hands in bloody imitation of Christ, about the jars of ears he saw in Vietnam, and his dramatic escape from Cuba — swimming across Guantánamo Bay under fire, dragging a rowboat full of relatives to the safety of the American base. I'd also heard about his Mookie-dog, part beagle, part Doberman, so smart she could carry an envelope to Severo's mother across a mile of Little Havana, or climb a tree to find Severo in a woman's apartment. When he said he'd shot this unbelievable animal, his dearest friend, there was a crack in his voice through which I could see him doing it, and suddenly I wondered whether everything else I'd heard from Severo might also be the truth.

We were lying in his narrow bed in a rooming house on Southeast Second Street in the City of Miami, near the river and the parole board. My dark angel's radio was tuned to the funky station; a ficus tree was attempting to crawl in the window with its round, leathery leaves. Far away to the north, my mother was killing herself by slow degrees, a fact that surrounded all my actions like darkness in a theater.

"Ay, Mami." Severo rubbed circles on my belly as he talked. How I loved his touch, and for him to call me that. "I'd just come home from Vietnam. I was so desperate, I knew if I didn't shoot that dog I'd kill my family, my wife and the two girls. I called La Mookie and put the pistol on her head. I looked in her eyes and said 'Dios, Mami, I love you more than God, and I know if you could understand me you'd say this was all right.' She looked at me and she told me she did."

Mami, Mami. Some rubbery column in my chest began bouncing up and down. I couldn't speak, so I pushed one arm under Severo's back and threw the rest of myself across the high mound of his chest. He'd been studying the black fiberboard ceiling, but now he started biting the side of my neck gently. "Marry me, Mami," he said.

"I can't," I said. "I'm taking care of my mom." I was grateful to have an excuse so I wouldn't have to say I didn't belong with Severo, who dealt cocaine and rode a giant black Honda motorcycle. I'd met him on my first night down here, doing a job for the Mach Corporation, selling pesticides to South American governments. I didn't belong in that line of work either, but I was proving something: I loved my mother so much that I was willing to exchange my fate for hers.

That night was the second time I heard Severo scream in his sleep, raw terror ripping the muscles of his throat. He was entitled to forty percent mental disability from the service but refused it out of pride. I wrapped my arms and legs around Severo as if I could provide him with safety. He didn't resist or wake up, but screamed again, and his nightmare sweat soaked both of us.

*

If a tree falls in the forest and no human being is near enough to hear it, then another tree falls in sympathy — across someone's car, or house — in a place where its death will register, even if it kills someone.

My father divorced my mother and married Marsha Simon, who did the accounts for his Talbots franchise. Marsha had exactly the same legs and cheekbones as my mother. My father was round and glossy and emitted the sheen of wealth. His bluff cheeks were polished by the wind that blows only across the decks of yachts, his belly's layers were as expensive as nacred pearl. Filet mignon, Clos de Vougeot, pies made from the tongues of parrots who've been taught to talk. I'd always been his special one, his diamond, his Schatz. When he married Marsha I felt less than human, like the residue left in a test tube after a biochemistry experiment.

I was twenty-five and living in Bridgeport, not doing anything except maybe trying to learn electric bass so I could move to Manhattan and be in a girl group. The Woman That Ate New York. Mom started calling me at all hours of the day and night, weeping. She couldn't live without him, she wished she were dead. Why didn't I come home? I could commute, as many successful people did, on the train.

Go to her, the voices in my head said, but I knew that if I did, she'd dress me up in Peter Pan collars and never let me leave. I suggested therapy and relying on old friends, advice that humiliated my mother. "I forbid you to mention this call to anyone," she'd say. Ten minutes later, she'd ring again, giggling. "Should I squander my alimony on a large-screen TV?"

Then the guest bath sink fell off the wall and onto my mother's big toe. I said get to a doctor, and she didn't call for a week. I confess I was so relieved that I didn't call her, either. Then the phone rang, and an accusatory nurse from Greenwich Hospital told me my mother was going into emergency surgery in order to lose a body part. She said the dreadful word *gangrene*. I knew, and I knew my mother knew, it was my fault for not calling. I got on the next train, with an army duffel packed for a hopeful maximum of three days.

Mom was on a high bed, zonked to the point of clairvoyance. She said, "Watch out! A man will sell you poisoned peanuts," and fell instantly back to sleep, her mouth hanging open. The hall nurse said the operation had been a success — the bone picked out and a chunk of flesh folded and sewn into a toe shape. My mother might even be able to appear in sandals.

By evening visiting hours, my mother was herself again. "A black woman came by and offered me a home in her church. I've never felt so loved. Where were you?"

"I was here at ten and you were raving. So I went to your place to unpack."

My mother's green eyes swirled corelessly.

"I'm going to nurse you back to health," I announced.

On Mom's night table was a funeral arrangement of orange gladioli, roses, daisies, and carnations. Seeing me stare past it, she cooed, "Daddy sent those. Aren't they nice?"

On her last day at the hospital, my mother waited for me in a wheelchair right behind the glass front doors. I progressed along the circular drive toward her as smoothly as one only can in a BMW. She grew bigger and more imposing between flashes of mirrored trees; by the time I'd stopped, she was the size of Abraham Lincoln in his monument. Dismissing the orderly, my mother rose from her wheelchair, resplendent in a chestnut brown Italian knit suit, and said, "I can't look at you in those clothes." I chauffeured us straight to Loehmann's, whence I came out wearing a black skirt, a yellow shirt with a lacy collar, and high-heeled espadrilles.

Then we went to fill my mother's prescriptions. Halcion, Xanax, Demerol. For sleep, for terror, for physical pain: the brown plastic jars were as thick around as sewer pipes. Within two weeks I was stealing pills from her. We drank quarts of Scotch to assist the pills, quarts of prune juice to combat the side effects. Every night at two A.M. we met, floating like specters up and down the steep townhouse stairs with our twin Lanz of Salzburg cotton nighties billowing behind us. During the days, I wore my mother's high-waisted underpants.

Next I was in white light above the clouds, drinking free mini bottles of wine. Overnight I'd become a two-hundred-dollar-a-day consultant; the sight of my arm in a J. G. Hook blazer no longer gave me the slightest pause.

If only I could have photographed the jellied chunk of time I spent under Miami Airport, waiting for the rental agency's minibus. Concourses coiled overhead like the labyrinth of an enormous cement ear; beneath them throbbed a greasy soup of air full of Cuban voices, diesel syncopation, rubber shrieks. The light, a fibrillating green fluorescence, was interrupted by slashes of void between which too-tan women walked past toward imminent reunions, with urgent expressions, toenails painted gold.

My rented maroon Aries weighed nothing and didn't touch the road. I got instantly, totally turned around. Flew over some causeway, drove past pyramids, wagon trains, blue mermaids three stories tall. Forgetting, remembering: where was my motel? I looped back onto dry land where the houses all looked like prisons.

A man ran out in front of me and said, "Don't go no farther this way, miss." I reversed and got even more lost in a crib of tiny streets near the river.

Broken drawbridge, one-way street. The crescent in the bottomless sky matched a piece of neon just then blinking on. Blue Moon. Fall evening in Miami, a perfection so acute it brought on the scent of danger, the sound of crystal shattering. I took a chance, opened the car door.

Tiers of bottles glinted onyx against the purple mirror. Whores on the first four stools, haughty and swollen as blood-fed Masai, kicked their feet in dangerous red shoes. But the bartender nodded at me. Gripped by that dreamy terror under which you cannot retreat, I walked to a stool far back, sat down, and ordered beer and chili.

Severo was already standing behind me, dressed in jeans and a white shirt the lights turned ultraviolet. His round face had an appealing, weary look. He said, "Severo Marquez, at your service. What you doing in here?"

"I got lost," I said. "I'm hungry."

"I can help you." He swooped onto the next stool and was quiet. Then, "Not afraid of her food."

He started telling me how the cook of this famous chili was ruining the life of a Coast Guard. "Basting." This Coast Guard's young wife came in yesterday yelling and waving the Visa bill. "Basting, basting, basting," Severo said tragically. He indicated two men in a booth near the jukebox, a black man with frizzy gray hair and an apple-cheeked blond boy. They looked as harmless as Uncle Remus and Beaver Cleaver. "Basting will ruin your life quicker than anything."

"Basting?" I said. Wet, glittering turkeys broiled behind my eyes.

"You looking for drugs? They told me talk to you, but I said no way. They said yes, sure. I said I'll talk to her myself. I only believe what I see." He peered into my face with the cocked and furrowed expression of a puppy hearing a strange noise. "You a good person. I see that much."

I preferred to be his good person than the low being who'd vowed to stop stealing Xanax from my mother but who somehow had ten of her Demerol stashed inside my purse. This, in spite of the fact that Demerol had no effect on any kind of pain, except for making me not care that I was feeling it.

Mom invited my father to dinner so he could see her plaster cast and blame himself — see that decorating the townhouse of divorce had maimed, was going to kill, her. So she said, out loud. Dad came to the door with two bottles of wine and a red heart full of chocolates which was as big and metallic as a shield. He didn't touch me, just wiped his heavy wingtips on the loon's head mat, his eyes moving from side to side like peeled eggs in a jar of oil.

"The rug color is Whispering Conch," I whispered as I led him through the living room. My mother had gotten her decorator's license, and she chose her colors by name rather than by examination.

My father and I exchanged the conspiratorial glance that said, "We, together, annihilate Mom." I knew the glance would not be repeated for the rest of the evening. I was glad. All my life it had called me into a terrifying existence, where I flew above sleeping villages on flaming, gnashing wings made out of razors. Or something like that.

We tossed his camel coat over the Blarney Green wingback and went into the kitchen. Mom was freshly permed and beaming like an advertisement housewife. In the microwave a chunk of salmon was revolving slowly, its naked pink flesh blasted by terrible rays. Tossing salad, Mom slewed her cast up onto the counter like a ballerina at the barre. Nearly at face level, it screamed "*See me! See me!*" I wondered if Dad noticed her steady pupils, slack jaw, or the tiny smear of toothpaste on her sweater.

It seemed he didn't. He uncorked a bottle, and he and Mom began agreeing. They were so glad I was staying home, taking some time to reexamine my future. I was a genius, I could do anything, I needed a job. Dad had the wonderful idea of setting me up with some interviews. Marsha Simon was going to pull these strings, I knew: she used to work in PR; but hers was the unspeakable Name. I said yes, yes, okay, good, fine, lubricating my throat's lump with Meursault Goutte d'Or.

After dinner Mom refused any valentine chocolates, announcing that she was on a diet. If it were just the two of us she'd chortle, as fat-cheeked as a squirrel, and pop them into her mouth. "What does it matter now? No one cares how I look." Tonight she sat, trapping her loveliness inside unyielding lips. Dad and I ate half the box. We nipped off the bottoms and traded fruit cremes, which he liked, for caramels, my favorite.

Next morning, the empty red heart, the brown crinkly wrappings that had protected each special morsel, turned the kitchen counter into a devastated countryside. Mom had come down during the night and gobbled the remains. Valentine's Day morning: I stood over my snoring mother in her bed, assessed that she'd be dead to the world till noon, crept past her into her bathroom, and stole a couple Xanax. If I started weeping, I'd only weep for years.

I'm eight years old, trying to sleep on the screened porch of our lake cabin. Chirring crickets, damp black smell of the canvas cot that sat folded all winter in a padlocked closet, crawling with silverfish. I'm terrified of the yellow bug light, which casts such black shadows that it turns summer nights into Halloween.

Inside, Mom and Dad are playing gin rummy with Ron and Connie Porter. They all laugh too loudly, ogres in their den.

I think I don't sleep, but I probably do. I wake into the other world when Daddy comes out and sits on the edge of my bed. Two black holes he has for eyes. He likes Mrs.

Porter better than he likes my mother, who's a bitch and doesn't satisfy him. Do I understand? His mouth smells lovely, like pine needles.

I pretend to be very sleepy, falling asleep, soft and boneless as an earthworm when he takes me in his arms. "But you, you're my angel. Mr. Peanut wants a kiss from you," he says. "Want to kiss Mr. Peanut's head?" His fingers, like pliers, break open my teeth.

I send my mind under the black water to the other side of the lake, where the Indians live. They'll steal me deep into the woods. Torture me, yes, but when I show my bravery they'll say: "Little Broken Paw, you're ours. You're an Indian now."

My job interviews were all the same. Dressed as someone else, I rocked gently southward on Conrail, peering down into Harlem's bitter canyons. "I'm fascinated by the (advertising, gallery, magazine, news, accounting) industry," I said to Jeanne Whittington at Beedy and Whittington, Orian Green at Channel Ten, Pablo Respucci at Fitch Gallery, Velta Cloud at *Children's Digest,* Hank Rosengard at Fuller and Peabody, David Fusilier at Asia Arts. "When I finish killing my mother I might want to work for you."

That's not what I really said, that last part.

"How was your interview?" she'd ask when I got home. She'd pour Beaujolais while I gave her Orian Green's lift of her plucked and penciled eyebrows, or Pablo Respucci's putting his fingertip into his nose and then looking to see if anything was stuck to it. We'd go upstairs, lie on her bed, and watch Judge Wapner on her huge TV. Some time before dinner, she'd stub her toe on the couch and scream, or slice her finger chopping parsley. We'd disappear to our separate bathrooms, tranquilize, and reconvene in the kitchen for dreadful confidences. She told me that whenever my father made love to her, he was like an avalanche that crushed her and kept on rolling. But she'd gotten used to him, she couldn't imagine anyone else.

"Come rub my back," she'd say when we had eaten. We lay together on the ice floe of her king-sized bed. Her shoulder, turned away, seemed as far off as a distant range of hills; as my fingers pulled at her dry white skin, she'd weep silently. When at last she began to snore, I'd creep off to my room and mount one of the guest beds. They were twins, so springy, high, and narrow that they seemed alive with a will to buck me off. And having absorbed my mother through my fingertips, I could never get to sleep. I'd made a point not to take her sleeping pills: something bad might happen if I slept too deeply.

Red dawn always found me half on fire. As the weeks passed, my eyeballs turned to steel wool; I forgot things, placed my wallet in the freezer, wore my sweaters wrong side out. I began to fear I'd go insane, like those prisoners who, deprived of dreams, begin dreaming awake, and permanently lose their reason.

The day my mother said she'd had an assignation with my father at a motel on the Merritt Parkway, I knew I had to get out. Her face looked like a test pattern; her brain emitted a hum.

My next interview was with Jim Banks at the Mach Corporation, an old friend of my father's. Jim hired the kid my parents always wanted — a perky, bright go-getter — to analyze the agricultural economy of the Dominican Republic. She'd produce a report full of graphs and tables, proving that Mach's nematicide would cause the countryside to bloom, dollars to flow in, and the national debt to vanish.

"Can I mention birth control?" I asked Jim.

"Heck, no. That's between them and the Pope."

He gave me an expense account number so I could buy a ticket to Miami, where Mach's Latin American archives were kept.

Business was much too easy; I felt like a robber.

"We're so proud of you," my mother said, "your father and I."

I rolled into Mach's Miami office at a quarter to eleven, wearing Severo's shirt. Some secretary in New York had screwed up my reservations, I lied to Pablo Maldonado, my new Dominican supervisor. He coughed and said he'd tried to reach me at the motel I'd never gone to. We had to fly to Santo Domingo that same afternoon because of last fall's hurricane and the death of the Liberator.

"My bag's in my car," I said brightly. I called Severo at the Fina station where he worked as a mechanic. European cars. He said, "You know where I live. Have fun, Mami."

Again I roared through white light. Once, I looked out the window and saw Severo's island lying still in the blue Caribbean, shaped like the Lacoste alligator. Pablo Maldonado talked a lot, his pointed tongue licking in and out of separated incisors. He had a cannibal's mouth in his wide, flat Indian face. After two glasses of Jack Daniel's, he confessed that today was his grandmother's ninetieth birthday and I was his excuse to fly home. Forget the Liberator, forget the hurricane. I nodded, as if I understood that family bonds were everything. Being who I was now, the child prodigy, I refused any liquor, drinking zesty blood instead from a thimble-sized can.

The airport lay close upon the ground; the Dominican wind was like exhaled breath. Ours was the only car on the narrow cement highway that led straight to the Maldonado family home. First, a wall glittering with fangs of broken glass. Next, a gigantic pile of dark mango-colored cement, its windows filigreed with black iron. In the patio a band played itchy music for a hundred guests who gobbled yellow rice. Grandmother sat in state, a bediamonded, black-clad mummy with a loud voice. We toasted her still endless future in raw red Spanish wine. From time to time she bent sideways and whispered to her middle-aged daughter, who sat beside her, also dressed in black. Against this morbid vision I took out two Demerol and swallowed them like vitamin C, right there at the table.

That night Pablo took me to a cement cave that smelled of mildewed air conditioning filter, where something electric kept making a sound like Band-Aids ripped from skin. This was the capital's finest restaurant. In the blue light his eyes were like more caves, or more mouths, more rooms within the artificial cave. I drank white Rioja until my blood screeched acidly, fingernails on a chalkboard. When the food came I could neither see nor taste it.

I let the cannibal intrude himself into my room, and into me. His back arched and hard as a turtle's shell, he pushed and moaned. "Ay, preciosa, ay, mi ángel." I stared past the hump of his neck, feeling utterly deadly boredom. Severo would understand all this; he grew up on a corrupt island not so far from here.

I woke alone, in a howling vacuum. During the night, some ghost had latched onto the back of my head and sucked out my brains, my soul, and my sense of location. I took two Demerol (leaving only six), drank four glasses of brackish tap water full of barely invisible worms, and then ventured out of my room.

I found the lobby's thin decor failing to keep at bay an impression of national poverty. Outside, a ribby white dog nuzzled a pile of garbage. People walked by, slowly; they were fat and shiny, like balloons, but I could see that they lacked purpose, energy, and motivation. After some time Pablo marched in, flanked by two murderers. He greeted me as a gentleman to a lady and introduced me to bodyguards Simon and Lucho. I was excited by the flat German pistols jammed into their back pockets, hiking the tails of their pale guayaberas. We drove to the Min-

istry of Agriculture in an open Jeep along an avenue of
crooked palms. The sky sang with yellow and green light.
I felt important.

Simon's and Lucho's hard shoes clopped up three
flights of terrazzo stairs to the air-conditioned office of
the Ministro. He was an enormous Fidel in tan polyester;
I stood before him in the rumpled clothes of my mother,
right down to the control-top panty hose that flattened
my pubic hair like run-over snakes. I wished I'd worn
panties; I felt less clothed than trapped in a dismaying
form of nakedness.

The Ministro sneered at Pablo Maldonado, so that I
felt a squirming sympathy with him and hoped last night
had shored up his honor as a man.

Timidly, I asked the Ministro about coffee production
after the hurricane. He ordered Lucho into the closet. I
registered that the bodyguards protected the Ministro,
not me. Lucho brought out five kilos of government pam-
phlets, according to the airport's baggage scale.

Severo wasn't at the Fina. I stayed at Mach until eleven
P.M. massaging statistics and then cruised over to the
Blue Moon. The bartender said Severo would be around.

Now that I'd returned to it, the Blue Moon felt like
home. There were the cook and his Coast Guard, still
looking like Uncle Remus and Beaver Cleaver. They chat-
ted awhile, then vanished into the back.

"Sad story," I remarked to the bartender, who was in
soapy water up to his elbows.

"*She* finally left him," the bartender said. "Got another guy."

"Smart," I said.

"Some are blind, others have eyes to see."

End of conversation. Was the heaviness of the silence
meant for me? It went on and on until its meaning, if it
had one, was exhausted.

Shortly I heard Severo's motorcycle. He came in,

headed for the back, and would have walked right past me had I not swiveled on my stool and stuck my leg into his path.

"Mami, I didn't expect you back tonight. Why did you come here? I didn't tell you to come here."

The bartender toweled his arms. He went out and fed the jukebox, which started twanking and insinuating. "We were talking. About the space between us all. And the people. Who hide themselves behind the walls. Of illusion!"

"I was looking for you," I said. Severo put his arms around my shoulders and twisted me from side to side on my barstool, tiny arcs. "This place is no good for a girl like you."

I shrugged, and pulled out a sheaf of photocopies I'd made of my naked body back at Mach after the cleaning lady left. "I was thinking about you."

"Ay, Mami," Severo said, riffling through them. "Meet me at home. Here's the key. I got to use the facilities a minute."

I went out into the dark like a lonesome experiment. When I opened Severo's padlock I saw his room for the first time, a plywood box painted with black enamel. The transistor radio was dismally playing. I lay on the bed and masturbated. Then I went out to the hall toilet, but an old man was standing there pissing with the door open.

There was nothing in Severo's drawers except a Gideon Bible and a slip of paper from the government saying Welfare would no longer cover abortions. When he came back we made love in seven ways, until I was tired.

Not calling my mother was like sitting on an overfull suitcase that had me inside it. Like trying to extend the clicking of a time bomb: the longer I waited, the worse it was going to be when I called. So I didn't call.

"I went to an island like your island," I told Severo in

a child's voice. "I saw palm trees. I smelled flowers." Severo told me that the town his family came from was divided in half like a brain. His family had started on the good side but moved to the bad side.

I felt as if I were in love with Severo.

My pesticide report sang out from underneath my fingers.

"It may surprise us to know that when it comes to agriculture, the force of life — as represented by fertilizer — can be less important than the force of death, embodied in pesticides. Kissed by Caribbean breezes and blessed by God with fertile mountains, the Dominican Republic has no need to call further upon the force of life. It has a powerful life force at its beck and call. But this life force carries liabilities, carries dangers. In the fertile womb of the tropics, a myriad of pests is engendered along with the helpful plants and creatures. Those who steer the Dominican Republic toward its future may wish to consider taking a firm hand to channel the force of life along productive and profitable courses. For this purpose, the Mach Corporation suggests its most efficient nematicide — Iratan."

Mom called Mach's office every single day, but I told the receptionist not to take my personal calls. No, not any, none. "It is only your mother," said the receptionist. She was a nice Cuban girl in a red cardigan with pearls. "My mother is a pill freak," I told her. "*Drogadicta,*" a word I'd learned from Severo.

I was wearing one of Severo's Indian cotton shirts again; they'd become a habit. They were always clean, ironed, but they smelled so sharply of engine grease that I couldn't walk past the receptionist without wondering when I was going to be found out. After what I'd said about my mother, she no longer looked at me, however.

The five days I worked on the report, I took one ritual

Demerol each morning, a placebo to forget about my mother. The day I finished the report and the pills, I called her, knowing it was her Tuesday hair appointment. Her machine said, "If you have any information about my lost child, *please* leave a message. If you *are* my lost child, *please* call. I've had a tiny accident." I told the machine I was still working, which was a lie, of course: I planned to spend a few days at the beach with Severo. "Burning in the sun," he said poetically, "then burning up some popcorn, then burning up in bed. I wish you was my wife, Mami."

I called my father, who said, "She had a fender bender. But why haven't you called? She's beside herself. She calls me every day."

"Now you see what it's like," I told him.

"I already know what it's like," he said.

Maldonado handed me a three-thousand-dollar check, which included a bonus. He loved the format I'd developed, and if I wanted to produce a series of similar reports for Mach's Third World clients, I was welcome to return. They'd even increase my pay.

Birds falling out of the sky, brown peasant babies sucking at the green lips of contaminated Coke bottles. I said, sadly, that I didn't know if I could do it again.

"It's been more than a pleasure," Pablo said. "I hope all goes well for you."

I bit my upper lip and pressed his hand, flesh known and used. Walking out of his office, I had an illuminating thought. "Can you give me this in cash?"

Severo met me at the Taurus Steak House, looking beautiful in his jeans, a tux coat, and a narrow red and black tie he'd bought at the Salvation Army. We ordered sirloins and champagne, food that means the good life. Everyone stared at us; I knew they must be envious of our sex. What else can people think of when they see a black man and a white woman together?

Severo told me someone was coming to meet him, but it wouldn't take long. We were having Martell and chocolate cake, and my bare foot was softly kneading Severo's crotch under the table, when the man in the yellow T-shirt arrived.

I put my foot back on the floor.

"Hi, Severo," the man said. "This your wife?" His eyes were blue, cold chips; his yellow T-shirt was a small, with French-cut sleeves, to show off his muscles. The man was a weapon, a Weimaraner.

"I wish," Severo said, meaning it. I rubbed his calf under the table. "What you need, Ernest?"

"I need you to start your motorcycle on the thirteen-hundred block of Tigertail tonight."

"Fine."

"Take your muffler off. I want it real loud. Three A.M."

"Okay, Ernest."

"Pretty lady," Ernest said, appraising me entirely in a glance.

He left.

I said, "What's that?"

Severo said, "If you don't know, don't ask."

A young man dying ugly. Black blood against the wall of some sea green cinderblock complex, cheap apartments with a name. Del-Mar. Maybe it was going to be the Coast Guard. Maybe this bad man was the wife's new lover.

"Don't you go," I said.

"Mami, it's my life," Severo said. "I owe that man a favor. Sometimes you have to take care of things before they take care of you."

A man with pliers hands. Who'd break my teeth, crack my throat, take care of me with a silent bullet. I'd be getting on a plane before I ever sat alone in Severo's room.

I changed the subject. "This money. I'd like to turn it into an ounce of toot, maybe I could sell when I get home."

Severo looked at me in disbelief. "You, Mami? That's a stupid plan. You just gonna to use it up. You better get away from your mother now."

I stared at him with righteous determination. There was a stony moment, which neither of us yielded. "This money is pure pesticide," I said. "I feel like blowing it."

Severo shrugged, blew through his lips like an exhausted horse. "*Claro,* go ahead and blow it. It's your life, Mami."

"Can we get it right now? Please?"

We rode a hundred miles an hour on Severo's black bike to a numberless house at the edge of the Glades. It was the first time he'd let me on his motorcycle; up to now, he'd maintained that I was too precious for the risk. A woman peeked at us through the chain lock and said, "What you doin', Severo. Bringin' someone here. He's not home."

"Tell him he's my brother," Severo said. "I'll wait."

"He ain't home, I said."

"Shit damn. Okay, I'll call you later."

Severo took me back to his place but said he had to go out again right away. "What a fucking night, Mami. Shit damn. My brother always come home by ten o'clock. He must have run into trouble. Or why she's not letting me in? I call you in an hour."

"Okay," I said, but as soon as he left, the air turned hydrochloric and I had to go. I left a thousand in cash on Severo's dresser because he was more trapped in his life than I was in mine. He must be back out there hammering on that dealer's door, with one thing on his mind: not to lose the contact.

In case I was wrong, I drove my rent-a-car to the Blue Moon to see if he was there. No, but the cook and the Coast Guard were in their booth as usual. I wanted to ask them questions, but the floor was melting and I might fall through it. Instead, I called some airlines from the pay phone.

So, I had two thousand dollars and a reservation on the red-eye to Manhattan. Not to mention the expense account number, the rented car, the key to a Greenwich townhouse, and one end of that fraying thread that anchored my mother's life. It all seemed like a lot, probably since most of it was things I didn't want.

I could get a room at the Chelsea, where Dylan wrote that famous song, sit in some room that smelled like cockroach poison. Hope that whatever seemed to be chasing me didn't catch up. Think what to do, besides go back to her.

LA VICTOIRE

The 707 bus is behind schedule and jammed with men from the downtown Buenos Aires racetrack, the kind of men who smoke harsh, short cigarettes and expose themselves to young girls. Victoria stands close to the driver, pressed among swaying bodies, wishing she did not have to breathe and that the bus would go faster.

A block ahead, she sees the railroad barrier suddenly fall across the road. That's it, she thinks, a sign. I will die before I see Paris. As the bus lurches to a stop, the slick-combed head of a seated man bumps against her fingers. He is blond; a book lies open on his lap, but he is gazing out the window with an expression almost of sadness. It appears that he has not noticed anything, so Victoria does not apologize.

A yellow train passes, but the barrier remains closed for the northbound express.

Victoria's first French lesson begins in ten minutes, and she will be late. She is wearing all new clothes for the occasion, and in her purse she carries ninety thousand pesos, full advance payment for six weeks of classes with Monique Gilbert, who holds a license from the French government. Sixty thousand of these pesos came from typing the manuscript of a dull book about multinational corporations; thirty thousand from a report about insect parts found in the tomato paste produced at a provincial factory. There were so many charts and tables that it took Victoria two weeks of nights to finish the work even though she has a year's experience as a typing teacher at the Pan American Academy of Secretaries and Office Workers.

Here is her dream: a man waits for her on the runway in Paris. He wears a wrinkled suit of white linen and a blue shirt; the breeze from jet engines has flung his thin tie back over one shoulder. She descends from the airplane and they kiss eagerly, using their tongues. Together they ride to the hotel in a shiny black car. Later, silver drops of condensation run down the sides of an ice bucket while they lie close together, touching each other's bodies under a thin sheet.

The bus ride lasts for an unbearably long time. Victoria and the man in Paris buy a house in the country and drive downtown each day in a Peugeot 504. They visit the Eiffel Tower and, at the top, he photographs her in profile as she looks out over the city.

Someone is breathing softly on Victoria's neck.

"Oh," moans a man's voice behind her shoulder, "oh, to be the sun and make you thirst for water." The voice gains volume. "Oh, to be a fork and pierce that potato." Victoria feels that her body has been instantly transformed into something as cold and deadly as the blade of a sword. These things do not happen to me! Without looking around, she pulls the bus's stop cord.

As she moves to the door, her skirt catches on the metal edge of a bus seat. She half notices but does not stop: her right hand crosses over the left to catch a handrail, her feet shuffle sideways like a crab's. Soft green fabric pulls, stretching along one thread into a mortifying line of puckers. Everyone stares. The bus driver races the engine and plays a few notes on his scale of electric horns. Someone, perhaps the young blond man, releases Victoria; she finds herself on the pavement, and the bus roars away, belching insolent fumes.

Alone on the sidewalk, she hunches, scratching one plum-colored fingernail along the pulled hem. Three weeks ago, her mother gave her two new outfits and said, "Happy twenty-ninth birthday. We were wearing the same styles when I was your age. Isn't that funny? You were just learning to walk." Victoria has forgotten what she said to her mother, but now in the empty street she continues the conversation as though her mother could hear her. "I know you want me to catch a man in these new clothes, Mama. I know you think it's too late. But what about you? Your husband has run away and you say you don't understand."

A woman pushing a baby carriage is coming around the corner. Victoria bites the thread, exposing for an instant the dark tops of her stockings. Brushing the skirt into smooth folds, she raises her head and hurries off down the pavement, her purse bumping, bumping away from her hip. She will have to walk six blocks to reach the French teacher's respectable suburban address.

There is no doorbell at Number 986, Street of the Viceroys. Victoria opens the front gate and walks timidly up a row of sandstones to knock at a heavy wooden door.

A tanned young woman's face appears at the open upstairs window.

"Monique is in the back," the woman says. "Go out again and in on the other side of the hedge."

Here, at a gate of twisted wire, is a buzzer. Victoria pushes the black button and then walks in, down a narrow muddy path between shoulder-high hedges. She steps over a child's stick horse and a little red shoe. In the back yard she can see a thatched hut, a few trees, and a beach umbrella. The hedge is infested with snails.

"Watch out for the dog!" cries the voice of Monique Gilbert. "Come here, Froufrou!" There are dog noises and scufflings.

"It's all right, now I've got him. I'll lock him up." The voice is hoarse, dark, deep for a woman's; it rolls *r*'s in a thrilling way. The long, fine hairs on Victoria's arms stand out. She wonders what French word she will learn to say first: the word for love? the word for the toilet? Good afternoon? She stands helpless on the scrap of lawn.

"*Bonjour, Mademoiselle Victoire*," says Monique Gilbert, emerging from behind the thatched hut. "Or are you *Madame*? I am Monique. You are late."

"Yes," says Victoria in a voice so meek it could have come from one of the snails. The French teacher is naked. No, the French teacher is wearing a black bikini, three tiny pieces of cloth connected by threads and gilded rings that cut deeply into pale, slack, aging flesh.

The French teacher is also wearing high-heeled slippers of gold plastic and an ankle bracelet. She looks fifty-five years old. Victoria closes her eyes and receives small dry kisses on both cheeks.

"This is how we greet in France," says Monique Gilbert. "Now, come in, sit down, and excuse me while I put on some clothes. I was just sunning myself; I thought you had changed your mind about me."

I think I am changing it now, thinks Victoria, trying not to look at the teacher's sagging buttocks. Have you no shame, to walk around like this?

At least, she thinks more generously, this Monique has the decency to pull a curtain while she dresses.

Sitting very composed in a canvas chair, Victoria inspects the hut's single room like a spy looking for evidence. The woman obviously lives here: there are win-

dow shades, and the thatch has been coated inside with
cement to keep out the rain. A small gas bottle with a
burner for cooking. Two canvas chairs, one wicker that
hangs by a rope from the ceiling; a couch that must be
used for sleeping, and a huge green and white map of
France. Except for an ashtray overflowing with filterless
cigarette butts, everything is very clean.

Books on a small shelf: *Madame Bovary,* dictionaries,
French books, *The Oriental Manual of Love with 57
Positions and Photographs.* The French teacher sweeps
aside the curtain. Now she is dressed in blue jeans, a
man's shirt, and the same gold sandals.

"*Voilà!*" she says. "Now, if my feet will kindly stop
hurting me, we can get down to business, Mademoiselle
Victoire Fernández." Victoria has never heard her name
pronounced this way before, with accents in the wrong
places and one syllable chopped off altogether.

"Is something wrong with your feet?" she asks politely.

"Oh, they are deformed," says the teacher, settling
heavily into the hanging chair. "They hurt all the time,
and the heels won't go down flat, see?" She removes the
sandals, one with each hand, and waves her legs at Victoria. "They don't look so bad. But I have this curse, that
I may never wear low shoes. At least I am not a man."

"No," says Victoria. "Should I have brought some
paper?"

The chair groans and twists on its rope; the teacher
throws down her shoes and places her feet in them.

"First you must learn to say your name, and then we
will have coffee, Victoire. Say after me, Vic-toirrre."

"Victwad."

"Veek-toirrre. In the back of the throat. As though you
were going to spit."

"Veek-twagh." Is this how people will say my name in
Paris?

"Better. Do you take sugar? I have no milk."

"Yes, please."

" 'Yes, please, Monique,' is easy to say."

"Monique . . . did you ever live in Paris?"

"Once, as a child." The teacher stands up, walks slowly to the sink, and begins filling a pan with water. "But I wouldn't go back for all the money in the world. Why? Because life is more interesting here."

Maybe your life is more interesting, Victoria thinks. I hate it here.

"Victoire, how old are you?" asks the teacher warmly as she settles again in her chair. "Myself, I am forty-eight. *Divorcée.* I have no secrets."

"I am twenty-nine and my boyfriend works in a bank," says Victoire, the lie rolling off her tongue of its own accord.

"Ah, you have a fiancé. Say it, *un fiancé.*"

"*Fiancé.*"

The word hangs in the air like a perfect rose.

"*Très bien!* And now I must grind the beans."

Victoria sets her purse on the floor. "Who lives in the front house?" she asks while the teacher's back is turned.

"My sister and her husband and the children live upstairs. My mother lives on the bottom, and she allows my father to use one room. She says he never takes a bath."

"Oh," says Victoria.

"Now. *Ma mère*, my mother. *Mon père*, my father. Say them. I will write them down for you. I do not use books because we learn, first, by talking. Like babies. *Comme les bébés.* Now say: *Ma mère. Mon père. Les bébés.* We are starting with the facts of life. And yes, you must bring a notebook next time."

At the end of three weeks, Victoria can see the map of France in her sleep. She can make sentences for combing hair, riding the bus, detesting tomatoes. At the Pan American Academy, she gives her pupils secret French names and thinks in French about them as she listens to their hesitant clacking on twenty-four ancient black typewriters: "*Je déteste Léonie. J'aime Suzanne. Hélène est belle.*" She finds it strange that the same word is used for loving a man, liking a woman, and liking to eat meringues.

Once, she calls her mother a species of hairy cucumber and then runs out of the room, choking with laughter.

Victoria also knows that Monique's husband was a secret homosexual for fifteen years before he asked for a divorce. She has seen Monique's nephews and niece prance naked through the yard on their stick horses. She has seen Monique's mother chase her husband out of the house, throwing shoes at his head and screaming things that Monique patiently translates: "Filthy beast," "Vile creature," "You stink of shit."

Monique had a lover who was a trade unionist, a martyr of the Communist cause in Chile. A poster of his face with one of his poems hangs in the hut: "I fight for my brothers, working like ants underground," it begins. "And for my sisters, flying like doves in the sky." Gerardo, Monique's newest lover, is a doctor with a heart condition. His skin has a greenish tinge, and he wears a large gold and silver crucifix around his neck. He comes to visit Monique one afternoon during the lesson and sits on the bed looking at magazines. He does not speak French. Victoria wonders how many of the positions Gerardo and Monique have tried, sure that they could not perform some of the contortions demonstrated in the manual by two, sometimes three, acrobatic-looking Orientals in leotards.

And somehow, with the regularity of taxis setting out from a crowded stand, lies upon lies have come out of the mouth of Mademoiselle Victoire. Her fiancé is named Ramón; he likes to make love with the lights on. Her father died accidentally while hunting boars on the pampas: he was shot by one of his friends. Her mother, no longer the principal of a grubby nursery school for the children of laborers, has become a pale wraith of a woman who spends all day at a wooden prayer stand, begging the saints to prevent Victoria from marrying Ramón. Ramón, who is growing a mustache, who has stopped wearing hair oil because Victoria said it made him smell like a prostitute.

It seems to Victoria that the more outrageous the history of Mademoiselle Victoire, the more eagerly Monique believes and presses for details. "But how can you go on seeing such a monster?" Monique demands when Victoria complains that Ramón does not want her to use birth control in order that she will become pregnant and force their marriage.

"He does not control everything I do," says Victoire, calmly blowing a smoke ring. "Besides, he is a fantastic lover."

That Friday night, Victoria and her mother decide to go out to dinner together at The King of Beefsteak, where they always go. Under the purplish neon lights her mother's lips look unnaturally bright, pinkish orange. Roaming among the tables, a scrawny photographer proclaims: "Everybody comes out good-looking!" For two thousand pesos, he takes their portrait with his American camera, mounts it on cardboard, and presents it to them with a flourish. Their four eyes have turned out red, like beasts'.

"I wish your father would come back," says Victoria's mother, inspecting the picture as though she might find him in it, seated at a table in the background. "I don't care if he has been living with naked Indians in the jungle." Victoria imagines her father sitting on a low wooden stool, smiling at the caresses of a dozen pygmy women whose bodies are smeared with different-colored paints. She places a hand on her mother's arm.

"Ah, Blessed Virgin," sighs Victoria's mother, dabbing wine and tears from her chin with a napkin. "Ah, Holy Heaven. He was a fool, but I loved him."

Victoria allows for a short interval of silence.

"Mama," she says softly. "I have always wondered whether I should tell you this. You never knew it, but Father had a lover. Here in Buenos Aires."

"What!" Her mother's face seems ready to break into several pieces. Victoria continues. "I saw them on the river beach one day. At first they were kissing on the sand, lying down. The woman had on a black bathing suit and gold sandals, but she took them off when they went into the water. Father was smiling. They played tag in the water, but they didn't see me."

Her mother draws a shaking breath; tears squeeze from under her closed eyelids and wash clean lines through the powder on her cheeks.

"You are lying to me," her mother says. "Take me home."

In the jungle, Victoria's father joins hands with the pygmy women and they all dance in a circle around his empty throne.

Set aside for conjugations, the fourth week of classes is the hardest so far for both teacher and student. Monique writes down all the tenses and persons for the verb "to love," because it is so amusingly regular in grammar at least; "to be" and "to have," which are very complicated; and "to suck," because Victoria wants to speak French to Ramón.

"*Ma chérie!* But you are funny sometimes," exclaims Monique indulgently.

Victoria takes the lists to the academy and types them over and over. She also finds more work to pay for a second six weeks: the studies of a woman naturalist in Tierra del Fuego, the new budget and bylaws of a small riding club.

On Thursday afternoon, Monique pronounces Victoire's progress extraordinary and says it is time for a little celebration.

"Some friends of mine are having a party Saturday at a club downtown. I invite you to come," she says. "All of them speak Spanish, so you can bring Ramón. And you can tell your mother you'll be spending the night with me: she'll believe that, won't she?" The two of them have discussed Victoire's difficulties in finding times and places to make love with her fiancé; in fact, Monique herself seems to have a talent for scheming, and together they have kept Mademoiselle's mother almost completely in the dark.

"Well," says Victoire. Luckily, that very day on the bus, she made a plan in case Monique should ever try to arrange a meeting with Ramón. "That would be, um, *merveilleux?* But I have to see if I can drag my fiancé away from his psychoanalytic theater group. They are meeting on Saturdays this month." She sets her mouth in a little smile.

"I would like to be introduced, so try," urges Monique. "Tell him he'll shrink his brains to the size of a raisin. But, if he insists, maybe you will meet someone who does not want you to have babies."

That night, Victoria locks herself into the bathroom at home while her mother is cooking. She takes off her clothes and stands on the toilet, inspecting her naked body from all angles in the mirror above the sink. She has never had a man. She wonders what she will say to Monique's French friends. I am not yet a woman, so how can I have children?

In the morning she stops to buy cigarettes at the candy stand across the street from the academy. Felipe, the owner, gives her a free packet of violet-scented breath mints.

"Such a lovely creature should not go around with

breath like anyone's," he tells her. "Suck one of these, and the men will come flocking around your mouth like bees around a flower."

"Thank you very much," Victoria says. "I will take them even though I do not need them. You see, I have been stung before."

"I see," says Felipe, leering. "At least you did not swell up." He laughs and makes a large encircling gesture with his arms in front of his stomach.

Je suce le bonbon, thinks Victoria in class, I suck the candy. It tastes like perfume, and she spits it into the wastebasket.

But I will keep the rest of the packet, she thinks, as a reminder of the sweetness we had together, my lover and I, before our destinies tore us apart. He was North Korean; he looked very much like the Indians of the southern Amazon. Last year his government assigned him to spend the rest of his life in Paraguay as an underground Communist agitator, and I refused to go with him. Once he wrote me a letter with no return address: he was spending his days in a village bar, telling the peasants about oppression. These were his favorite candies, but he could not get them there. Now I do not know where he lives, or even if he lives. This is how I was stung. This is why I must go to Paris and forget.

Just then Lourdes, the shorthand teacher, comes to knock at the open door of the typing classroom. "Would you like to have coffee after work?" Lourdes asks. "I am meeting my new boyfriend, a Sicilian, a sergeant in the army, but he can't come until four-thirty and I want someone to sit with me till then."

"All right," says Victoria. "I should be finished here at a quarter till."

At the sandwich shop next door, she and Lourdes chatter and laugh over cups of syrupy, bitter espresso. Lourdes is the biggest gossip of all the academy teachers.

She has just found out that the owner of the school, a plump and balding man in his late thirties, is probably having an affair with Leoncia Jiménez, the tallest of the students and one of the least intelligent. What is more, Lourdes is having an interesting time with the Sicilian: he is married, and he says his wife always undresses in the closet. Victoria agrees that nothing could be worse than that.

"I think it is better not to get married, ever," Victoria is saying as the Sicilian walks into the restaurant. "You should have seen the way my father behaved. Is that your boyfriend? He's handsome."

The Sicilian introduces himself as Luis, orders a coffee, and then lapses into an awkward silence.

"What were we talking about?" Lourdes says. "Oh, your family."

"Yes," says Victoria, tossing her hair. "It's just that my father was always giving things away. He gave everything away."

"Really? Like what?" says Luis.

"Oh, he would come home in winter and take away the gas heater for a friend he had met in a bar the night before, things like that." Victoria takes the last sip of her espresso and then places the cup carefully back on its saucer. "No one could make him see reason until the day the living room couch disappeared. That night my mother kicked him out of bed and he had to sleep in the armchair. In the morning he spat on the floor at her feet and announced he was taking the car on a trip to the north, to sell a load of plastic-coated tablecloths. We didn't know where he got them."

"How awful," says Lourdes. "And you haven't seen him since?"

"No," says Victoria. "He called my mother up from a public telephone to say the car had blown up and he had sold it. Nothing after that, and that was two years ago."

"How awful," Lourdes repeats. "And your poor mother!"

Luis nods.

Sometimes I go beyond myself, Victoria thinks. "Not really," she says. "She was glad to get rid of him. My mother is easily bored. It is a trait I must have inherited from her."

"We have to go," says Luis.

"See you Monday," says Lourdes.

"I hope you two enjoy yourselves," says Victoria. As soon as they have disappeared she walks to the counter and asks the waiter for a glass of mineral water. She chooses a seat near the wall and begins reading a row of signs posted above the menu: "Mother, the only light in the dark clouds of this world." "May God give you twice what you desire for me." At the pay telephone next to her, a young man is shouting into the receiver with one finger stuck in his ear.

"Listen!" he screams. "You can't do this to me! It's barbarous!" He slams the telephone into its cradle and stands still for a moment, looking around at the tiny tables. Most of them are occupied. He sits down on the stool beside Victoria and orders a fried steak and a beer. Victoria tries to read more signs through the water in her tilted glass, but the letters are wavy and indecipherable. The young man is blond and bearded, like Ramón: like the young man who helped me get off the bus that day of my first lesson with Monique, Victoria suddenly remembers. His eyes are wide and blue, and the white shows all the way around, as though he has just had a surprising idea.

Suddenly he hides his face in his hands. "I have been betrayed," he moans so that Victoria can hear. "Beasts in human form." Victoria reads through the bottom of her empty glass: "Cash only." "I love the tango because it tastes of Death."

The young man clutches her arm. "Tell me," he says. "Have you ever given everything you had for something? And then . . . and then been crucified?"

"No!" shrieks Victoria. "What do you want?" The young man blinks; slowly, he releases her arm. There is bitterness in his smile, Victoria thinks.

"I have made a fool of myself," he says, and turns his head toward the wall. "Two plus two is four, but the heavens are empty." The waiter brings his beer, and he takes a large gulp. Victoria lifts the strap of her purse over one shoulder.

"No, please, wait," says the young man, grabbing her arm again. "Will you let me explain? I don't always behave like this." He stares at Victoria. He is a well-bred man caught in some desperate situation. He is intelligent and deeply emotional; he has values. Perhaps his fiancée has left him.

"I should go home," she says, looking pointedly at the hand on her arm.

"I'll come with you. I have to talk to somebody. I can't sit here alone just now."

Victoria places her purse on her lap. The young man releases her arm and places his two hands side by side on the counter, palms down; his long fingers dance in order, as though he were a piano player gently practicing.

"My name is Raimundo," he says. "I have just suffered a tragedy." He pauses, looking up from his fingers into Victoria's eyes. "Will you listen to me?"

"I guess so," says Victoria, thinking: yes.

The young man continues slowly. "A political tragedy. Personal, in a way." I was wrong about the girlfriend, Victoria thinks, and wonders whether she should ask if he is a Communist. He looks like one, she decides: his hair is not quite combed and he wears a dark blue military jacket that once had insignias sewn on the sleeves. The jacket is too big: he is on the thin side, Raimundo.

She notes, too, that he looks five or six years younger than she; this fact is somehow reassuring.

"It was something like a coup d'état," Raimundo begins, slicing off a bite of steak and stabbing it with his fork. "Conspiracy among the lieutenants." He puts the meat in his mouth and chews it gloomily. "Am I boring you?" Victoria can think of nothing interesting to say.

"Are you a Marxist? No, I am not bored," she says.

"Not exactly," he says. "Are you?" Victoria shakes her head. She is watching the motion of his lips. Like bees around a flower, she thinks.

"Yesterday I was the chairman of the Union of Radical Students at the National Faculty of Agronomy and Veterinary Science," he says. "Today I am nothing. I have just been deposed."

"Monstrous," Victoria says. "Why?"

Raimundo's pink tongue darts out to lick the golden hairs of his mustache. He makes a small, exasperated smacking noise, then sighs, and says, "They are calling me a revisionist. I thought we could get what we want by talking." For a year now, he explains, veterinary students have been agitating to get a new laboratory and buildings of their own. He himself had reached an understanding in private conference with the Ministers of Education and Agronomy. But his followers were not convinced: and this very afternoon they have called a student strike.

"Even now," Raimundo says, "the Radical Students are slaughtering a sheep on the steps of the university and building a fire to roast it. Oh, the thought is unbearable." He pushes his plate away. "Do you want to go to the movies?"

"I should go home," Victoria says without conviction.

"I'll pay for you. Please? I am in your debt."

"Well, all right." Victoria's heart beats very fast. I like you, Raimundo, she thinks, even though I know what Felipe would say, I know what my mother would say, I know what the waiter must be thinking. She imagines herself at the party telling someone that she has found a new lover, a man whose kisses are like apricots.

As they walk to the cinema she remembers something Monique has told her: that for the past hundred years, architects in Buenos Aires have been copying their designs from Paris.

"Buenos Aires looks a lot like Paris," she says in a conversational tone.

"Have you been to Paris?"

"I lived there as a child," says Mademoiselle Victoire. "But I wouldn't go back there for all the money in the world."

"That's interesting," says Raimundo. "Why not?"

"Bad things happened to me there," she says.

In the darkness of the movie house, the face of John Wayne looms on the screen like a huge moon. Raimundo's elbow touches hers on the shared armrest; Victoria cannot pay attention to the film. She sighs and moves lower in the seat.

Somewhere in a red canyon he kisses her. His mustache prickles softly on Victoria's upper lip; it smells like new shoes. Behind the barrier of her teeth, his warm tongue surprises her own. Raimundo's eyes are closed; his long eyelashes rest like a flickering shadow on his cheek. Sweetness, thinks Victoria as Apaches begin to yip. She trembles. Raimundo puts his arm around her shoulders.

"You have a wonderful mouth," she whispers.

On the way to the lobby they hold hands. It is dark outside; under the blinking neon he says, "I always feel strange when I come out of the movies and find that night has fallen, don't you? It's as though a part of our lives has been lost and we can never get it back."

"I never go to the movies at this time," says Victoria. "I like to be outside at the hour when you can't tell if it's night or day. When the sky is light, but it's dark down here."

"I am falling in love with you," Raimundo says. "Can we go have coffee somewhere?"

"Yes," says Victoria, "but not right now. I really have to go."

"Do you have a boyfriend?" he asks. "No? Can I have your telephone number?" On the back of a bus ticket, Victoria writes her name, her address, and, for no reason, a false telephone number.

"Come to a party with me tomorrow night," she says.

He agrees to pick her up at eight, at her apartment. They will have dinner together and then ride downtown on the train.

At ten minutes to eight the telephone rings. Victoria is standing on one foot, then the other, in front of her mother's full-length mirror, trying to decide whether her black pants hang better over a high shoe or a low one.

"Vicky, it's for you," shouts Victoria's mother from the living room, where she is watching the Saturday night soap opera. "I think it's your French teacher." Victoria turns down the volume of the television set as she hobbles unevenly into the room.

"The high one," says her mother as she hands Victoria the receiver and turns to look out the dark window. I know you are pretending not to listen, thinks Victoria.

"Hello, Monique?"

"*Allô*, my cabbage, yes, it's me." The connection is bad, crackling and tangled with many voices.

"I can't bring my lover," Victoria says loudly. "But I can spend the night anyway." Her mother's shoulders rise and stiffen.

Through deepening static, Victoria strains to decipher words. Monique sounds very small and far away, as though she were a dwarf shouting across the central hall of an airport. She seems to be saying that she has arranged for Victoria to meet one of her friends, a young man, tonight.

"Can you hear me?" Victoria shouts. Monique's voice dissolves into a roar. It is the sound of airplane engines, Victoria thinks: I am landing in Paris. And my shoes are mismatched. She wants to laugh.

"You see, Ramón and I had the most awful fight," Victoria says into the deaf receiver. "He didn't want to share me with anyone else, and I wasn't about to adopt his politics. Plus he never gave up about the babies. So it's over, what can I say? He told me he's going to join the guerrillas because he doesn't want to live anymore. But wait until you meet Raimundo."

"What lies you tell," Victoria's mother says.

Suddenly the teacher's voice speaks, as clearly as though she were standing in the same room.

"*Allô? Allô?* Who is there?"

"*C'est moi, Victoire.*" The French *r* comes smoothly, with a little rasp.

"You are coming tonight, aren't you? Oh, I have had it up to here with these telephones! Did you hear that Jules is dying to meet you?"

"I am coming at ten or so," says Mademoiselle Victoire. "But I will probably be bringing someone, if that's all right."

"Who? Not Ramón? Oh, Jules will be so disappointed! But I am pleased anyway, the whole world knows that Ramón is a pig. And you have just told me all about the other one while I was listening to an old lady complain about a sick canary. I tell you, I will never be like that."

"Someone is at the door," says Victoria. "I will tell you everything tonight."

"I refuse to open the door for a terrorist," says Victoria's mother.

"Good," says Victoria.

As Raimundo helps her put on her coat, Victoria looks into the living room. "See you tomorrow," she calls to her mother.

Walking down the hall to the elevator, Raimundo takes her hand.

"I have a confession to make," he says.

"Already? What is it?"

"I'm not really the chairman of the Radical Students. I mean, I never was."

"Then why were you shouting at the telephone?"

"I wanted to meet you," he says. "Do you forgive me?"

"Never," says Victoria. "Yes, on two conditions."

"Anything. I submit to your mercy."

"I will tell you the second condition within six hours."

"Agony is delicious," Raimundo says. "Tell me the first one now."

"You must promise in advance."

"I do."

"That we shall always lie to each other."

"I am telling you the truth right now," he lies. They kiss while the elevator rises to meet them. They kiss again inside, descending.

URBINO

When I was a teenager I
lived in Buenos Aires, in a cubical brick mansion with
three acres of grounds. It had a low, thick wooden
gate where a guard sat in a folding chair; behind him,
you could see the house at one end of a vast lawn tra-
versed by the inch-wide highways of leaf cutter ants. On
weekends, widows came to snip leaves off the lindens
that overhung our fence, for a tea that soothed the
nerves.

We lived there from 1969 to 1974; my father was the
U.S. ambassador, appointed by a friend of his parents' in
return for Democratic favors. He'd worked for a bank in
Baton Rouge; the posting came as a surprise to him and
my mother, who went around the house for weeks saying, "Buenos Aires. My, my. The good airs," which is a
translation of the city's name. They certainly never asked
me if I felt like moving to a deeper South, another hemi-
sphere. We got on the plane New Year's Day of 1969 and
arrived in Buenos Aires sometime before my birth, in the

flower of my parents' youth — the midsummer of 1952, or even 1940. Men wore their hair slicked straight back; the cobblestone streets were full of boxy black cars with their steering wheels on the wrong sides and headlights like frogs' eyes. I saw one car driven by an old woman whose hairdo was barely visible over the dash; on the passenger side sat her pet Great Dane, looking as if he were the driver. I, who'd been waiting to be old enough to be allowed to go to Dead and Airplane concerts, went straight to the record store in the basement of our hotel. There I learned that records down here were sold in plastic bags. Bands had dumb names, like Almond or Fresh Paint.

My parents were glad I'd been removed from the influences that were ruining my generation: pot, sex, long hair, rock music. Argentina was wonderfully soothing in comparison, placid and prosperous under its elected president. Housing was a little short, so all the parks were full of lovers, rolling over and over each other under the so-called "drunken trees." Still, Dad used to say the Argentines didn't expect too much from Presidente Onganía: they were happy if they could just eat their two steaks a day, the best beef in the world. Eating so well, they couldn't understand how we Americans got so upset over the inconsistencies of our own officials.

There was a German war criminal hiding up in the Chaco. My father sent a CIA agent after him, a blue-eyed man who could shoot wild parakeets out of eucalyptus with a pistol. The war criminal was caught, and my dad's name came out in *Reader's Digest.*

His salary was paid in dollars, and due to the exchange rate, he and my mother's lives were magnified, far beyond what must have been their wildest imaginings as they grew up in ordinary suburbs, north of Baton Rouge. The Residence soon was full of my mother's purchases: Inquisition chairs, pink urns, writhing Laocoöns of brass, heirlooms sold for cash by European immigrants, and their children and grandchildren. Our chauffeur drove it all home to us in a huge silver Cadillac imported from the States. Dad used to say, "You got to impress the locals": as if our lives were a pile of glass beads or a box that made a coin materialize and disappear.

Of course, it was he and my mother who were the most impressed. They took up tennis; they inherited the American Club theatricals, held on the raised cement deck behind our swimming pool, which did well for footlights, lit up at night. My father's tenor got him leads in *South Pacific* and *Oklahoma!* He was tall, with thinning, curly blond hair, like Ashley Wilkes. He looked extremely dashing in a suit, and people said he was popular among the Argentines — that even though he was bad at tennis, his Southern manners charmed.

In our downstairs bathroom he kept a wooden tray, full of all the bottles of cologne he got as official presents. When tennis guests came out reeking of Brut, Chanel, or Drakkar Noir, my mother and he would judge their taste and their discretion. In our dining room, a big silver radio talked in code all night. "This is Balloon. Calling Chocolate." Candy and circus clowns; and so it went, through several bloodless revolutions.

Mom worried about my social adjustment, about the way I avoided American kids and instead sat around the kitchen socializing with the servants. How could I tell her that I was embarrassed about our home because it was nicer than anyone else's? She'd be hurt; she'd say I ought to be proud of family achievements. Worse would have been to explain the nature of my initial faux pas — my mother liked to call it a "fox paw," quoting a joke of her father, Daddy Bob. Instead of a hand, I'd extended this red, hairy thing with claws.

It was our first official barbecue. Striped canvas tents floated like spinnakers across the lawn; a strolling *gaucho* band played armadillo ukuleles while steaks, blood sausage, sweetbreads, and whole split-open goats sizzled over fire pits as long as bowling alleys. Dozens of kids were in the pool, Americans doing cannonballs and playing Marco Polo. My mother had invited them for me, but with thighs and belly still U.S. winter–pale, I refused to show myself in a bikini. She put me in charge of tots instead. Brats from oil, Army, beef byproduct, Christian families.

"Remember that you're always an example," she told me, pressing the sharp points of a barrette into my scalp. "Ambassador's daughters keep their bangs out of their eyes."

The Argentine women were all in maroon bell-bottoms that year, wearing eyeliner that was half an inch wide and swept up in black commas to the hairline. As soon as my mom got into a conversation, I pressed a maid to keep the tots away from the edge of the pool and sidled up to the other kid who wasn't swimming. He was the son of Embassy Security. His name was Bram Sorensen; he had zits and lank black hair to his shoulders. He was sitting on a recliner looking snide. Already, by my mother's orders, I'd marched up to him and offered my dad's bathing trunks. He'd refused the loan, as I'd known he would: too cool to get in water.

Argentina had made it possible to skip winter, to turn back twenty years of time. Now I believed I might venture a small leap forward. I asked Bram did he have any weed? I leaned my head back a little, so that my eyelids would slide half down and make me look already stoned. Habituée.

"Sure, man. Kif." We went behind the empty pony stable into the bamboos, and he pulled out a tiny, heavy, silver metal pipe.

"You go," I said.

During my second turn he suddenly exclaimed, "Man, don't tell me you don't *inhale?*"

I hadn't imagined I ought to, but I nodded yes, indignantly.

"Prove it."

I gulped, choked, gaped. Tears came.

"Oh, wow," Bram said, taking back the pipe. "I've been saving this stuff from Beirut."

I didn't get high at all.

After everyone had left, my mother came to my bedroom and asked me if I missed Louisiana. I told her I'd forgotten it: whether to spite or appease her, I didn't know. I was fifteen, unable to give words to my understanding.

So I went native, then, that first year. The servants taught me Spanish and the language of *maté*, bitter tea they drank from a gourd with a sieve-tipped silver straw. Cinnamon means "I love you." For an enemy, serve the *maté* cold, or pour boiling water down through the *bombilla*. We had three guards and seven, or eight, servants. It depended how you counted Sandro, the cook and the maid's son, who was ten when we left Argentina in 1974. He didn't have to work, but he wore his school uniform all the time, and shared with me a lack of visitors. Besides him we had his parents, Urbino and Edelmira; a laundress; a gardener; a woman for heavy cleaning; a seamstress; and my father's chauffeur. Some came only once a week, and so, of course, very few lived in. Only Sandro and his parents: they had two rooms and a bathroom up the back stairs. The guards outside stayed all night, but they weren't supposed to sleep.

From the servants I learned about Peronism, trade unions, strikes, and the Montonero guerrillas — all the reasons why we had guards. I noticed that the Residence was built for a siege. You could lock a single door upstairs and isolate half the rooms.

*

"Claire, how would you like golf lessons for your birthday," my mother asked from her end of the breakfast table. "At the Jockey Club. Since you refuse to have a party." I was to be sixteen.

It was the day Urbino had made us brains and eggs because I'd asked him to.

Brains had no taste.

"I hate golf."

"But golf's a sport that lasts you all your life. It's something you can play when you're old and you can't do anything else. You'll be grateful to me then." Her sad, dark eyes looked into mine. In them I saw the two of us walking arm in arm, laughing across the links of the internationally famous Jockey Club in matching lime green golf skirts, and pink socks with bobbles.

For an instant I wished to be a different child, the one she should have had. But I made my heart hard, and said, "The only worse present I can imagine is an invitation to be in your bridge club."

"The pro is wonderful," she said inexorably. "He's young and handsome." She giggled and waved one hand, impersonating the elegant woman she had so recently become. Urbino, walking behind her with pots of coffee and hot milk, was impassive. I thought, how he must hate us.

"*Más café, Señorita Clara?*"

"*No gracias, Urbino.*" I smiled intensely at him and was rewarded with a nod, but no expression.

"I'll make a deal with you," my mother said, accepting more coffee. "If you'll take a golf lesson once a week, you can take a riding lesson once a week." She knew I couldn't refuse.

"I'll think about it."

"*Quieren que tome clases de golf,*" I announced that day at dusk, at the servants' gathering; there were five of us.

"They want me to take golf lessons." I made a face and leaned back in my folding chair, awaiting comment.

We were sitting outside; the breeze was soft in the lindens and the eucalyptus. Urbino was sharpening his kitchen knife, which he did every day for an hour at least.

I was angry with them: I could feel them all retreating into the labyrinth of servants, where they understand nothing, have no opinions, always agree. Edelmira's pet finch hopped neurotically back and forth inside its tiny cage.

"*Qué bien,*" Edelmira said. "How nice."

Sandro was kicking his soccer ball again and again at a chalk **X** on the wall of the garage. "*¡Goool!*" he shrieked, forgetting himself.

"Sandro!" his mother cried, fiercely.

"It's okay, my parents are getting ready for a party and can't hear anything. Don't you think golf is really bourgeois?"

Urbino straightened himself and picked up the cigarette he had left burning on the table's edge. With the cigarette hanging from his lips he shaved a hairsbreadth of skin from the side of his thumb. "Depends," he said. "Maybe you'll like it."

His eyes were soft, pulling on me.

"I won't like it," I said quickly. Urbino shrugged. "Well, maybe," I said.

"It's bad for the lawn when your father practices," the gardener ventured. He was a Basque, fearless and irascible, with a blue beret, suspenders, and the longest fly I'd ever seen: it curved at least a yard over his belly.

"Give me a smoke, Izaguirre," I said.

Deciding not to talk about the riding lessons, I sat smoking and listening to the gritty, satisfying sound of steel against the oil stone. It was a beautiful knife, Japanese, a quarter inch thick and slightly curved: when he wasn't using it, Urbino kept it wrapped in a cloth inside a wooden case. To sharpen, he'd told me, you pretended the stone was cheese and carved from its top the thinnest slice. But he made me practice with a different knife — for this, like some knife in the words of a tango, was all that remained of his past.

Urbino was from Tuscany, a stocky, vehement man, with sandy hair and blue eyes; he was fairer than my father, which was strange to me. He'd been shellshocked fighting for Mussolini in North Africa. Later he'd owned a restaurant in Rome that had just been getting famous, Urbino said, when his partner ran off with the money. This topic made me nervous: whenever it came up, Urbino's pupils contracted to the size of ice pick points, and in a loud, hard voice he would recite the menu of his restaurant, starting with Carciofi Crudi. But I believed him about the fame: Urbino was the best cook I've ever known, an artist of veal, of pastries and *paella,* too good to be working for one family. The knife had been a gift from a patron of his restaurant; Urbino brought it with him when he emigrated to Argentina, where he'd first gone "into service." He and Edelmira had met when they'd both worked for the German head of Pepsi — I don't know where I got the idea they'd been fired. Edelmira was tiny and kindly, from the Chilean Andes. I loved her, but she also frightened me, with her round, pale green cheeks as soft as talcum, the bruised bags under her eyes. Her feet, in cloth slippers, pointing inward, the size and shape of mittened hands.

At nine o'clock I stood at the banister railings in a flannel nightgown, looking down as my father helped my mother into her silver fox stole. I'd just smoked a big joint in the bathroom, covering the smell with Flit. Bram Sorensen and I were friends, ever since last Thanksgiving when we'd gone for a bike ride together, brandishing enormous turkey legs to shock the neighborhood. The

Sorensens lived just behind us. Since he was a grade younger, the boyfriend notion never crossed my mind, but Bram did give me free pot.

In this condition Dad looked to me like a portly Fred Astaire. I don't remember which outfit Mom wore that night: her kelly green sequined sheath, her mauve taffeta gown with thunderclouds of net, or her narrow black suit of unborn lamb with mink buttons and a matching pillbox hat. They were going to some Ministro's house and wouldn't be back till one or two. I liked them best this way, dressed up, and in the process of leaving me alone. I could go down and listen to my Buffalo Springfield record on Daddy's Voice of the Theater speakers. I could lie on the living room shag and watch movies on the insides of my eyelids. My parents dancing tangos in a red mist. All the people on earth marching into the maw of a giant, upright Hoover vacuum cleaner, whose red light blinked happily as it ground us into burger meat. My favorite was the flat green and white jigsaw puzzle that represented everything in the universe as interlocking frogs. When the frog that was me jumped out of place, unbearable brilliance blasted up through the hole.

"There's a horse for sale," I burst out. "It's only two hundred American dollars. It's a really good horse. You'd save money in the long run over rental." I fell silent, frightened that I had revealed too much of my desire, but I couldn't stop. "Board is only twenty dollars a month."

"What's this about?" my father asked my mother. "Her birthday present?"

"We'll discuss it in the car," my mother told him. "Claire, have you done your homework?"

"He's got a nice build," my father said, as the orange gelding stood blinking mildly at the clouds, his shaggy winter coat half-shed. His freshly oiled hooves had bits of sawdust sticking to them. A former polo pony, he was named El Cana, Argentine slang for "The Cop." I described him silently, in the horse words I'd learned: chestnut, cobby, blazeface.

Mr. Rossi put his fingers in the space behind El Cana's teeth and twisted. "Ten," he said, running his index finger over El Cana's jonquil-colored fangs. "A good age for a beginner's horse." El Cana jerked his head up, out of Mr. Rossi's reach.

The riding instructor smirked. "*Un caballo mansísimo. Sano también.*" Tame and healthy.

"*Muy bien,* I guess," my father said. We went into the clubhouse, and my father wrote out the check, leaning on the snack bar. As I watched the top of his head, pink scalp showing through curly blond hair, I was swamped by grief. I wanted to cry out, No, Daddy, it's okay, I don't have to have a horse. But I didn't, could not.

My father put his arm around my shoulder. Usually he was jumpy in his touches, but now pride had made him confident and I felt the density of his flesh. I shrank the tiniest amount, which he nonetheless felt. Lifting his arm quickly, he said, "Happy birthday."

"They've bought you a horse?" Urbino said. "*¡Maravilloso!*" He smiled, showing an eyetooth rimmed in gold.

"But I still have to take golf lessons." I hiked myself onto the marble counter and sat swatting my riding boot with my new crop, looking down with pride at the reddish saddle stains inside my knees.

"You should be grateful to your mother," he said. "She does her best."

"If I should, you should," I answered sourly. "Why doesn't she get Sandro a horse?"

"Don't talk like that, Señorita Clara."

"Why not?"

"I'm Sandro's father." Urbino unwrapped a package containing three raw squid.

I wasn't sure what he meant. "What are you making?"
I asked, to change the subject. The kitchen was full of
white butcher's packages, piles of vegetables, lobsters in
the sink trying weakly to crawl out.

"*Paella. Mira, pues.*" He laid the squid on the counter
in a row and sliced off their tentacles with a single stroke
of his knife. Then he picked up one of the bodies and
turned it inside out, with a sudden wrenching motion. A
whole dead fish fell slapping to the floor.

"Eeeh." He was pleased. Grinning, he held it up to my
face. "We can put this in the *paella* too," he said. "Remember, squid eat any garbage, so clean them always
well. And when you put them in the boiling pot, dip them
three times before letting go."

He demonstrated in the air, his big pale hand rising
and falling. At the moment of letting go, he hissed loudly
between his teeth. "*¡Zás!*"

"They're not alive, are they?"

I was considering vegetarianism.

We had *paella* a lot that winter. Congress had passed a
law to protect exports: beef could be sold only every
other week. My father exploded at the table. "I've got to
live by this *veda* nonsense because I'm supposed to be the
ambassador of goodwill. But any Argentine who's got a
butcher for a friend, any Argentine buys all his meat for
two weeks, then gets the guy to keep it in the locker. You
know they're all friends with their butchers."

One Saturday, my mother bought some plants with purple leaves. She went out and dug around the flagstones,
giving the front walk a purple edge. I could tell that she
enjoyed putting her hands in the dirt; it felt to her like
home, like Baton Rouge, where she'd complained about
having to do everything herself.

When Izaguirre came on Tuesday, he pulled her plants
up, and left them slaughtered on the flagstones as a warn-

ing. This was his garden. He'd worked it twenty years, through many varying appointments.

He refused my mother's order to replant. "Even God cannot make me put ugly plants where they should not be."

As soon as the front door closed behind her, my mother burst into tears; she ran upstairs and flung herself on the bed. She was all but screaming. My father stood over her, piecing together her story. "Well!" he said at the end. He grabbed his pistol and went out in the yard to look for Izaguirre. In fact, he'd never used this gun; it was a present from the man who'd caught the Nazi.

"Plant those plants," he ordered, in his rotten Spanish.

Izaguirre grabbed both his suspenders. "No." My father raised the pistol; Izaguirre stared, and resolved himself. "Go ahead and kill me."

My father didn't.

The guards were watching, Edelmira said, including the fat one who didn't like anybody. "Your father should take care."

I told her that my dad was harmless, living in a movie about the Old South part of North America. I explained about slaves and plantations and said it was all different now, except in certain people's minds, where there was a war they hadn't really lost.

"Here it's the same," Edelmira said. People still followed the dictator Rosas, who'd died in 1877. And in the forests of southern Chile, she'd seen buses full of blond children singing the Horst Wessel song on the way to private schools.

The golf instructor had Welsh ancestors and spoke English with a distinguished accent. Albert. Black wavy hair combed straight back without a part; blue eyes; and a pink V-neck sweater, all the rage in B.A. that year. When he put his arms around me from behind, to demonstrate proper grip, he had a fatherly smell, of Williams Lectric

Shave. I drove a dozen balls straight down the fairway.

"Beginner's luck," said Albert.

After the lesson we had espresso in the clubhouse. He said my parents were the first U.S. citizens to be invited to join the Jockey Club. The way he said Ameddicans, I could tell he didn't like us.

"I know," I told him. "They can't stop bragging. That's why I had to take these lessons."

He laughed suddenly, so that a snort of coffee went up his nose and he had to wipe it with a napkin.

The more lessons I had, the more confused my body became. After four lessons I was either missing the ball entirely or burying the club head in sod. I tried getting stoned to see if I improved, but it didn't work.

One Friday, Albert again found it necessary to correct my pinky overlap. "Your slice is incurable." His warm breath condensed inside my ear.

"I hate these lessons anyway," I said. "Let's just go in and have coffee."

Albert ordered us peach brandies, as hot as fire.

"I bet you've tried drugs," he said.

"Not me. But there's a lot of kids at school." I was torn between prudence and the desire to impress him. "I could probably get you some grass."

"Minx." He'd been appalled at my brand of cigarettes, too, the same ones our gardener smoked. "We've got an hour. Let's go down to the Costanera and get a steak and papfrits."

I was in love with El Cana, though not as much as I would have liked. There was an absent-minded, apathetic air about him; he refused to learn to jump, which was what I wanted most passionately in the world to do. Even the instructor had given up on him — this was why he had been sold to us. It was his neck, incorrigibly stiff, the thickest, strongest part of his body. He carried it so high he couldn't see what was in front of him.

"Go! Go!" I screamed as El Cana cantered leadenly toward the jump in the middle of the ring. The instructor stood by, poker-faced, hiding the whip. When El Cana slowed to a trot, ignoring my flailing heels, my cries, the teacher ran out behind us.

Whack!

Upright, jelly-kneed, my cheek pressed against El Cana's lathered chest, I recalled catastrophe in patches — the horse bunching himself, tiptoeing in place, suddenly springing straight ahead. Striped poles scattering. My nose banging on the hard, dandruffy brush of his mane, the slow spiral downward until my boots touched dirt.

The teacher's laugh.

El Cana's thousand-pound head went down, ripping my arms from around his neck. He lipped at the ground, blowing dust away with his nostrils, until he delicately found a tiny wisp of dead grass.

After this I remained earthbound, galloping as fast as I dared around the circumference of the ring, while in the center, other kids bounced neatly over the bright barriers, their horses' tails flicking.

Yet when I appeared at the stable door, El Cana would kick at the back of his stall and whuffle impatiently until I fed him a carrot. He took it in his bristly lips, and afterward licked my fingers with his thick, pink, frothy tongue. He gnawed gently at my chin with his dull incisors; I put my arms around his neck, breathing deeply his innocent, vegetarian smell. "You remind me of Albert," I'd say. Parked above the Pan American, I was getting kissing lessons now.

Edelmira and Sandro were Peronistas, along with the rest of the servants. Only Urbino was against. As rumors began that Perón was coming back, the kitchen became the scene of arguments. Every night now, I could hear voices rise and fall when I stood at my window after dark, letting thin clouds of bluish marijuana smoke complicate the patterns of the trees.

Not a shot had been fired when Generals Levingston and then Lanusse had taken over, but the peso had been devalued many times, and every week now, there were strikes. No bus, stores closed, no light. This or that leader, this or that form of government, was being suggested. I'd never heard anyone get really excited about politics before, and often I was drawn downstairs to watch, to join the arguments myself. The only opinions I had were ones I'd heard from my parents, and they sounded reasonable, so I repeated them. This put me in Urbino's camp. Perón was a crook. He'd come into office a penniless lieutenant and left the ninth richest man in the world.

"He'll fix everything, you'll see," one of his supporters would say, the laundress or the seamstress or Edelmira, and another would add: "He gave my uncle a job, a car."

"To distract you while he robbed the treasury," I'd retort.

One night, Izaguirre stayed later than usual. He said, "Foreign companies are strangling us."

"Ah, no!" Urbino said in sudden, shocking rage. The veins on the sides of his forehead went blue and bumpy. "How can you say that when the *señorita* is here? Perón is the devil. And his wives, both sluts and harpies."

"Evita was a saint," little Sandro said piously.

"Go to your room," Edelmira told him.

Everyone was staring at Urbino. He took his knife again and stroked it softly on the stone. "Listen to Señorita Clara," he said. "She knows, she has an education." Then he laughed, once, bitterly, like a dog barking. I'd have said something about the bleeding veins of Latin America, but I didn't dare.

Soon, an oilman in my father's poker club was kidnapped. Our radio squawked then, quite a lot, about "the package." I shuddered guiltily, remembering how I hadn't liked the oilman, nor his particularly noxious tots, whom I'd had to babysit at several barbecues. Bram told me that my father was taking the hard line, saying don't pay any ransom money. He didn't need to tell me. I'd heard it all at the dinner table, how this was blackmail and if we started giving in, we'd never stop; how in any case terrorists were after publicity and they'd get too much bad press if they actually killed a U.S. hostage. But Bram's father had been Security in Lebanon and believed in terrorist threats. Bram's family laughed about the time when a station wagon had blown up right in front of their house in Beirut: the terrorists had driven by and thrown a grenade against a window they'd forgotten to roll down.

In the end, the oil company paid twelve million dollars to get their hostage back. Bram recounted embassy gossip that compared my father's strategy to his tennis game. He didn't really know how to play, but stood at the net calling out "Good shot," while his partner ran himself to death. If a ball came at him, he pretended not to see it coming. Or maybe he wasn't pretending.

The rescued oilman came to dinner before flying home to Georgia, where his wife and children had already gone. He'd become a Christian in captivity. I was ashamed to listen to him; I'd never heard a man be vulnerable before.

After he left, my father said the man's company had put him out to pasture.

I thought of what Bram had told me. Now my father sounded like a fading radio station.

There began to be bombs downtown. Anonymous callers at the office threatened my father with assassination; he went to work by a different route each day, followed by an armed escort in a Fiat 600, the model known as "the marble." Bram said that if my father had personal enemies, he was more likely to be kidnapped. That's what CIA research had found all over the world. I considered Izaguirre: but he had a saintly wife. Edelmira: she was too soft. Urbino: he was too loyal. But the fat, mean guard was troubling; and I even came to wonder, strangely, about myself. If I didn't respect my father enough, his weakness might increase, make him more vulnerable to attack.

More guards came to the house. They worked two at a time and carried pistols. They were retired cops, or younger men who had failed the police exam. I liked most of them. One old guy had worked for many years at the racetrack; he brought me a horseshoe, as light as Cinderella's slipper. Another claimed telepathic communication with the trees; yet a third picked out Bible verses to describe each member of our family: he said I was "bright as the sun, clear as the moon, terrible as an army with banners." I liked that.

My mother ruled that I must travel everywhere by private taxi.

I argued. "I'd be safer in a bus. I have black hair, no one would recognize me as American. The people wouldn't let anyone drag me away." When I tried to discuss this with Urbino, he cut me off. He was no longer willing to teach me any cooking, and often spent whole evenings upstairs while Edelmira, Sandro, the rest of the servants, and I sat down in the kitchen, talking carefully about pleasant subjects, Urbino's silent brooding hanging over us like the shadow of a wing.

The political situation was troublesome for Albert, who wanted to spend more time with me and to go out at night. I was willing to conspire with him. With him I had learned to enjoy the contact of another human tongue; his kisses made the bottoms of my feet itch with pleasure. In exchange, I endured aspects of Albert himself — his use of the hair grease called Gomina, his insistence that I never make eye contact with other men, never order for myself at a restaurant or leave the table without his express permission.

One day in November I told Albert we could go on a real date and stay out after dark. My parents were going to a military ball in La Plata, sixty miles away. Albert said he'd come for me at ten, after Mom and Dad would be surely gone.

In case of some emergency, I decided to tell Urbino. I found him in the kitchen, alone, sharpening the knife by the last of the daylight still coming in the windows. He asked me what I wanted for dinner, and I said I wasn't going to eat here. I said I had come to him because I trusted him.

"I'm going out with a guy tonight," I said. "I don't want to tell my parents because he's Argentine and they're prejudiced. But I'm telling you just in case they call or something happens."

He didn't say anything or even look up, but kept slicing imaginary cheese from the oil stone. I filled the silence.

"We're just going out to eat and for a drive along the river." Why was Urbino so quiet? Was he going to tell my parents? "If they call or come home unexpectedly, just say I'm with a friend from school. Heidi Scruggs" — whom I'd just called on our tapped phone. She was another marijuana head; she lived in a boarding house and could do anything she wanted because her parents were in the provinces.

"Who is this Argentine?" Urbino said, still not looking up.

"My golf teacher from the Jockey Club."

I could see the vein jumping again. He ground his teeth and finally looked up. There was a yellowish crumb in each corner of his mouth. "*Yo sé lo que vos hacés,*" he said. "I know what you do. What all the women do. But I'll keep your secret, ah, *sí, muy bien, señorita.*"

That night Albert drove far out, beyond the army camp. As he chattered on, I thought about Urbino, what he'd said. It made my stomach feel cold. Finally I said, "Where are we going?"

"I know a tearoom," Albert said, "where they serve ice cream in a very private booth. You can eat ice cream and kiss at the same time."

"Hah," I said.

"Get down," Albert said a minute later. "A bunch of people who know you live here."

I shrugged my shoulders but nonetheless made myself a tiny bit smaller. I tried to believe that Albert was a sincere human being.

Our destination was a motel; Albert left me in the car while he went into the office, to order ice cream, he said. I was repenting, but I had no options. No money; I didn't know the bus routes out here; if I called one of our private taxis, word would surely get back to my parents.

In the room, Albert made a show of locking the door behind us and put the key in his pocket.

"I don't like this place," I said.

"The ice cream's coming, my little hippie," he said. "Give me a kiss."

I couldn't tell if I had wanted this or not. Albert felt like a hot brick ripping open my lower body, breaking into places I should have known for myself first. Right then I would have given anything to go back to Baton Rouge, to my mother's idea of home.

Afterward Albert said, "You love my penis, don't you."

I turned my back on him and began forcing myself to go to sleep. "You wake us up at three or I'll make sure you get fired," I said.

"Oh?" he said. "Are you going to tell your daddy?" And he forgot: the pale dawn woke us up. I washed the blood off my thighs with cold water and cried in terror all the way home. Albert dropped me off at the corner, so as not to be seen.

"Until Friday," he said.

The fifty yards to the house, I felt my belly crawling up my throat. It was seven-thirty. If the old racetrack guard still was there, perhaps I could sneak in, and he wouldn't tell my parents. I could still say I'd been with Heidi.

But the gate was unmanned, the house empty but for our German shepherd, who came toward me cautiously, wagging the heavy sickle of her tail. There was a note in my room in Edelmira's writing: Your parents don't know. Call the Sorensens.

"Far out!" I said aloud; but my voice sounded thin and false, wandering through all the rooms and coming back to me.

Bram answered the phone. He said my parents were at the hospital with Edelmira, Sandro, and Urbino. Urbino had been shot in the spleen by the fat guard.

"I heard the shot," he said.

"Where's the blood," I asked helplessly. "I didn't see any blood."

"I don't know. Come on over."

I smoked a joint so that I would be able to take whatever came: Cuddles, the Sorensens' horrid beagle, or anything worse. The bullet wound, a black hole surrounded by a bruise. It would look just like Edelmira's eyes.

The Sorensens gave me breakfast. I gobbled eggs, bacon, yogurt, toast with cheese and honey, toast with just jam, fruit, café con leche: trying not to think. Afterward I wanted to take a nap, but I was afraid to. The raw ache between my legs felt visible: as soon as I fell asleep, Bram might start thinking about me in ways I didn't want.

They took out Urbino's spleen, but he died anyway, three days later. For reasons I couldn't name, I never went to visit him in the hospital. Dad sat me down in the living room and gave me a talk about the incident. Insane jealousy was one of the results of Urbino's shellshock. He accused Edelmira of sleeping with other men. The night I'd been gone, he chased her and Sandro with that knife. The two of them were afraid to stay in the house alone with Urbino, so they spent the night with our heavy-cleaning woman. Their absence confirmed his suspicions: he sat all night in the kitchen, sharpening the knife. When Edelmira returned in the morning, he chased her out into the driveway — with the knife drawn and waving in the air, the guard said. Leaving the knife in the kitchen, said Edelmira and Sandro.

Edelmira ran out the gate, and Urbino attacked the guard instead, so that he had to defend himself — the guard said. Edelmira said the guard stepped back at his ease, took aim, and shot. She claimed he'd asked her once how my father might feel with a bullet in his head. She asked my parents to prosecute the guard for murder, but nothing ever came of the case.

Before she took Sandro back to Chile, she told me that Urbino had loved me very much. "I know," I said, feeling terribly uncomfortable.

I never went back to the Jockey Club. Albert drove past the house and called twice on the phone. I told him to be careful: the phone was tapped, our guards would suspect him if he lurked about. Eventually he gave up.

I lost interest in El Cana, too. "Sell him," I said one day to my mother. "I hate the way he holds his neck."

Six weeks later, my horse still was unsold. Perón returned and seven people were massacred at Ezeiza Airport. Death threats were made against my father. Security ordered us out of the country. We left El Cana in the hands of my riding teacher but never heard any more about him, nor received any money.

My parents went back to our old house in Baton Rouge, which had been rented that whole time. It was the end of their diplomatic service. Their horizons having expanded, they visited Europe and even Thailand, where everybody smiled so beautifully, my mother said.

It was time for me to go to college. I met a guy at a freshman mixer and we went to bed. I fell in love, and decided I was cured of Albert. Ten years later, I married a Milanese architect named Ignazio, who said he liked to commit Catholic sins with me, not because of their being sins but because of being with me. We took our honeymoon in his country, in January, to avoid crowds of Americans. I found Italy and Italians astonishingly similar to Argentina and Argentines. In a freezing hotel room in Pisa, I told Ignazio the story of Buenos Aires. When I got to El Cana I started crying, crying loudly, smearing his chest with snot, saltwater, and the slimy red of a nosebleed. Of all things, it felt worst to have left my horse alone, a loyal heart defenseless in that place.

When I'd calmed down a bit, Ignazio said it made him feel strong and mighty to hold me against his chest and listen. He said, too, that someone must have loved El Cana after me.

JUDGMENT

When Mayland Thompson dies he wants to be buried with the body of a twelve-year-old girl. "A fresh one," he says. "Huh! Just toss her in there and let her keep me company till Jesus gets here."

As for his wife, Linda, he'd like her to wait for judgment in a mass grave with all of her boyfriends. He threatens to write their names in his will: two deputy sheriffs, a detective, a railroad switchman, bartenders, motel owners, pavement repairmen, drunks.

"You'll have some real winners to cuddle up to," he tells her. "They're bad enough alive. Just imagine what they'll be like, full of worms."

She holds up a dead mouse by the tail. "There was three of these in the basement. Reminded me of you. Time I get old enough to die, you won't be able to make me do nothing."

His hair turns a shade grayer in the afternoon light. It's just that he wouldn't want her to be lonely either, he tells her.

Her expression is blank, the muscles of her face completely relaxed. She has Indian blood, and Irish. Once a month, she uses a special wax to remove fine black down from her upper lip.

He's known Linda since she was eight and her mother used to roll with him naked on the musty box spring in the attic. Right on this very porch, he would sit the two of them on his lap, Felicia Biggins and her daughter; they would each put an arm around his neck and fill his ears with tongues. He pinched here and there, gave them sips of Schlitz. The three of them were the talk of Rampart City, Kansas. At least once a week there would be a preacher or a juvenile officer or a member of the Ladies' Benevolent knocking on Felicia's door, until she borrowed Mayland's Goose gun and started to wave it around. That stopped them. She was his kind of woman.

The day she died of the liver, Mayland felt a natural responsibility arise in his heart, so he kidnapped Linda away from her uncle Clyde and the custody girls. Through one moist night he drove, Linda curled snoring beside him, her face stuck to the plastic seat. At dawn, a sleepy Mormon gave him the key to Room 206 of the New Paris Motel outside Provo, Utah. Three weeks he hid her there, feeding her ice and double cheeseburgers. She took two baths a day and watched the TV news in color. She cracked the enamel of her molars and grew as plump as a broiler.

They were married, which made Linda the third Mrs. Thompson. He waited six months, until she was of age, before bringing her back to her mother's farm.

Did marriage agree with her? She was as silent and distant as the moon. Each night as she lay under him in bed, she seemed plumper and more mysterious than the night before. By the end of the year, she was pregnant.

Wild with joy, Mayland bought two used pizza ovens

at an auction and resold them to buy her a color television set. It had no knobs; he placed it on the coffee table and turned it on for her with a screwdriver. It refused to turn off again, but Linda didn't mind. She watched it for two days straight, changing channels with a wrench, until one morning the tube burned out in the middle of a program. Then she sat up on the couch and announced she couldn't stand the feeling of being overweight. Hitting her stomach with her fists, she walked out into the dusty yard, climbed into Mayland's pickup, and drove to town for diet pills. That night, and for two days afterward, blood came out of her in clots that filled Mayland's two cupped palms.

The doctor shook his head. He gave her a shot.

When Linda woke up, she would eat nothing but celery and carrots.

Now she won't let him touch her, so what has he got? A ninth-grade graduate with a magazine figure who sleeps in cotton underwear, and a hundred and twenty acres of her land to take care of. He has done as much as he can, as much as his wife and the farm will let him, but in four years he hasn't scraped together a hill of beans. How much can you do with forty acres of river bottom full of dead trees and another eighty oversprayed? What can you do for a girl twenty years old who can't make change for a dollar?

These days he wakes up, the backs of his legs red from the heating pad, and he has the feeling that there is something he doesn't want to remember. He leaves the house quietly, very early, and goes to talk to high school girls waiting for the morning bus. If he can't get any of them to play hooky he'll spend the rest of the day in town making deals.

In the river bottom, another man's horses graze, standing with their tails to the wind. On the northwest corner of the property, Roy the sharecropper sweats over the broken windmill. Mayland wants to get somebody out there with a metal detector: one of the milo fields is supposed to have been an Indian battleground.

Noon. Linda straightens her legs under the electric blanket. Sunk in the mattress, her body seems boneless. Blue veins show through the skin of her neck; she is no longer asleep.

Behind the toolshed, in a square plot Mayland made by wiring four yellow gates together at the corners, there is a tablet of slate over Linda's mother and a small aluminum marker that says BABY but doesn't have anything buried under it. Linda keeps the weeds out, and she's collecting rocks from every state in the union to decorate the graves.

Rummaging in the bottom of the closet, she finds a pair of blue stretch pants and a T-shirt with a silvery photograph ironed onto the front. She dresses, puts on her eye shadow, and goes out to stand on the road. The man in the red car sees her from a distance and takes his foot off the gas.

Wednesday Mayland traded a hundred junk cars to the dealer for eighty dollars in cash and a purple boat with an outboard motor. Thursday he traded the boat for twenty dollars and a four-wheel drive truck that was missing one wheel. Today he is making arrangements with his pal Frank about the metal detector: they'll split anything Frank finds, fifty-fifty.

"It don't matter who holds the title when it comes to something buried more than a foot," Frank says. "This'll be in your name for a change, how do you like that?"

The two men smile at each other across the counter of Frank's Shoe Repair Salon.

"How is that wife of yours, anyway?"

"Oh, you know her," Mayland says. "Pushing the legal limit. And you know me. When the two of us comes to town . . ."

In that white Lincoln or the blue pickup: Frank knows all about it. "The mothers lock their girls in the closet and they push their sons out the back door."

"You got it."

"No, you all's the ones that's got it." Frank pushes away the display of rubber heels and leans across the glass. "And you deserve every bit of it you get." He slaps Mayland's shoulder and the two of them laugh. "It's just too damn bad you can't sell the place till she's twenty-one. I hate to see a friend scratching in the dirt like that."

"You bring that machine out and it's finders keepers," Mayland tells him. "Anyway, we'll sell that farm next year and be in Florida with water skis on our feet."

As Mayland gets ready to leave, Frank says, "I'll remember what you said. If you can sell that dump I'll have a pig roast for you."

"Pigs is free at the 4-H farm. If you go at night."

Walking out in the thin autumn sunlight, Mayland wishes he were in Florida. Some of his children are there, including Junior. The only one of Mayland's kids ever to try to walk the straight and narrow: turns Jehovah's Witness and a week later he gets shot in the head at a rally. Junior's alive, but he'll never be the same. Some things just go to show you, Mayland thinks, they just go to fucking show you.

He decides to check at the bar to see if Linda and the sharecropper are having a beer. But she's not there.

It is too dark to see. There is a smell of frying onions.

Mayland comes up the steps and sees Linda inside, standing in the yellow light of the kitchen, slicing. The tip of her tongue is out, she is concentrating on a potato. He bangs the door and she looks up.

She flicks a strand of black hair behind her ear. "You

left the refrigerator open this morning," she says. "I could have drank the spread, it was that runny."

"I want you to tell me where you was this evening and this afternoon."

"Roy came over and we went down for a beer. You said that was all right, Mayland."

Roy the sharecropper, Mayland thinks disgustedly, she's named eighteen guys after him just because she knows I know she thinks he's ugly. And Roy will usually tell me whatever she says to. But today at six o'clock, Roy told Mayland there was a red car parked all day in the driveway, and Roy didn't know whose it was.

"'Went down' might be the truth," Mayland says. "But you wasn't at the bar and you wasn't with Roy either."

She smiles faintly at the cutting board. "How come you know so much? You been following me?"

He wants to hit her. "No, it ain't worth my time. I want to know where my three-hundred-dollar ratchet set is and my seventy-five-dollar power saw."

"Ask somebody else. I ain't touched nothing of yours."

"You had somebody over and they took it." He steps closer to her, and she shrinks back against the wall, her lips shaking open to show her teeth.

Now she's scared of me, Mayland thinks, damn it. That's all we need for her to think. I never hit a woman in my life. He turns away and walks back toward the bedroom, clicking on light switches as he goes. There are three beer bottles on the table, and an ashtray. As he tears the sheets off the bed, he notices Linda standing in the doorway, watching.

"The trouble with you is that you don't know how to judge people," he tells her. "You might be real pretty, but that ain't going to stop you from getting a disease. You might own a farm, but you'd get yourself in a lot of hot water real fast if it wasn't for me."

"But all my blood relatives is dead except for Clyde, and he hates me because of you."

"I got a lot more dead relatives than you do. That don't mean you can't make something of yourself." He throws the sheets on the floor. "Better make sure them onions don't burn."

She runs back to the kitchen. Look at her, Mayland says to himself. Pounding through the house like a three-year-old. I guess I can't leave her out here by herself no more to moon over them graves and attract the lowlife.

"I got you a job," he says as the screen door slams behind him.

She is standing in the middle of the kitchen, staring out the window. "Somebody ran over that spotted horse," she says. "It's in the road."

"I saw that this morning while you was still asleep." He walks around in front of her, hoping she will say something.

Linda looks down at the floor. Her small bare feet look cold, bluish against the dark linoleum; there is fresh persimmon-colored polish on the nails of one foot. "It screamed," she says finally. "Before the sun came up."

"I'll sell it to the dog food factory tomorrow," he says. "Now listen up. I'm taking you to town at seven o'clock A.M. tomorrow morning. You're going to wash dishes at the café for three-fifty an hour."

"You just want to make me pay you back for that saw," she complains. Turning her back on him, she walks past the refrigerator into the living room. "I guess I better get some rest then, huh."

There is nothing in the refrigerator except fifty-two-percent oil spread and an empty cardboard box. The first time he tries to close it, the rubber cord they use to keep the door shut snaps back; the metal hook flies past his ear. He goes in to look at his wife on the couch: she has covered her face with a sheet of newspaper, which blows gently up and down with her breath.

She can sleep more than any human being, until four in the afternoon sometimes. In his opinion, she's still suffering from that brain fever she had when she was two, three years old. At least she reads. She reads the newspaper every day, and she pays attention to the radio.

"There's a man in Colorado who was teaching his dog how to shoot a gun," she will say, excited. "It picked it up off the table and it fell out of its mouth and onto the floor and now he's in the hospital!"

No way would Mayland let her near his guns. The ones that aren't at the pawnshop are locked in a closet in the basement.

At the table, her mouth full of store-bought chicken, she tells him she doesn't want to go to work in the morning. She'll do something wrong the first hour and then she'll want to quit. He answers that he'll lock her in the toolshed and hustle her to niggers if she wants to stay home.

Linda giggles. "It wouldn't be no worse than nothing to eat but this greasy fucking chicken," she says. "But I tell you what, if you do that, I'll get one of them niggers to kill you and then I'll bury you with a goat!"

"Greasy chicken is your own fault," he says. "You should have asked that guy to take you to the grocery store at least."

Both of them laugh. After dinner, he tries to give her a lesson in case Mrs. Folsom wants Linda to work the register.

"Here's a dollar. Coffee's thirty cents," Mayland says. "Plus tax."

She counts the change in brown coins, big silvers, medium silver, one small silver coin.

"Good," he says. "Now, pie."

She throws the money on the floor.

*

Her breathing is slow and quiet, her back curves away from him like a train track. He watches her body rising and falling, its edge against the dark. The October moon is cold in the window; a shaft of its light falls across the rumpled blanket, the gray carpet, the gray wallpaper with its gray roses, now pink.

His arthritis is bad tonight; his legs stick to the heating pad. If he touches her now, she will roll away, even in sleep. She will mutter in her sleep and roll away.

He tries it anyway. She lets his arm stay for one second, and then says, "Quit." For a year now she's been saying he's not her style in bed. It was never good except for once upon a time when she had a couple of other guys on the side, who paid her probably. She was hot for Mayland then. It lasted one month. He didn't understand anything about it, but it was nice while it lasted. Nowadays they have an understanding about sex. She's not jealous about Mayland's little girls, and he doesn't ask her questions very often. She will even call the girls' houses and say she is a classmate when the mother answers.

If you consider the difference in their ages, Mayland figures, if you consider everything together, they are two people who can live with each other.

He'd like it to be different.

It's not as though he is the type to be found on the bottom of the cage with his feet in the air. When he was her age, there were women who would pay him fifty, a hundred, just to feel his body heat. He rubbed up against a woman eighty and a girl thirteen; he spent himself on a pool table, in church, and in the Sears furniture department.

He used to pick locks with the ace of spades — snap, like he owned the place, that fast. Like he was John Doe, picking up the mail from his mailbox and going inside to read it.

There are at least eight of his sons and daughters scattered over the nation. Rosalinda, his Mexican ex-wife, Junior's mother, still sends him religious postcards from Florida. His first wife, Belinda, is dead. Funny how he ended up with three Lindas. The other two had longer names, but this one's as complicated as half the letters in the alphabet.

"Linda," he whispers.

"Huh?"

"Once for old times' sake?"

She groans. He remembers the horse outside, its brown legs as stiff as an inflated toy's.

"A man has his needs," he says.

"I'm trying to sleep, please."

He stands back and sets fire to a whole book of matches.

It lands on the horse's shoulder. For an instant he can read the words "Purina Feeds" printed in red on the white cardboard. Then there is a thumping sound and a huge yellow flame. It smells terrible, the gasoline and burning hair, and Mayland yells in delight. He sees Linda's white face at the bedroom window, then her fluttering nightgown as she runs along the driveway toward him.

"See!" he shrieks. The carcass is burning ferociously. Several yards behind him, out of reach of his jerking shadow, Linda comes to a stop. Lifting one foot, she shakes a stone from her slipper.

The two of them stand in awe until the burning stops. This happens sooner than Mayland would have liked. In the dark, the dead horse hisses and crackles like a doused campfire. Mayland can tell that only the hide is really burned, but the horse's lips have broken and stretched back horribly, so that its teeth gleam in the moonlight.

Linda covers her eyes. A small cloud of black smoke drifts eastward across the stars. "What did you go and do that for?"

"Saturday night's all right," says Mayland. "That's what we used to say in Texas."

"Texas," she says. "You're out of your mind." She giggles. "Let's go to Texas. Then I won't have to work tomorrow."

"The dump's as far as I guess either one of us is going unless you sell the farm for me in town."

"Guess so."

Later, as they lie in bed staring at a string of water spots on the ceiling, he feels Linda's fingers brush his shoulder.

"Look," she says. "A crocodile trying to eat a duck."

The water spots on the ceiling. Mayland chuckles, air pushing through his teeth. Thick-fingered, he touches her hair where it lies dark against the pillow.

"That plaster needs to be fixed or it'll fall in on us," he says. She turns halfway toward him, so that he can see the moonlight gleaming on her teeth, in her eyes. Suddenly he rolls his big body on top of her and kisses her, holding her arms down. She squeaks a little, tries to bite him, but he doesn't give up, and soon she is just lying there, staring past his face.

"Fuck you. Fuck you," she says as he begins to grunt. He thinks he feels her spitting. "Fuck you, old man."

A crocodile that ate a duck, he thinks afterward.

The walls of the house dissolve in moonlight.

After some time there is the sound of running water. The radio's digital clock says 6:38. Through the window, the plains are a mild gray-blue; the huge loneliness of the sky is disguised by a thin ceiling of clouds. He has dreamed, he suddenly remembers, that Linda's mother was in the attic calling for cake and ice cream.

His body aches.

Wrapped in towels and a cloud of steam, Linda appears in the doorway to announce that she can't find any underwear. "I guess nobody's going to know the difference."

"I bet you tell six people, time I come get you. I bet you let them look."

"Shut up," she says. "Pig."

"Sorry," he says. Then, "Do whatever you want."

She stares at him.

Ahead, on the road, they can see the dark silhouette. Two buzzards are walking around it in the dust. The birds look awkward on the ground. Linda peers down at the carcass as Mayland drives around, his left wheels almost in the opposite ditch. The buzzards fly up. He accelerates to forty-five.

Linda pulls down the visor and leans her head back on the seat, narrowing her eyes against the sunrise. "I didn't get no sleep at all," she says. "I don't know if I can work today." The muscles of her neck tighten as the truck bumps up onto the highway pavement.

When they reach the café, she won't let Mayland come in with her. He doesn't insist; he watches as she inspects herself in the rearview mirror, tucks her purse under her arm, and is gone.

As she walks into the building, she waves at a long-faced young man who is eating an iced doughnut at the window table. Mayland recognizes him as the operator of the truck scales at the Pearsall grain elevator, the half brother of a fat girl named Minnie who once let him kiss her breasts.

In the window, Linda holds up three fingers. Three o'clock. He makes an okay sign with one hand, and she disappears into darkness behind the counter.

The young man's name is Gene, and he changes seats so he can watch Linda's head and shoulders through the foot-high opening in the wall behind the counter. He orders another doughnut; when it's gone, he wipes his mouth with a napkin and goes to the cash register to ask Mrs. Folsom for a loan of her ballpoint pen.

On a napkin he writes: "Winter coming. Last chance

to get out! Meet me at 2 P.M. at Fast Gas, reg. pump if you want a ride to sunny Arizona. Yr pal, G. Friddell."

He folds the napkin and waves it at Linda; he points out the window at a black Pontiac with fiery wings painted on the hood.

Some in jeans, some in Sunday clothes, half a dozen teenagers are sitting on the city park benches near the monkey cage. They smoke, and look Mayland up and down.

"Playing hooky from church?" Mayland calls to them in a friendly tone.

"What's it to ya?" asks one of the girls. Her hair is dyed blond, showing black at the roots, and it stands out in pointed wings on either side of her face.

"Want some beer?"

The teenagers drift over. They know him, Mayland Thompson, lives out west of town on Route 6. Mayland invites them out to his place to see the ugliest thing in the world, but first they have to stop at the hardware store to get some kind of pulley rig. The blonde and a redheaded girl sit with Mayland in the cab, along with one of the boys. The redhead's arm is squashed against the side of Mayland's chest. Her name is Diane; Mayland tells her she's a little fatter than he likes them, but he bets she'd be a whole lot of fun if she'd just relax.

He tells them the whole story about the horse: about lying awake in bed, about his old lady, as cold as a piece of liver out of the icebox until he did something to light a fire under her. They would see it in a minute.

The boy named Fuzzy makes a joke about barbecue.

"We had some of it for breakfast, yeah, but we left the rest of it for company like you," Mayland says as the carcass comes into view.

"That's the rudest thing I ever saw," Diane observes.

"You bet, honey," Mayland says. He turns the truck around in the road.

Diane stays in the cab, playing the radio while everyone else goes out to sit on the tailgate and look. A tall boy takes out a pack of cigarettes and offers them around. Fuzzy pokes at the carcass with a stick.

"Believe it or not," Mayland says, "that thing right there used to be spotted. A spotted horse. That was even its name, Spot." He wants to put his hands on the blonde, but she is sitting on the tall boy's lap. On her arm is a homemade tattoo, the initials E.G. inside a heart. The horse smiles hugely at Mayland, making him feel uncomfortable. Something ain't right here, he thinks, checking his fly. No problem.

The beer is gone. "Okay, boys," Mayland says. "Time to load up. We've got to take this sucker to the dump."

"Listen, old man," Fuzzy says. "Not so fast." He puts his hands on Mayland's shoulders. "We got our good clothes on, man."

"I was wondering if you'd say that," Mayland says. He smiles slowly. "You can walk back to town if that's how you feel."

Fuzzy's not a bit surprised. "We don't want to start no fight here. Give us ten bucks each and everything's cool. Okay, Grecian Formula?"

Mayland sees the boys' legs arranged in a loose arc in front of him. One of them could hold my arms and then the rest knock my teeth out, he thinks. I should have seen it coming. "Fifteen bucks for the four of you boys."

"What about the girls? You a chauvinist?"

"Twenty."

It's a deal; Mayland pays in advance, a ten, a five, five ones. The boys take off their jackets, roll up their sleeves. Mayland lets down the tailgate.

In ten minutes the horse is loaded, covered with newspapers and canvas, and tied firmly down.

"You can drop us off at the pinball parlor," Fuzzy says. "Everyone in front this time."

The teenagers sit on top of each other; no one talks. Diane has changed all the button settings on the radio to rock stations. Sharp bones press against Mayland's arm. Once, he is obliged to wave and smile at the driver of another truck, who has pulled off the road to let Mayland by.

Finally they stop across the road from the Balls of Steel.

"See you around, man," the teenagers say as they untangle themselves. They dance through traffic and away.

Two-thirty by the clock on city hall. A new rattle in the engine. Mayland decides to stop at the café on the way to the dump. If Linda isn't finished with work, he'll have a lemonade and figure out what to tell the owner of the horse. He hopes Linda's not going to be mad at him still.

"I bet you can't guess my secret," Linda says as Gene's car reaches eighty miles an hour.

"You ain't got any underpants on."

"You're too smart," she complains. Her bare feet push against the dashboard, her right hand dangles against the window. She starts to tell Gene about her rock collection: she's got a lot from Oklahoma and one each from Texas and Arizona, but none from New Mexico.

"Rocks," he says. "That's a new one on me. Well, where we're going they have all the rocks you want." He laughs. "All the rocks you want."

Mayland never noticed before that the crickets still sing in October. They make a crazy sound in the trees as he stands at the foot of Linda's mother's grave, telling the whole story out loud and asking Felicia for advice.

Yes, he wanted Linda to pay for those tools. Yes, he made her do a lot of things she didn't want to: made rules, gave lessons. Partly he did it because he thought it would have made Felicia happy, partly because he judged that Linda needed it. She wasn't smart enough to get along by herself, but maybe she knew her own mind better than he did. Maybe she was too old to have a husband who acted like her daddy. About what happened last night, he guessed that was the last straw for her. He can't say why he had to set that horse on fire, but he knows he couldn't stop himself. He couldn't stop himself from rolling over on top of Linda either. He still can't keep from feeling like her husband.

"Tell her I ain't going to chase her down," he says. "If this was the old days I would. But tell her I'm right here. Bring her back if you can." This seems to be the end of what he has to say. His arms hang loose and heavy at his sides. He starts to cry. The crickets keep making their screamy noise. Finally he goes back to the house, careful to step over Linda's curving rows of colored rocks.

Everyone, even the bartender, is out on the sidewalk. The squad car is making a right turn into the parking lot; the siren dies suddenly, with a strangling sound. The car stops and three Oklahoma state troopers get out.

Grim, pale, silent at the center of a fury of sparks, Linda is ripping the neon off the front of the Sportsmen's Lounge, by hand.

No one wants to get close for fear of being electrocuted.

Chrome stripping hangs crazy and twisted from the side of the black car. Gene Friddell stands under the blue mercury lights of the parking lot, drunk, telling the trooper it's not his fault. Yes, he pushed over the chair. Yes, he called her a whore. But it was only because she kept talking about her dead mother. No, he didn't slap her, she slapped him.

"The witnesses say different," the trooper says. "Put one hand on your head. Good. Now the other one." Handcuffs click twice, surprising Gene.

"I got business in Arizona," he says.

"Too bad," says the trooper, leading him to the black and white squad car. He locks Gene inside and goes to help his buddies subdue Linda.

The three of them tell her she'll set her hair on fire if she doesn't stop, but she won't listen. Suddenly they're holding her arms in a grip she can't break. She goes limp. The troopers call for another car.

Mayland is at the county jail by midnight with two hundred dollars' bail money he borrowed from Frank. Linda comes out of her cell in an orange jumpsuit that flaps around her ankles. She looks happy to see him.

"It was cold in there," she tells him. "I didn't have no socks."

"You don't look so good," he says.

The jailer gives Linda her clothes, and she goes into an empty cell to put them on while Mayland pays the bail.

"Drunk and disorderly," the jailer says. "Destruction of property. You got a handful there, mister."

"There's going to be some new rules around the house starting tomorrow," Mayland says, without knowing what they will be. The jailer tells him that Linda will probably get off with a light fine because it's a lady judge and because of Gene hitting her.

When she comes out in her clothes, the men in the big cell whistle and wave good-bye to her, sticking their hands through the bars. Except for Gene: Mayland sees him reading a magazine at the cement table in the middle of the cell.

Outside, in the parking lot, Linda hugs Mayland. She still smells like beer. "You know what?" she says. "I knew you wouldn't like it when I ran off. I was going to come back anyway in a couple of weeks."

"You should have left me a note," he says.

MANIKARNIKA

First day in Varanasi: Martina had seen the red ball of dawn rise upon the sacred river, the yogis erupting from the water beaded and panting like champion Labradors. She was walking back from breakfast at the Baby Krishna Café, babbling uncharacteristically about the undividedness of food in India. The breakfast had gone to her head: *pooris* and *channa* and yogurt, lots of sweet *chai*.

There were no calories here, no vitamins, she said. Food was simply food, whole and undivided in the mind — but no one was listening; they were all talking at once, weaving through the alley's boil. Dead rats, beggar widows, young men on shrieking scooters. Shit; garbage; sacred cows lying with their front legs tucked under, as compact as cats. An old man in a dhoti carrying brass pots down to Ganga. Five Westerners: Martina, Sandra, Jean-Jacques, Viv, and Stuart.

The Viswanath was their hotel. They veered into its outer courtyard, a sudden whiteness tiled in yellow.

Empty, but for the owner's temple, a marble cow wistfully facing a shut door painted silver.

"He's *there*," Jean-Jacques insisted for the umpteenth time: he was speaking of his guru, and his British girlfriend Viv's; they'd brought Martina and Sandra up from Calcutta to meet him. Hari was his name; it meant "light." He saw through all appearances. He had the powers that were the reason why charlatans existed.

They were going to meet him now; according to Jean-Jacques, Martina could be enlightened by lunchtime.

Martina felt sure that her skepticism would repel any of Hari's emanations. Still, she was dying to meet him. She'd read Nagarjuna, Krishnamurti, Ram Dass, and Annie Besant. To know the reasons for everything — why red is red and black, black; why human eyes see only the colors that objects have rejected — and then, to know what lay past reasons. Emptiness? Such notions drew her heart like iron filings.

The Viswanath's owner was lolling behind the front desk, fresh from his morning dip in Ganga, his Brahmin string still wet across his naked breasts. The Westerners passed by, nodding but not quite seeing him until he stopped Martina. "Madom! Miss Martina Sachs!" She made ready to produce her passport, or insist she'd paid for the room, but he handed her a folded paper.

"Telegram. Farword from Calcutta guess how." Forwarded from your Calcutta guesthouse.

CARR DIED IT SLEEP 2–11 HAARF ATACKT CALL ME JANE.

The paper was fibrous, gray; the type wavered.

Martina remembered reading somewhere that your heart is the size of your fist.

Odd — or not? — how shock made things seem foreordained. Over here, causality was cooked up in one's blind spot. Martina couldn't get this through her head, so India's surprises still surprised her.

Even coming to Varanasi had been a coincidence. Three days ago, she was sitting with Sandra in the Blue Sky Café on Sudder Street in Calcutta. They were deciding where to go next, wavering between Rajasthan (camel trek, uncut gems) and Poori (beaches, the original Juggernaut). The decision was more Sandra's, since this was her fourth trip to India, and only Martina's first.

"Really I should take you to Varanasi," Sandra was saying. "It's, like, essence of India. But the religious energy there is so heavy, I don't know if I'm up for it."

"Heavy? What do you mean?" Martina was intrigued. Sandra grimaced, shrugged.

Cubes of pure noise were smashing to pieces all around them. Still, Martina thought, Sandra might have taken the trouble to explain.

Now someone tapped Martina's shoulder. A stranger, Jean-Jacques, asking if he and Viv might share the table. Maps and guides were swept aside, and the travelers' conversation began. Where have you been, where are you going, is it good there? Why didn't Martina and Sandra come and meet an enlightened being, and maybe spend the hot season up in Rishikesh with him?

Who could refuse?

Martina couldn't help feeling smug when they said the guru stayed in Varanasi, where she'd wished to go.

They took the train, Martina, Sandra, Jean-Jacques, and Viv. Stuart, now the group's fifth member, happened to be staying at the Viswanath. He came out to the balcony last night while the rest of them were watching the stars through monkey-proof wire. Stuart was from New Zealand and hadn't been home in six years. He was really interested in gurus, and all spiritual things.

*

The Viswanath's owner clasped his hands together, making a sad face, as if he were looking into a baby's crib. "Relative?"

Martina heard some garble —"Dellatiff?"— and said, "No," automatically. Yet the landlord's English was making its way through the folds of her brain; as soon as she'd spoken, she understood what he'd said. "No, I mean yes. It's my father."

Carl told her last year that the next time he tried to kill himself, he'd do it with phenobarb and Scotch so that it would look like a heart attack in his sleep. "It's my father," she repeated. She examined her companions' four bland faces. A month ago, she'd never seen them. "My father just died." Well, not "just": the news was two weeks late, ancient light from a star that had exploded. "I mean, he was alive when I left."

She handed the telegram past Stuart to Jean-Jacques.

"Parents always die when their kids are in India," Stuart pronounced. "It never fails."

"Poor baby," said Sandra, throwing her arms around Martina, who stood stiffly, resisting. She was a little attracted to Sandra. Furthermore, she wasn't ready to become the designated object of pity. Already she had too many identities: the youngest, the least experienced traveler, the lesbian, and the one most prone to digestive trouble. (Diarrhea, continuously, since her second day in Calcutta.)

Handing the telegram back to her, Jean-Jacques said, "You must have missed the funeral."

Martina felt guilty about how glad she was. "I guess I have a good excuse."

Standing up, the hotel owner waved a fistful of smoking incense sticks. "Indian people try to die in Varanasi so as to go straight to Heaven. Varanasi is our Jerusalem. Best, pray for your father." He began shuffling around the room, offering smoke and garlands to his 3-D Shivas.

"Oh yes," Jean-Jacques said. "She will go to the guru this afternoon."

"I don't know," Martina said.

"Heart attack. Was he a smoker?" Sandra was a nurse, from Noe Valley. Pre-Raphaelite reddish hair, the type who would, and did, go around all in white clothes; she was an incongruous companion for Martina. Martina wore a lot of black and was taking a year off from the graduate program in computer animation at NYU. A mutual friend had hooked them up, insisting Martina not come to India alone. She'd acquiesced, taking the long route from New York through San Francisco so that Sandra could get on the same plane. Martina was condescending until they landed at Dum Dum Airport and she realized what India was.

Sandra knew how to get a taxi; Sandra had spent her last three vacations working at Mother Teresa's.

They'd stayed with an Indian family, the Baruas, friends of Sandra's from the last visit. The father was a journalist and the mother owned sari shops. Sandra went off to Mother T's, where Martina was afraid to work lest somebody die while she was shining a penlight into their pupils, a thing that had happened to Sandra. Instead, she stayed home with the two Barua daughters, eating sweets, smoking, and answering questions about America. It was fun for a while, until Martina grew weary of sidestepping the topic of sex with men. She'd begged Sandra to make an excuse so they could move to the travelers' quarter. Based on the Barua girls, Martina had decided that Indians were the most intelligent people on earth. They had the least illusions. Still, she couldn't figure out how their cynicism reconciled itself with their perfect faith in invisible forces.

She could hear the Baruas now, commenting about her father. "Everyone is miserable in America, except the Indian immigrants!"

Martina described Carl's health habits to Sandra. "He'd smoke a joint once in a while, but no cigarettes. He drank, but not that much. He was fifty-two. It's not a *total* surprise though, that he would die."

The others waited for her to explain, but Martina wouldn't. Feeling perverse and powerful, she asked to be left alone. No, she didn't want to meet Hari today, nor have one of the men accompany her to the post office to place a call home.

Like a chunk of radium in a vault, she sat in the blue room she shared with Sandra and listened to them clatter down the stairs. Talking about her, no doubt. After they'd been absorbed in it, the noise from the alley got louder, and the toilet's smell more insistent. A long brown stain on the wall next to her bed seemed to be preventing Martina from crying. Automatically, she reached for her *Survive India Guide*. Its creased spine fell open at the page describing the most famous thing in Varanasi, the burning ghats, where Hindus cremated their relatives on expensive piles of logs. The group had discussed taking Martina down there, this afternoon or tomorrow, as soon as they'd figured out Hari's schedule.

It was all right to watch the cremations, as long as you didn't take photographs.

Martina had seen an accident victim lying in the street once, but covered with a sheet. The sanity of Indian burial customs now impressed itself upon her. I'd know Carl was really gone, she thought, if I watched him burn to ash.

Last night, Stuart had been pontificating on the corpse meditation practiced at a wat he'd visited in northern Thailand. Monks spend a year watching a dead body bloat, turn black, and decompose. You don't know the nature of life, he said, until you've seen the nature of death.

Why do I dislike him so much, Martina asked herself.

He is so often exactly right. Well, yes, because of that. But why should I care?

Unable to enforce any positive feeling toward Stuart, she sprang up from the bed and assembled supplies for going out. Water, guidebook, sunglasses, money belt. Everything but the camera, even though her vest pocket was big enough to hide it.

I hope my mission is pure enough to prevent its being stolen, she thought, stuffing the big Nikon under her pillow. It made an obvious lump, but she didn't want to leave it at the desk.

Walking downriver, she found herself at Manikarnika in ten minutes. Four corpses were in various stages of cremation, each releasing a braid of black smoke straight up to Heaven. No wind — intense transparent heat, like vaporized quartz.

She chose the corpse closest to the water, the least burnt, a woman, and stood six feet from the pyre, clasping her hands together to show an attitude of reverence. The few live Indians, all men, standing and sitting around, ignored Martina thoroughly.

The ashy ground was so hot it nearly melted her rubber thongs.

The corpse was economically fleshed. A small cigar wrapped tightly in red silk and garlanded with tinsel and marigolds. Her son sat up the bank, as thin as Gandhi, with a newly shaven head.

She smelled exactly like broiling steak.

Martina's face tightened in the heat.

Impossible to think of Carl, or anything else:

First the marigolds wilted, blackened, burned. Then the shroud evaporated, revealing a shapeless brown flank that spoke the woman's whole life: squatting at a kitchen mortar, turning on her haunches. Bearing children. Lugging water jars.

All at once, a flock of blisters rose. The skin crusted

white, then blackened in patches. Her flesh opened; muscles burned in layers like the pages of a book.

The thigh split, showing yellow fat, white tendon, bone. Ribs appeared. The hands puffed up like rubber gloves, but the fingers were still slender, human.

Never emerging from its tight wrapping, the face resolved into three holes. Eyes, mouth: around the mouth, an oval ring of muscle. The universal face: I, you, me. Carl. No one.

A Dom came out with a bamboo pole and broke the leg at its charred knee, flipped the unburnt foot into the heart of the fire. His skin was the color of eggplant, so dark that Martina could barely distinguish his coarse, drooping features. What did he think of her? She could not know. A pink, enormous female from the land of wealth.

Carl was underground, in pinstripes, whole. He'd been lowered into the frozen ground in a coffin like an ocean liner, a shining ship of death. How would they dig a grave in winter in Connecticut? With ruby lasers?

CARR DIED IT SLEEP 2—11 HAARF ATAKCT CALL ME JANE.

The dead woman's gastric juice shot up in a bitter, yellow fountain, and fell back hissing on the coals.

Reality hits you in the face, Martina thought: What opinion could I possibly have?

The flames were dying; under white ash, Martina could no longer tell limbs from logs. The woman's son came down the bank, dressed only in two squares of unbleached cotton. Using the Dom's long pole, he stirred the ashes until he came up with a black lump the size of a small cabbage, the hips that bore him. Waded ankle-deep into the river and, with a jerk, pitched it in. The lump bobbled, then sank utterly and at once. The son walked up the bank smiling, not looking back.

"Good-bye," Martina said to the woman. If Carl could

have become part of a sacred river, would he have killed himself sooner or not at all?

She turned away and began walking upstream along the low, glittering river, back toward the hotel. It must have been one o'clock. No shadows; a pinpoint sun blowtorched the ghats to white. A family of women wailed, squatting far enough from Manikarnika for their grief not to draw the dead back into life. Good, Martina thought. Not everyone is smiling about this.

A too handsome young holy man paced in a shady sandstone alcove; moored below, his ocher-tented house-boat bobbled on the stream. Farther along, skinny, desperate men picked at Martina's sleeves, crying: "Bwoot, bwoot, madom, my bwoot! Hunderd rupee! Burning ghat! Twenty-four hours get body fire!"

She plowed through them, shaking her head no. No, no, no, no, no.

The water's edge was clotted with roses, marigolds, and plastic bags like man-o'-wars. This, *this,* Martina thought: sun, river, fire, stone. This is what religions tried to get to. Still her mind remained frozen, impenetrable, its darkness the only cool for a thousand miles.

"But why *India?*" Carl had asked her over the phone. "Are you into poverty, filth, and crowds?"

She said, defensively, "It's the oldest civilization, Dad." She could have said, I want to understand emptiness, but emptiness was no longer a topic between them.

Two months after Jane divorced him, Carl invited Martina up to Connecticut for Sunday dinner. He didn't meet her at the train, so she took a cab to the house. He didn't answer the door, so she took the key from under its fake rock. His car was running in the garage: odd. She found him in it, quite conscious, waiting for death — or for Martina? — with the vacuum cleaner hose duct-taped to the exhaust pipe. He said he'd forgotten she was coming.

They talked until one A.M. in a Greek diner on I-95. Carl drank one Miller after another, wanting her to listen. Life had no meaning: he hated the emptiness of things just going on and on. Martina was starting to be interested in Eastern philosophy then. She was reading Nagarjuna and painting white canvases with pale, almost indistinguishable objects. She could tell him emptiness was how it was, and that you didn't have to hate it: in fact, the sages called it blissful. If everything was empty, nothing could be taken away from you.

She remembers feeling quite desperate, telling Carl that.

Carl said there must be more than one kind of emptiness. For his kind, he should have used pills and Scotch.

Martina said, "It looked more like you wanted me to find you." Carl admitted he was lonely. Martina stayed the night in her old room. It didn't feel right, but she couldn't think of anything else to give him. Soon, he was involved with Shastine, a blond dental student and born-again Christian. Shastine had been in the army and had a disciplined fanaticism that Carl seemed to depend upon. She started taking him to church; he'd call Martina on the phone and praise the sermons' intellectual depth, but when he repeated the preacher's arguments, Martina could hear nothing but thunder and threats. She wondered what had gotten into her father, yet she allowed herself to feel relieved.

At six the Smallpox Goddess temple swung into full charivari: bells, horns, and sirens summoned Sitala to protect babies from disease. And someone was pounding on Martina's door. Yelling, "Martina! Are you in there? Let me in!"

Sandra. Martina rolled over till she could reach the door and with effort slid back the iron bolt. "Sorry."

Sandra rushed in, her long limbs whipping in all directions. "I couldn't get in! We were worried about you," she said, sitting on the edge of Martina's bed. "Wow you're pale." She placed a cool hand on Martina's forehead. It smelled of spicy Ayurvedic soap: miraculous how clean Sandra could keep.

"Yeah, I feel pretty sick."

"You would. You're not feverish, just kind of clammy. What's wrong?"

"I've got a migraine. My stomach is upset. I spent all morning on the burning ghat." Martina closed her eyes. Her hair still reeked of corpse smoke; next to Sandra she felt fat, as big as a man. Sandra was asking how many times did she use the toilet today, but Martina overrode her. "My dad killed himself. I'm pretty sure."

She was almost gratified to hear Sandra gasp.

She talked, keeping her eyes shut. A disembodied voice spoke into a night sky, telling the incident of the car exhaust. Carl. He couldn't be happy with his money or his career as a doctor. He wanted to heal others but saw patients as cases, not as human beings. He'd abolished inwardness very early in his life. Several of his aunts and uncles had disappeared in northern Poland; as a young man he'd changed his name from Sachs to Sax. Martina had changed it back, for herself, unofficially.

Poor Carl, if he could hear his pain so horribly oversimplified. "Sorry I didn't say anything this morning."

"Don't apologize. You had to be with it." Sandra fed Martina two Motrin with Bisleri water. "Seems like your father had more spiritual perception than he was willing to live by."

For once, Martina was glad Sandra wasn't ashamed to talk this way. "I want to watch the sunset," she said, letting herself sound a little babyish.

"Honey, you've got to eat. Come to Hari's. He's invited us for dinner."

"So, yeah, how was he?"

"I think he's the real thing." Sandra shrugged, pushed her lip out. Eyes wide — who knows? — affirmed solidarity with Martina; but she was brighter than usual, lit up. Something had happened to her while Martina was out on the ghats.

"Then I guess I can eat his food," Martina said. Earlier, Sandra had told her that the Indians drink straight from Ganga and don't get sick, so powerful was their perception of its purity. "Let me wash my face."

The far riverbank was cirrus-pale as the five Westerners strolled past the dhobis folding stiff pants; past the home of Tulsi Das, the poet-saint whose name means "Servant of Purple Basil."

Stuart was discoursing about mystical tests. In cliff monasteries in Sikkim, for example, the young monks had to go down to the river and get a cup of water before the abbot's cup of tea got cold, sitting out on the stone floor. "I mean, this is a very high cliff. By road it would take ten hours. They have to fly."

Sandra was nodding in a continuous way that seemed odd, until Martina realized she was attracted to Stuart. How could she be, when he was so pompously taking possession of these magical things and places and powers? She still didn't like him. At the first lull Martina preempted the conversation. "You know what? The day we landed in India? I think was the day Carl died." She counted back on her fingers to January 29, and said, "He was dead the whole time we were in Calcutta."

"Wow," Sandra said. She looked at Stuart. "And hey, today is Valentine's."

Obviously, her case was beyond hope.

"It's incredible. The illusion of coincidence," said Stuart.

"I *know*," Sandra said, beaming at Martina. "You're going to fall in love with Hari."

Oh, glop, Martina thought, wishing their attention had stayed on Carl; but she was unwilling to pull it back there.

Stuart pointed upward, touching Martina's arm. "There's the place Hari stays. It's an old maharaja's castle that's been divided into apartments." He pronounced Hari as "Hairy."

"It looks like the witch's castle in *Sleeping Beauty*," said Martina, hoping Stuart would disapprove of pop comparisons. Then guilty over her pettiness: Carl was dead. Dead, dead, dead. And Martina herself was next, the next row of wheat to be scythed. The image gave her an exhilarating sensation, as if she were about to leap into vast, clear space. No one was in her way.

The castle's river wall was blind, as high as a cliff, with yellow lines marking famous floods. Two hundred feet up, pariah kites wheeled from a large tree growing out of the parapet. A narrow, piss-stinking stair led to the street level; Martina gave a rupee to a woman beggar at the gate. Her baby's head had rolled sideways, but its raccoon eyes, decorated with kohl, focused on Martina with interest. Martina hoped the baby would live a long time. On one rupee? Next time, if the mother was here, she'd give more.

Hari sat on a hard Indian bed next to a window barred against monkeys. He was bald, with a powerful, handsome head, and wore Western clothing, a collared shirt buttoned tightly at the neck. As the Westerners came in, he nodded and smiled in a delight that seemed genuine.

Jean-Jacques touched the small of Martina's back. As she sank onto the matting, the room's dark green walls slid upward around her, so that she sat into a darkness. Next to her, Sandra and Stuart closed their eyes, so she did, too.

Silence. She still could hear, faintly, the wild harmonium that played on Dasashwamedh at sundown, the intoxicated baritone singing his opera of gods' names. She kept her eyes closed.

Hari intoned, "Who is the experiencer?"

More silence. No one, Martina thought, but she was afraid to speak the wrong answer.

Stuart said, "I see no boundaries. Boundless field. Everything . . . is the field of the witness."

"There is no witness," Hari said firmly.

"The witness is very subtle," Stuart said. "Almost not there."

"So put yourself in that place," Hari said.

Martina peeked. Seeing Stuart's eyes clenched shut with effort, she almost forgave Sandra for liking him.

"Very good, Stuart," Hari said. "Stay in that place."

Now Jean-Jacques was introducing her. "Hari, this is Martina, who we told you about, whose father died this morning."

Hari said, "Welcome, Martina. I am sorry to hear. Is there anything you would like to ask me? As Stuart said, there are no boundaries here. You can say anything you like, for you are free."

This is my moment, Martina thought. I'm standing in the secret heart of India. "So why do people kill themselves?"

Collective inbreath, collective sigh. Viv jumped up and clicked on the overhead tube, which stuttered grayly, making everyone look half dead, like people waiting in a waiting room.

"They are imprisoned in the thought, they cannot get what they want."

Very true, Martina thought, but how mild it sounded. How much too broadly applicable. She tasted Carl's bitter specificity: What had Carl wanted?

She imagined her father's last night on earth: Shastine putting fresh sheets on his bed while he was in the shower. When he came out, she brought a tray with one silver-rimmed tumbler, one brown plastic prescription bottle, and Carl's bottle of Dalwhinnie. And a rose in cut glass.

Everything resolved. Everything smooth, finished.

Hari was saying, "Your father was a suicide?"

"I think so. But I haven't talked to my mom yet."

"You must call her tomorrow morning. Jean-Jacques will go with you." He then inquired about Martina's health, her studies, and whether she had brothers or sisters? When Martina said she was at NYU, he said he had lived in Greenwich Village for a year once. He found it very interesting. Manhattan reminded him of Calcutta, action without stop.

A stout middle-aged woman brought food on round steel trays. Martina finally wept a little when the pudgy, brown hand entered her field of vision, placing the tray of white and yellow food before her. Hari was sipping *chai* from a steel glass, observing her over its rim. With as full an intention as if she were drawing aside a curtain, Martina allowed him to watch her cry. "You are very innocent," he said. "Take little yogurt and rice. The *dal* is *saadi dal,* without spice. Good for stomach. It is how I eat it myself."

While they were eating, Sandra asked, "Why are we here?"

"You must tell me."

Sandra said, "I don't know."

"Very good, this don't know. Only That can know enlightenment."

"What is That?"

"That is you only. Try to identify." Hari smiled broadly. Then he fixed his gaze at his own foot, except that Martina had the impression that he was thinking too intensely to see anything. He seemed a little embarrassed.

Sandra stopped eating; her face was pale, saintly. Glazed, as if with finest sweat. Her soul shone out.

Eventually Hari said, "All right, enough. Sandra, come back to us. All of you come back tomorrow."

In the rickshaw home, Martina felt strange, as if she were floating in a pleasant soap bubble. Time had stopped: she said so to Sandra, and Sandra's eyes gleamed. "Hari." She was still shining, essential.

Unmoving, unseen, they passed brightly lit market stalls that emitted loud Hindi opera; they squeezed past a wedding procession. First twenty men, two rows of ten, each holding a white porcelain socket on his head, each socket supporting two green, neon tubes that stuck out at angles, like antennae. Loops of extension cord linked man to man, and the men to a humming generator on an oxcart lumbering behind them. Last came the bride and groom, riding a decorated elephant.

If the world were real, India would not exist. Some sort of prayer formed in Martina's mind: actually, an effort at communicating with the dead.

"I won't go home. I never want to see his grave," Martina groaned into Sandra's clean, wadded shirt, which was saving her face from the hotel pillow, as stiff and greasy as a dog's bed. "Dog's bed": when Martina had said it, a couple of minutes ago, she'd dissolved into hysterical laughter. So Sandra gave her the shirt.

Now she sat on Martina's buttocks, digging her thumbs into Martina's occiput. Migraine massage. Martina was to release her mental pain, too, by speaking it. This was difficult with her face muffled by the soft shirt, and the intermittent shocks from Sandra's thumbs. Sandra was stronger than she looked; her massaging contained a merciless element.

"Grisly. Selfish. Violent. Bastard. I can't afford a plane ticket for his funeral. I already feel like it's my fault. Ow! If only I'd been better." Martina stopped, closed her eyes. She wasn't sure whether these were her real feelings, or things she would expect herself to say as a psychologically literate person.

Darkness with red aureoles of pressure. Sandra persisted, pushing the headache's poison up toward Martina's forehead.

Martina, too, pushed stoically forward. "If I'd stayed home. I got too far away. But it was his own choice. Nothing I could do. And that's the worst. I guess, but I don't really *feel* helpless. I feel. Lonely."

This, at last, was real.

"Good, good." Sandra dug so hard, Martina saw a lime green network. "Ouch!"

"Sorry."

"He killed himself," Martina repeated. "His own decision." Heat was coming out from between Sandra's legs. Martina let out all her breath, a final deflation of resistance. Sandra's ischial tuberosities pressed into Martina. Deliciously. "Now I'm too bereaved to get enlightened. And Sandra has a crush on Stuart. They'll run off to Goa and leave me." She started giggling.

"Is it that obvious?"

Martina flapped her arm to make Sandra stop rubbing. She rolled over, sat up; her eyelids were raw, all around. "I don't trust Stuart. Stuart looks like a junkie."

"Lots of travelers look like junkies."

"He lay around drunk in Piraeus, that's what he said. He probably has some horrible disease."

"I won't leave you. I won't go off with him."

But you already have. "Promise?"

"Promise. We'll be with Hari for a while, right?"

"Right. I could hug you, but it wouldn't be decent."

Sandra's eyes widened. "Well. Um. I mean, that's okay. You can hug me."

"No," Martina said.

Late that night, she heard her friend quietly lifting the bolt; but she only went out to pee.

*

Kik-kik! Shadows flitted across the barred, grime-frosted window as rhesus families woke and scampered along the high wall. Monkeys! Martina was stabbed with joy. How could a person not want to live?

The headache still lurked, a poisonous deposit behind her right ear. But she was dressed and eating fried potato *chai* in the courtyard by seven-thirty.

Jean-Jacques popped in and out of his room like a clock's cuckoo, brushing teeth, putting on a shirt, forgetting something, coming back out. He was robust, bearded, fifty, stylish in baggy military shorts and an old woven shoulder bag that said "Tibet." His skin was incredibly smooth except for a massif of varicose veins on the back of one calf.

"All set? What are you eating?"

"*Chat* with mint sauce," Martina said, smirking.

"You're gonna make yourself really sick," Jean-Jacques said. "Take it from me. Ever since my first trip I've got no stomach lining."

"But rice is so boring."

"Suit yourself." Of his French accent only the faintest buzz remained; he'd been with Viv, who was British, for ten years. He started for the main road at a pace that required work to follow.

Martina's stomach burned from the spicy *chat*. Under the archways, the poor were beginning to stir under ragged cotton quilts. Children, widows, *sadhus*. Jean-Jacques gave ten rupees to one leper who raised his Kewpie face to the sky.

"Ten rupees!" Martina had thought she was generous yesterday, giving the woman a whole rupee.

"That guy, three years ago, I was trying to give him just ten paise? He had fingers then. He grabbed my hand, very rare for a leper in India. Looked into my eyes, like, what was I holding on to? I gave him everything I had in my pocket."

"But you were still yourself," Martina said, meaning that Jean-Jacques and the beggar could not actually have traded places.

"Yes," said Jean-Jacques. "I remained myself," and she saw that he meant something different, perhaps that one could give without losing.

Another beggar was following them, a man with a withered arm. He pinched his aluminum plate against his chest, and with the hand that was whole he touched Martina's upper arm softly, insistently. His fingers were sticky, damp. She gave him four rupees, but he was not satisfied. He touched her arm again, not smiling. His eyes were bloodshot. The touch traveled inward, deadly, seeking her heart.

Carl. Carl. The worst time, when he got her attention at a party by coming up behind Martina and pressing under her breast with the flat of a steak knife. His forearm around her throat, like an assassin's. She was seventeen, a senior in high school; Jane used to pay her to serve at social dinners.

Carl had made some joke and asked her to refill the ice bucket; Jane had been across the room, acting brilliant.

Martina hurried to catch up with Jean-Jacques, who was now buying a banana for a filthy little girl. "My father was so crazy," she told him. "I could spend the rest of my life in therapy getting over him. Millions of rupees." Jean-Jacques told her that the word *therapist* meant "friend of the rich" in Greek. A joke, she realized, too slowly.

"Not possible," said the postal clerk.

"Her father, he has died," Jean-Jacques shouted, retroflexing his *d*'s to be understood. Martina almost giggled.

"I am so sorry," the clerk said. "What can I do?"

"She must speak to her mother!" Jean-Jacques's outcry to universal feeling was not lost on the crowd that waited to call Bubaneshwar, Delhi, and Patna. Men pursed their lips and waggled their heads. A wealthy lady in a purple sari cried, "Yes, yes. Put hah through."

"Wan Howard," the clerk said resentfully, indicating a row of chairs. One hour. "Sit down."

Martina was ready to obey, but Jean-Jacques stood glaring into the wire cage. She wished she could hold hands with him.

"Farm," Jean-Jacques insisted.

The clerk shoved a pad through the grille. When Jean-Jacques had filled out the form, the clerk examined it and said, "Okay, pipteen minnit. Sit down!"

They stood. Jean-Jacques entertained Martina by reading the list of money-saving telegram codes painted on the wall. The one she should use was 03: "Sadness for your grief."

Soon the clerk cried, "America, America," and pushed a green receiver out the grille hole. The holes and creases in its mouthpiece were clogged with black, organic gug. Martina squeezed through; the crowd leaned inward, like interested relatives.

"Jane! *Hi!*"

Jane sold real estate in Cambridge now. "Hello, honey. How *are* you?"

"Fine! You? I mean, I'm sad, I'm kind of in shock."

"Me, too. I've been waiting on your call. Three days before . . . indecent! . . . at the funeral."

"What? I didn't even get your telegram till yesterday!"

"*Sh! Sh!*" Fierce-eyed, the woman in the purple sari calmed the crowd.

"Hell yes," Jane said through sine waves of static. "I built that medical practice. I worked for him for years."

She's not in the least concerned with me, Martina realized.

"Why? A savings account bypasses his will," Jane continued. "She had to strike at the right time."

Martina started shouting into the receiver, to get her money's worth. "Sorry I missed the funeral. I feel close to him. We're the same, in a way. Look, I just hope he's found some peace."

"My God!" Jane's voice was fading. "Don't you . . . ?"

"I'm with this fantastic guru. I'm not coming."

". . . memorial service . . . clean out the house."

"Can't Tom and Barbara help you? I can't afford another ticket. We can have a memorial in May."

Somewhere in space, the telecommunications satellite turned its good face toward India. Blip of clarity: "No darling! I need you here."

"I don't know if I want to know what you've been telling me," Martina said. "Anyway. I'm not coming right now."

The screaming of postal customers rolled like thunder around the high British-built barrel vaults. The bodies pressing Martina heaved with life. They'll all end up at the ghat, she realized suddenly, black and flaky, like burnt croissants.

"I'm not coming," she said again.

"Line is cut," the clerk enunciated. He slid out a form covered with ballpoint curlicues. "Eight hundred rupee." Everyone watched Martina count out enough mildewed bills to keep a family half a year.

Jean-Jacques made Martina send Jane a telegram with the teacher's address in Rishikesh. They'd be leaving in a week. Up in the Himalayan foothills, they'd bathe in Ganga where she was clean enough not to give you typhoid: and be saved, Hari had said, but laughing. Ganga was a river of nectar that came straight out of Heaven. Martina was quite prepared to jump in it down here. Carl, she thought, you were almost right.

She hoped his ghost was hovering around her; but realistically, it probably couldn't deal with the squalor.

Jean-Jacques said, "Let's get milk shakes, and you can

tell me about your father. Vanilla milk shakes are one good, bland thing we can eat." He kept her out all afternoon. Among other things, she was surprised to learn that he taught sociology at a small university north of London. She asked him, then, for help with her theory about Indians, how their cynicism fit with faith. Jean-Jacques said, "In a different way, they're just exactly like you."

For the evening session with Hari, Martina put on a white silk-cotton *kurta* she bought after admiring Jean-Jacques's: he showed her the shop in one of the narrow lanes near the hotel. It made her look wide, but the fabric was soft and light against her skin.

"I'm glad you're not going home," Sandra said, twisting on the bed. She was always doing bits of yoga. "There's so much potential here. Hari was talking about you this morning. I think he likes you. He said you were very intelligent, very pure." Martina gave her a funny look, but Sandra refused to be made uncomfortable. "I mean. Whether your father got killed or he killed himself, or whether he really had a heart attack, it doesn't make any difference, right? So you still might as well come to Rishikesh. At least until you get ready to face things."

"Yeah," Martina said, "live forward." She could hear a deadness in her voice. "But don't you think it's uglier to be murdered for your money?"

Sandra turned her slim foot in a circle, then stopped. "I don't believe that," she said. "Sounds like Jane's making up things."

By some slight margin, Martina preferred to agree: if suicide, she'd know where Carl was. When she was twenty and Kurt had broken up with her, Martina bought enough heroin to die with. Looking at the needle, she'd stalled out. Left it loaded on the table and gone outside in the rain, Manhattan November, trying to gather courage and despair into one momentous lump. Imagining, after a pinprick, nothingness, the perfect dark. But the sky was a pretty, toxic pink, and she'd become interested in a row of raindrops hanging off the accordion wire at a parking lot. Watching them slowly gather weight and fall, an austerely orchestrated tone row, she'd clung to existence for five whole minutes.

She'd kept the heroin for about a week, thinking to take it in recreational doses; in the end, she flushed it. After that, whenever Martina thought about killing herself, she always told herself she could do it anytime.

Since the burning ghat, she saw no difference between life and death; no reason to die before it simply happened. Martina could imagine becoming Hari's attendant, living a simple life, dressing in saris and watering his hibiscus. Which is, in fact, what she did, six months later. After going back to the States for Carl's memorial service, cleaning out his house, she returned.

Tonight they had to eat their own dinner before going to Hari's, so the five Westerners walked south along the riverbank toward the burning ghats, intending to climb out at Lalita Ghat.

There was a mild breeze; the sky was the color of tamarinds and mangoes. Approaching Manikarnika, the smell of meat came to them on the wind, and Martina could see many more fires burning than she did yesterday morning. Ten at least. She got out her camera. There was something she wanted to hold onto from those flames, something film would reveal. The actual light rays, registering on emulsion. Five years from now, she might be an artist again and use it.

She was far enough away to take a photograph unnoticed, except that in the dusk, the automatic flash went off, a sudden burst of light that caused a furious young man to materialize.

"No photo!"

"I'm sorry," Martina said.

"Give camera! American bitch!"

"No," Martina said. "It's not even going to come out. I'm much too far away."

"Bitch, you come to break our religion."

"Throw in Ganga, throw in Ganga. Purify," a second young man demanded, plucking at Martina's sleeve. His teeth were bright red with betel juice; he had a six-hair mustache. Several others appeared, too, hopping in Martina's peripheral vision. One of them carried a stick.

"I won't," she said. "It's my camera. I have a lot of pictures on there."

"Hey look, they're getting heavy," Stuart muttered.

"Bitch! Bitch!" the men yelled. Dark was falling, the orange fires leaped, greasy smoke enveloped the five Westerners. Of her friends, Martina could see nothing but the whites of their eyes. Jean-Jacques was pleading with them in bits of Hindi.

"Give it up," Stuart said suddenly. "Give him the camera. We're going to get hurt."

A squat, ugly man slapped Martina on the ear, hard. Ringing brass. The edge of her ear went huge and hot as the ball of the descending sun. She was trying to twist and run when Stuart grabbed her arm, as roughly as any of the Indians might have; he twisted the camera from her hand. Slow motion: with a pitcher's windup, a gesture containing thousands of lines of apology, he threw Martina's Nikon out over the river. Black. It hung over the current and fell in with a sudden, deep suction.

Four hundred dollars. The young men were temporarily impressed. "Sorry, sorry," Stuart said turning back toward them. "*Chalo.* C'mon guys. Let's go."

Still excited, the young men blocked their way: but they were hopping up and down, so their line was porous.

"Sorry," Martina said to the first young man.

"All right." He stepped aside. "You, stupid girl, never come back here. Never come back."

The young men went off, talking and gesturing savagely.

"God, I am so stupid," Martina said. "I can't be left alone."

Sandra said, "You didn't know. See what we meant about heavy?"

Jean-Jacques said, "Varanasi is the worst. You can't smell the flowers or people get angry. But it's okay. Just wait a few days before coming again. Wear different clothes. All Westerners look alike to them."

Stuart was already walking back in the direction from which they'd come; Sandra was hurrying to catch up with him.

When they told Hari, he was incensed about the incident. He said it illustrated the evil of organized religion. "And Sandra," Hari admonished. "You should take care of her. Martina is like a very young child. Too much has happened to her."

"I learned a lesson," Martina said, and shivered.

"You both will stay with me in Rishikesh," Hari said. "If you like. Not in hostel."

"Yes, yes! We belong together," Sandra said. Martina gave her a quick grin, full of sexual wickedness that was all but lost on the beaming Sandra. Oh well.

That night she dreamed of fires, corpses, war. She lost her black shoe in the river and had to dive in after it. The shoe traveled swiftly along the bottom, in deep currents; she could not catch it, so she came up next to a café where Stuart was reading a newspaper, waggling his bare foot. A nice, French place with a stone floor (like the ghats). Her hair was full of mud and shit. Large blue-black storks came to feed on it; they preened Martina's hair with big, stiff beaks until it was clean again. The storks were sort of Hari, or belonged to Hari.

In the morning, she was so happy about her dream that she woke Sandra up to tell her about it. Martina didn't usually remember her dreams. It felt good to dream about the people she was traveling with. It let her know she was connected.

MY MOST RECENT, PERFECT KNIGHT

Frank Bennett called just after New Year's, having tracked me down through Information. He'd married again and was living in Paris, two things he'd wanted to do ten years ago when we were lovers.

"I'm still a lawyer," Frank apologized, "but I've been helping Cambodians get into the States. I'm in New York taking a seminar on how to fill out immigration forms." He chuckled. We hadn't talked in three years, but I still remembered how Frank saw himself from two points of view: the man he wished to be, and the man he'd avoided becoming. And I still found it charming, the way he could laugh at himself.

How was I? he wanted to know.

I was glad to be able to tell him some European news of my own. Ellis, the head of my dance company, had suddenly gotten a MacArthur, and so this spring the Rhino Dance Company was going to tour Frankfurt, Rome, Avignon, Madrid, and Prague. I had two chorus parts: an aged Rockette and a nymph in the *Rite of Spring,* but I'd lost the solo about women's subjugation. Company politics. The piece involved ripping apart a naked baby doll, so I was halfway relieved. But it was so in-your-face that reviewers were likely to single it out.

Frank said the reviewers would be talking about Ellis's choreography anyway, not my performance. "Cara Doyle, you're the bravest person I know. You live by art, by what you believe." He'd always considered himself a sellout for not writing his poetry. "That's sort of why I called. I'd be honored if you'd consider being my son's godmother."

Somehow I'd known about this child. "I'm not such a stable figure," I said.

While he reeled through further protests, I examined my forearm, turning it gracefully over and over. Light fell through the rice paper I'd taped over my windows, snowy light so stark that I expected to see my bones shining through flesh and raspberry-colored cotton. Radius, ulna. And fibula. That's Freudian for the holes in my life. When Frank and I were lovers, he was married to Barbara Rhys-Davies Allen, the great-grandniece of the inventor of anesthesia. I used to call her Madam Novocaine. They'd had a son who was now in prep school in Connecticut. At barely forty, Frank was one of those powerful old lizards whose older children are the same age as their newer wives.

It made me feel old; lots of things did now. It had started four years ago, at thirty. To be perfectly fair to everyone, Frank's current wife was a ripe twenty-seven. She had ancestors too. Her name was Marie, as in Antoinette; one ancestor had escaped the guillotine, if I remembered right.

"But what about Marie? What does she think of this idea?"

"She's into it. I've told her all about you. We're both so sure you'll strike a chord with Alexandre, I'm calling to offer you a round-trip plane ticket to come and meet him."

"But I'm going to be in Europe anyway. I guess I could take the train from Berlin to Paris. We have a few days off during the last week of March."

"Perfect," Frank said, "but we'll still buy your ticket. The train's expensive, you know." Alexi was a terror, he went on, but very spiritual. He thought I'd understand that.

I hoped I did. I'd always admired Frank's judgment of people.

I got off the train at Gare de l'Est, rejoicing. When I'd left France after my junior year abroad, I was sure I'd never be able to come back here. Looking up at the pigeons in the station's metal rafters, I felt as passionately open as I had at twenty, when Bohemian Paris redeemed my childhood's hardships. Memories of Fall River stank of the kerosene my mother used to clean the bathtub, claiming we could afford no better. Ah, but in Paris, when the landlady turned off the hot water with the same unnecessary meanness, I could think of Malte Laurids Brigge, the sensitive Dane. The day I broke up with my Brazilian boyfriend, I went walking in the Luxembourg Gardens, letting my tears mix with drizzle and run, brackish, into the corners of my mouth. Between sobs, I quoted Baudelaire out loud. *Je suis la plaie et le couteau, je suis le soufflet et la joue.* Sonorous, painful, depressing. Perfect.

My main cultural input now was to watch Vanna White give away money on "Wheel of Fortune" once a week while I waxed my legs. This was good, I thought, since I was about to visit my life's major heartbreaker.

None of the pay phones took coins, but a guy was

standing there renting out phone cards. Seeing through this scam, I decided to go straight to Frank and Marie's on the *métro*. I took the pleasure of reporting the scam artist, in French, to a policeman who was standing by the stairs looking world-weary, just like a *flic* in a film. He complimented me by not answering in English: shrugged and said it wasn't his *affaire* if people were idiot enough not to buy their own phone cards.

Don't ask me how I ended up at Guy-Môquet; I got absorbed in people watching on the subway. Once I knew I was lost, I still wasn't willing to examine the maps carefully and got on a few trains in the wrong direction. Finally, I came up for air into a street full of Algerians, West Africans, and Vietnamese in cheap windbreakers, hurrying home. The evening sky was shutting down like an enormous, sad armoire, the buildings looked peed-on. I searched under the skin of blank, defended faces for inward expressions I might recognize, but I saw nothing. I bought a *Petit Plan de Paris* and hurried back underground. Climbing down the broken escalator, I stifled the unworthy thought that I didn't want people like this filling up my country. I'd tell Frank he was more idealistic than I was.

It was dark by the time I arrived at Frank and Marie's apartment near the Invalides. Nonetheless, Marie was still alone with my potential godchild. "Welcome, welcome, Cara," she cried, leaning out so I could see her as I climbed the marble stairs. She spoke perfect English, being from a branch of the family that had lived in the U.S. for generations; still, her Gallic nose divided her face into vertical halves, giving Marie a look of bewilderment that didn't seem to express her personality. She and her younger brother had come back to France when their great-aunt died, leaving them this apartment, plus a vineyard in Burgundy which the brother took over. "Frank's sorry he couldn't be here to meet you, but he's just left the office. He should be here any second. This is Alexandre."

He straddled Marie's hip, an elfin, frowning baby with blue eyes and lots of shiny dark hair — Frank's colors. Marie was olive-brown. Alexandre was not in the least interested in me, or maybe he was making sure I understood his priorities. I'd have exclaimed that he had Frank's mouth, loose and generous, except I didn't know if lips were a safe topic. My current self-improvement project was managing my tongue. My current boyfriend said I talked too much, about the wrong subjects; just now, I could see his point. I liked Marie; I wanted to be friends. Chattering, she preceded me down a narrow hallway lined with watercolor landscapes. She was wearing black linen shorts and pretty shoes, but she was not at all the willowy aristocrat I'd envisioned. I was sexier and more inventively dressed, and would have been a hundred-percent glad about it had I not also felt that these were the qualities of an ex-mistress.

Halfway down the hall there was an enormous black mastiff lying on the floor, its jowls oozing across the floorboards. Marie stepped over it. It was the ugliest dog I'd ever seen, with bits of mucous membrane showing under its eyes and at the corners of its dribbling maw. I'm not afraid of dogs, but I hesitated to approach its hideous head.

"That's Cerbère," Marie said. "We call him Frank's *bête noire.*" It was obviously Frank's dog, Frank's joke. Marie's French pronunciation wasn't half as good as mine. "He's harmless, but don't pet him unless you want your fingers to stink. He has this skin thing. It rots in the folds of his coat."

I petted Cerbère anyway. He seemed grateful, rolling his eyes up at me so that the whites showed. "Frank always talked about getting a dog," I said. Only dogs and babies love you unconditionally, he used to say.

Marie showed me the apartment, a string of high-ceilinged rooms opening off one long hall, a standard design for European palaces. No sign of infant squalor. Did they have a maid, or had Marie cleaned in honor of my arrival? The first room had maroon walls and very little furniture, just a Khmer Buddha's head and several mounted stone friezes of dancing goddesses. Enormous plants, and a sofa that looked imported from the planet Mars.

Alexi was taking cautious peeks at me. His eyes were indeed extraordinary, the hottest blue I'd ever seen. When I cooed at him, he stuck his head into his mother's shoulder, but soon popped up to flirt with me again.

"Yes!" Marie chirped. "She's your fairy godmother!"

"Pawn dack!" Alexi yelled, delighted.

Fairy godmother? Eek. I hadn't brought a single gift.

In Frank and Marie's bedroom, the walls were black and a huge abstract painting hung behind the bed. Frank's study was ocher and cluttered, full of exotic things I wanted to examine, but Marie stood hovering in the doorway as if this were some kind of sanctum. In her arms, Alexi stretched as if to fly in my direction; Marie held him tightly while explaining that she and Frank could never afford this place except that they paid no rent. It had been deeded to one of her ancestors who'd been Napoleon's marshal. She and Frank sold most of the furnishings except for that campaign chair, which Frank had kept as a throne for his study.

"We were totally broke when we came," Marie went on. "Anyway, ormolu doesn't fit our style. We sold things one by one and stripped all the wallpaper ourselves. A lot of our stuff is gifts from Frank's clients, too. Did you know he had to take modeling jobs when we first got here? A Katrina agent scouted him on the street. I was working under the table at a gallery. Did you know the French pay you to have a baby?"

And so forth. She must be trying to put me at ease in these opulent surroundings. I wondered what class of immigrants Frank was helping who could give away paintings and museum-quality friezes. I grabbed Alexi's foot, intending play, but he let out a lung-rending scream.

Marie just jounced him and talked louder, telling me how much Frank had hated modeling. He'd decided to go into the immigration business after a Polish poet had begged his help. Tons of refugees came through Paris, not only from the former French colonies, but from South America and Eastern Europe as well. Since French society was relatively closed, many refugees were desperate to move on to the States, where they could get decent jobs.

Scream, scream, scream.

"Is he okay?" I pointed to her beet red child.

"He's teething," Marie explained. "I was trying to keep him up till Frank gets home so we could put him to bed and have some quiet. Hey, Al, want some juice?"

His screaming made me want to imitate him. Clearly it had been too long since I'd been around a baby.

We walked quickly past Alexi's room and the dining room into the kitchen, the end of the line. The kitchen was white and rather grandly unassuming. Marie asked if I wanted some Evian and then forgot to serve it. Alexi, hideous with rage, was refusing to be appeased by juice or milk.

"He thinks I'll nurse him, but I don't like to since he's grown his teeth. Okay, Alexi babes, you're going to bed."

His misery diminished down the hall. I sat there wanting the Evian, wondering where I was going to sleep. In any other house, I'd have served myself, but Marie's self-possession had unbalanced me. I was afraid to do anything she might think coarse.

"I've got to apologize for putting you in the maid's room," Marie said, coming back. "At least it's quiet." It was just off the kitchen, a room only as wide as its window, furnished with an iron bed. The mattress was horse-hair and wretched, Marie said, but she came in here when she had insomnia. "It's not the worst. The worst is that you have to share our bathroom." It had a door from the living room, but unfortunately the wall that sepa-rated the bathroom from the master bedroom was all glass brick, one of Frank's major construction fantasies. He'd insisted on doing the work himself, to the horror of their French friends; he'd made endless mistakes with the metric measurements.

"We can't really see you except as kind of a pink blob," Marie remarked. "You can turn the light off, or else Frank and I will try to stay out of our room when you need to be in there."

I said I'd be fine; I'd be here for only two nights. "Living in Paris, it might be wise to make your house-guests a little bit uncomfortable." This was too much for Marie. Her expression hardened, and we were at a loss when Frank appeared.

"Yo ho!" His voice came booming the length of the hallway. "Alexandre? Do we have a guest? I brought food. Burmese." He hove in, walking fast. "Cara? Hi! Do you eat chicken? Hi, honey," and he pecked Marie on the cheek. "Where's Alexi?"

"I'll get him," she said.

"Love that baby!" Cerbère ambled in and leaned against Frank's thigh. He rubbed the beast's ears ener-getically, so that a long tendril of dog drool swung onto his pants. I cringed for his beautiful suit, blue pinstripes with a daring European cut. "I think I need some more dogs and children," he said, as Marie put the conked-out Alexi into his arms. "Don't you?"

I shrugged, feeling too poor myself to grant him any further expansion.

I was slightly surprised to see that Frank was still the same person. He hadn't even aged much. Standing at the center of his family tableau, he looked bewildered for a minute, as if he'd just woken up to find he'd sleepwalked into this. "You're not fat," I said. "You said on the phone you'd gotten fat."

"I'm fatter," Frank protested. "I've been on a diet." Our eyes connected, and I was sure we both remembered things Marie couldn't. How sharp Frank's pelvic bones became when we trained for the marathon, for example. I got the flu at the last minute and didn't run; I remember feeling relieved that I wouldn't see Frank's wife hugging him at the finish line. More than one man would have been happy to rub my legs for me, but I wouldn't have wanted Frank to witness that.

My life was complicated in those days.

"You should have seen him last fall," Marie said. "His eyes were getting little, piggy. Too much wine and pâté."

"I was not," Frank said.

This wrangling made me nervous, since Frank was too vain and high-strung ever to gain weight. "I have this truly massive boyfriend," I cut in. "One of the few straight male dancers. Ellis keeps him on for sheer magnificence. His body never runs out, but mentally I think he's starting to. Run out." I stopped short, wishing I hadn't introduced this topic. About a week before we left Manhattan, Nick told me I was keeping him from seeing two other women he was interested in and that monogamy was a social form forced on men by women. I'd avoided hearing his message then, but now it seemed to have sunk in.

Dinner was exquisite. Frank described its delicate harmonics, a balance among five tastes; then the conversation swung to my romantic problems. Maybe I overemphasized that I was a decent woman who wanted a real commitment, but in truth, I was proud of this new, healthy phase. Trite as it may sound, I'd begun to feel that I deserved someone to love me.

Frank said, loyally, that if the guy was that scared, I probably had him. "I'll do it," Frank said. "I'll call him and say, 'You could wait your whole life for someone like Cara.' "

I wanted to collapse under the table.

Marie glanced at me, and said, "Men are such fools."

After dinner, Marie went out to walk Cerbère; I had an espresso so I could stay up and visit with Frank. We sat in the living room admiring photos of Frank that had appeared in *Uomini* and *Vogue*. Frank in thick-rimmed Italian glasses; Frank as a joyous lumberjack; Frank leaning over a secretary's desk, reminding me of how we met. "I wish I could have kept that suit," he said.

"It's foppish," I said, to keep from being too charmed.

"So?"

When I saw *La Dolce Vita* at age twelve, I hoped I'd one day experience fits of passion. If I could only fling an ashtray against the wall, or scissor some man's clothes to ribbons, I'd be a proper woman of my heritage. Remember what Saint Theresa said about answered prayers? My affair with Frank was melodramatic and heartbreaking. I have Irish nerves, too delicate for an Italian heart.

I had a dance scholarship to Newton College, with a minor in the equally useless field of French literature. When I finished, I went to work as a researcher at Frank's law office, where one partner was an NC alumnus. Every woman at the firm had a crush on Frank but me. I was too young and shy — and Catholic, and working-class — to fantasize about a man who had graduated from Harvard Law School, who had a British wife and a son in private kindergarten.

Then I gave the firm six free tickets to a dance performance. Afterward the lawyers took me out for drinks, and Frank gave me a ride home. In front of my building, he cut the engine and asked if he could come up. "What for?" I asked. Men in the office propositioned me fairly often. I was a dancer full of naive, just-back-from-Paris airs that must have made me look like easy prey. "I'm in love with you," Frank said. He put his hand on his lower abdomen, on exactly the place I tried to dance from, and told me you had to live from your gut, no matter what the consequences. I was impressed with his perceptiveness. Watching me dance had been an epiphany for him, he said. He was a kid from New Jersey who'd been intoxicated by Barbara Rhys-Davies Allen, until he heard the great chord that rang when she walked into a department store. How had they become entangled, how had they had a child? "Please let me in. Just for a cup of tea. I want to be with you."

Shocked, I got out of the car and went around to his window to apologize for hurting his feelings. I found myself kissing him instead.

Three years later, on a bright sunny morning a million miles from Boston, I was rolling on the floor, weeping hysterically as I begged Frank not to leave me, not again, not to move back in with Barbara Rhys-Davies Allen and sensitive little Oliver. I was halfway through my dance master's at Cal Arts. By then we'd enacted many versions of this scene, but this was the first time I'd literally crawled. I grabbed Frank's ankle and let him drag me across the floor as he walked out. I remember thinking that being dragged wasn't as degrading for me as it would be for someone who wasn't a modern dancer, since dancers were always writhing on the floor.

Soon Frank wrote that he was filing for divorce and moving to New York, and I was often in his thoughts. I didn't answer the letter, but a few months later I was in Manhattan for a movement workshop and couldn't resist phoning to say hello. Frank insisted I stay over. "On the couch," I said. "Of course," he replied, lightly, as if it was presumptuous of me to assume any other possibility. In the morning, he made me an omelet with mushrooms, cream, and lemon. I felt disappointed: the old Frank had been helpless in the kitchen, but this food seemed like what a man learns to cook when he wants to impress women.

But why shouldn't Frank see women?

As we ate, he asked my advice about Marie. They'd been seeing each other for a year; just then she was in Paris, visiting her great-aunt. She was an artist, like me, he said, but a painter interested in grids and repetition. He'd met her at a night class he took to cheer himself up during the early postdivorce period.

At that time I only understood abstract expressionism, large gestures whose meaning you could never establish. I told Frank that Marie sounded kind of limited. Of course, I meant in comparison to me, but I don't think either of us noticed.

I slept dreamlessly in the horsehair bed and woke up in broad daylight. My potential godchild had crawled over and pulled himself up to stare into my face. He was panting, tiny breaths, from the effort. I looked into his extraordinary eyes and saw the human creature, absolutely wild. He opened his mouth in an enormous, soundless laugh, showing two serrated incisors as wide as my own.

How could I refuse him?

"Don't wake up Cara," Marie cried, swooping in. "How did he get in here?"

"It's fine," I said, but she'd taken Alexi away and shut the door behind them.

How could I accept her?

Let her be possessive, I thought, admiring my body as I dressed. No stretch marks: a leopardess.

Frank was still asleep. Marie gave me a big bowl of café au lait while she made Irish oatmeal, the kind that takes half an hour. Where had they gotten it, at an expensive British shop?

Alexi was on the floor, happy with the wooden spoons and spatulas.

Marie stirred the pot and asked about the yoga class she had been taking. She'd forgotten the instructions, whether to breathe in when she raised her leg and out when she lowered it, or vice versa. Yes, I told her: imagine the air inflating her leg. I asked how long she'd lived in Paris, and she said she'd been here five years this time, and before this, she'd come to art school for two years.

Could I see her paintings? No. They were all in storage in the States. The watercolors in the hallway were Frank's.

I could never be any man's wife, I thought, if it meant having his baby, stirring his oatmeal, and hanging his paintings while mine rotted.

Not any man's wife, I corrected myself, Frank's. Would it have been different if it had been I who'd married him?

I announced that I didn't want any breakfast and went out into the living room to stretch.

"Can we watch?" Frank was standing in the hall in jeans and no shirt. He and Marie brought in Alexi's high chair and sat on the couch, three feet from me, to eat their oatmeal.

"See that? Cara's antigravity legs," Frank said.

Marie said, "She's inhaling."

"She can put both feet behind her head, too."

Okay, I would perform, though not that particularly exposing move. I concentrated, slowing down my gestures as though I were swimming through honey. I felt all the life force coiled inside me, and more that I could gather from the air; Frank and Marie became irrelevant. Deep in my own center, I felt the room move with me when I turned and crossed the space in a series of cart-wheels and jetés. As I fell into a back bend, preparing to pull myself slowly up and over, Cerbère ambled up and stood in the way. He was smiling, breathing rotten dog breath into my helpless face.

"God, what a mouth." I laughed, collapsing. Frank and Marie clapped loudly, the sound sparse in that huge room.

"You should have gotten that solo," Frank said.

"Oh, I did, I didn't tell you. She pulled her Achilles tendon."

"My prayers worked," Frank said. "I was doing voodoo on your behalf."

"It was excruciating to dance it," I said. "And no review. Nothing's extreme in Berlin." I recalled jerking naked under a red strobe. I told Frank that it was the first dance Ellis put together after getting his award.

"Sick," Frank said.

Marie's uncomprehending eyes moved back and forth. Frank didn't explain, just pointed to Alexi and said, "Babies are disgusting, aren't they?" He had covered his entire head with oatmeal. Frank asked if I minded staying here alone with him and Alexi while Marie went out for Saturday lunch with friends. I said of course not, Alexandre was after all my godson. "So you accept?" Frank said, noticing.

"Maybe I speak too soon? I don't know what's involved. But he's really great, Alexi. He remembers how the gods laugh."

I knew Frank would save that up as an important statement; I didn't look at Marie. How do people ever get along, I wondered.

Frank said my only duty was to emanate moral radiance.

Marie said, "There's a church thing. But no rush. I might not do it if I were you."

"I don't know why you want me," I confessed to Marie.

"You're very important to Frank."

In her shoes, I'd never go out and leave me alone with her husband. But then, I wasn't in her shoes, so I didn't say anything.

"You'd make a great mother," Frank observed.

We were in the study; I was shamelessly currying favor, helping Alexi toss Frank's books onto the floor. Lots of Simenon and used paperbacks in English that must have come from Shakespeare and Company. Alexi would grab a few and fling them behind his back; then I'd put them up again, meanwhile perusing Frank's knickknacks arranged above Alexi's reach. A fist-sized uncut emerald. An ivory netsuke representing a bag of rats. A tiny wooden goddess riding on a mythical bird.

As Alexi's crashes grew more and more satisfying, I saw him edging toward nervous overload, but I didn't know how to stop the game gracefully. He could hardly believe that I was letting him run wild like this. He'd squeal and glance sideways at Frank, who was sitting in his campaign chair, his hands resting on its two carved lion heads — the thing must have taken a mule to carry.

It was odd, this scene of apparent domesticity, when I'd come so far to meet Frank; like a duet in the hurricane's eye.

Marie came to say good-bye. She twirled before us in a red silk *cheongsam,* pale makeup, and very red lips.

"Honey, you look great."

"Fantastic," I added.

Ignored, Alexi began hooting, pulling against the bookshelf hard and dangerously. "Okay," I said, "one more." I set up a dozen books and he shoved them off, shrieking in glee. Marie gave me a look of disapproval, so I didn't set the books up again. Alexi had a conniption; she picked him up; he was instantly calm. They stared at me out of the heart of their mutual love.

You're turning him into a repressed Parisian mama's boy, I thought.

She kissed the baby, handed him to Frank, and left. We went out for supplies, pushing Alexi in a pram. The March light fell flatly on the lovely, imposing buildings. This neighborhood was truly civilized, its men in cashmere coats looking sleekly dissatisfied, its women in furs lifting their chins to face the ravages of spring.

Frank brought up my problems with my boyfriend, saying that if Nick missed this chance he'd probably never have a real relationship.

I could hear Nick laughing at the notion of a real relationship. I wondered what he was doing now. Rhino had arrived in Rome without me. Tonight or some night very soon, the curve of Nick's thumb surely would run along another woman's flanks.

Frank was saying men like Nick waited until they were sixty to admit that they were lonely. Then they married the first young thing that came along and lived unhappily ever after.

If it's possible to be married for one instant, that's the instant I was married to Frank Bennett. "I hope so."

When I told my father Nick was into other women (I don't know why I did that; Poppy must have called right after some evil conversation), my father offered this advice: "Men have no incentive to get married when the women sell themselves as cheap as you do, Cara. Don't hang onto him, at least."

"I'm not," I whined to my father, only the first of the unsuitable men who had paraded through my life.

Alexandre was sleepy in his carriage, so we put him to bed as soon as we got home. Frank stood over his crib pointing at the objects in the room, promising Alexi that each thing would still be there when he woke up. I envied Alexi his loving parents and his expensive toys, especially since he seemed to ignore the latter.

When he was asleep, Frank said again, "You'd be such a great mother."

"Yeah?" I said, absently. He'd caught me suggesting that whether I thought about it consciously or not, I'd always be emanating goodness toward this child, so that Alexi would fly unscathed through all the things I'd flunked: kindergarten, love affairs, the battle to take oneself seriously.

I made joke passes toward the crib.

"What are you doing?" Frank asked.

"Casting a spell."

Nick would have grabbed my wrists, pushed my palms down to my sides, kissed me to shut me up. Frank just said, "That's what we hired you for."

We went into the dining room. While Frank uncorked the wine, I spread out the bread, the salads, and the cheeses we'd bought at three different stores. This was the meal I loved more than any other. Frank felt the same. He'd splurged on a Romanée-Conti.

"To all our picnics," he proposed. "At Walden Pond, and the time we drove all the way to Maine so we could go to a beach where no one recognized us. To that poor chicken you tried to roast on driftwood, remember?"

"To picnics," I toasted, not perfectly comfortable with this line of talk. "Tell me about your work." Instead of letting Frank answer, I described the immigrant neighborhood I'd gone to by mistake. "You know, it's funny. I'd love to be rich and live in a fancy place in Paris, and if I had all this, I'd never once look back at where I came from. I know it's wicked. But I'm for euthanasia, too."

Reintroducing myself as a stranger to a stranger. I

poured myself a second glass of wine, not waiting for Frank to offer, and spread Brie on a hunk of *boule.*

Frank took a big glug from his glass and then said he was helping a different kind of immigrant, political refugees who were not easy to place in any country.

I couldn't understand his embarrassment. "But Frank, that's great. I mean, they need someplace to go. Isn't that what the Statue of Liberty is about, huddled masses yearning to breathe free?"

"That's the liberal point of view. But I think Miss Liberty is talking about people expressing their opinions, not behaving like savages and getting away with it courtesy of the U.S.A. But I'm a lawyer, and I must believe, I must believe that I believe in the law more than I believe in my own opinion." He finished his wine. "Besides, I have Alexi. Maybe he'll go to college on Marie's money, but I can't just sit back and let her take care of him until then."

I'd always hated seeing Frank uncomfortable. "Look," I began. "I hated dancing 'Love You, Babe.' But I did it because I think it's the best way for me to get ahead. And I've done some other despicable things, including wrecking your first family. Not that I should be an example."

"My divorce had to happen."

"Okay, well, what about after you left me in California? I went through this weird klepto phase? I stole a load of wash, cans of tuna, really minor stuff. Eventually I made myself stop. I never think about it now, but it was a bad time." I hadn't realized how much I had wanted Frank to recompense me for what I'd suffered: it made me a little frightened of myself.

"I think about it every day," Frank said vehemently. "You don't want to know this, but among the people who might want to kill me should be you."

"What are you talking about?"

"You're a remarkable woman, you're the love of my life, that's what I mean."

"That's so nice. Why should I want to kill you?" I'd definitely had too much wine; things were happening faster than I could account for. I told Frank I was feeling insecure about Nick and that I needed to know I'd been somebody's princess, at least once in my life.

He gave me a dark look.

My brain was murky, roiling. I wasn't absolutely sure we weren't headed for the bedroom. If Frank wanted to, I knew I could not refuse. In a flash, I saw us overshadowed by that painting, Frank and Marie's conjugal abstraction — no, I'd insist on the horsehair mattress, the white room. Cold light would fall on our bare bodies, like making love in a hospital.

But Frank didn't move to touch me. He just sat there looking at me with the eyes of the same burning blue as his son's.

None of my minor confessions having worked — and why should they have, I thought, since I didn't feel profoundly bad about any of those acts — I felt driven to tell Frank something that would genuinely bring catharsis, healing. The ammunition was close at hand: I'd lied. I'd slept with tons of men while Frank and I were lovers. Only during periods when Frank had gone back to Oliver and Barbara, stricken by guilt and vowing to be a good husband and a faithful father — only during those unbearable periods. Then, as soon as Frank came back to me, I'd dump all the others. At the time it had seemed a fair and necessary way of keeping my mental balance, except that I knew Frank believed I'd waited for him in my Brighton apartment like a virgin princess in a tower.

"Don't feel so guilty," I began. "Maybe I wasn't ready for a real relationship."

"You didn't have to be. You were in love, and that should be enough."

I was living disproof of that particular theory, but I couldn't go ahead and say so. I was remembering something I'd forgotten, something that was pressing me into the chair cushion, locking a brace around my jaw. Slowly, I began making another sandwich using all my favorite foods. Fresh basil leaves, Saint-André cheese, moutarde Pommery. Whether I ate this or not, it was going to be a work of art.

Frank saw me concentrating, and said, "I want us to agree that it was all very long ago. I love Marie and Alexandre. They're my life now."

Capers, Brie, pâté. I took a huge bite. Delicious.

There'd been a law firm party once, at someone's big house in Waltham. Barbara stayed home with Oliver, but Frank brought along a bunch of his Yale pals from his undergraduate days, all guys, who were visiting. They stood around together, a circle of manly backs in rugby shirts, all clutching cans of beer. I couldn't bring myself to walk up and say hello, so I got drunk instead and went off with Antonio Perez, a lawyer we'd recently hired. I talked to Antonio, the first time I'd revealed my love affair to anyone at the firm. Antonio agreed to take care of me. First we did a little coke, then we locked ourselves into the family room and put on "Everybody Must Get Stoned" eight times in a row. This seemed really funny. Then Antonio came upon Shostakovich and said it was the perfect music for my state of mind. He put it on full volume. As disastrous chords rained down on Leningrad, the party hosts came to the door, shouted, and tried to get in, but Antonio and I were dancing. I was howling in circles, and he was jumping on top of me, when Frank put his fist through some French doors that led in from a porch.

Frank let Antonio walk out of the room and stood there like Frankenstein, his right hand dripping blood onto the hosts' wall-to-wall. "So," he said.

"It's the music," I explained. "I love you."

Frank grabbed the neck of my blouse. "Why didn't you say hello to me?" I couldn't answer; I couldn't even say, Don't hurt me. He jerked me to my feet; a button ripped off, making a small sound, as final as the ligament I tore once onstage. It seemed to me that my life was tearing and would never come back together. In the aftermath I saw how ugly existence really was, had been, was going to be.

Frank dropped me suddenly, with a kind of shove that threw me flat. Catching my breath, I raced after him onto the porch, my shoes crunching on broken glass. The garden was full of mute wreckage. Apparently everyone was still in the living room, wondering what happened. The music was still blaring.

Frank knelt in the street and started beating his fist on the pavement, the same hand he'd used to break the door. "You couldn't say hello to me," he kept repeating.

I could have reminded him that I was the one who was at a disadvantage — he hadn't introduced me to his friends — but I was so scared I didn't even think of that. I just stood there, out of range of his attack. Soon his friends came out and surrounded Frank; I walked back toward the house. They glanced at me, obviously not registering my significance.

On my way home, I drove into a parked Jeep on purpose.

Antonio called my place to see if I was okay. I said not really, so he came over. We talked until the windows grew pale. He felt it was his duty to tell me I was in a sick relationship and I should get rid of Frank. No, I said, this was passion, love. Even if, Frank scared me sometimes. When I closed the door behind Antonio, I slid the chain bolt, wishing I'd asked him to stay until full daylight.

Two plates, two glasses, an empty bottle, butcher paper: easy cleanup. Frank washed.

"What's Cerbère up to?" He was blocking my way to

the garbage pail, shaking his head in fast arcs. "Mice," Frank said. "His only talent. He doesn't eat them, he just breaks their necks and lays them in a row."

Frank dried the *ballons* carefully with a linen towel. I envied Marie then and dreaded the moment when she came home to see my face flushed with wine. He'd had me again: not that we'd even touched. I vowed on my honor not to meet his eyes.

We checked on Alexandre, still sound asleep, and then went to sit on the Martian couch. I didn't want to think about a thirty-six-hour train to Rome. "Okay," I blurted. "This Buddha, for example. Who gave it to you? Can you ever sell it?"

"André Malraux pried it off Angkor Wat," Frank said. "It was a famous scandal. The Cambodians got it back and put it in the national museum. Then, well, it came from a client of mine."

The Buddha smiled its mournful, feminine smile, but the corners of its stone eyes were upturned in amusement.

"I see these destitute widows paying you with family heirlooms they pull out of their bras," I said, remembering the small treasures in the study. "Do you make your clients give a pound of heritage before you'll ship them to the melting pot?"

"I couldn't be unscrupulous in that particular way," Frank said. "These things are my revenge." The uncut emerald was from a Colombian drug dealer. The man who gave him the Buddha's head might have been Khmer Rouge. They were terrible to their own people about art treasures, but when it came to dollars they had no scruples at all. They had large-scale operations in the States, siphoning money from Cambodian temples.

Frank didn't always want to know who his clients were or what they'd done. He simply sent them to computer courses or set them up with people in the States who were willing to say they needed an expert in some esoteric skill, like orchid cloning. He was known as a miracle worker, the best immigration lawyer now in Europe.

I suddenly understood that he'd invited me here to ask for absolution. In exchange he offered legitimacy, a ceremony in church; and his child. I couldn't imagine Frank and me standing at an altar with Marie, but I still wanted to save him from his inner demons.

"I will take on Alexi," I told him solemnly. "But no church. I might not be seeing you again too soon, but I'll think about him." I told him I was tired and starting to feel nervous about the Rome performance. I should leave this afternoon instead of tomorrow, so that I could rest for two nights in the same bed before dancing.

Frank said, "At least wait for Marie."

"Of course. We have to say good-bye."

"You should pull your own Achilles," Frank said. "Get out of that solo. Get out of the company, in fact. Ellis is an egomaniac."

"I will," I said. "In a year."

"I mean it. Start your own company. You're as good as he is. Take it from me, I know."

Marie came home. We got Alexandre out of bed; I rolled around on the floor trying to make myself interesting, but his face wrinkled up and he started weeping in rage.

"We're teething," Marie apologized.

I stood up, slapping dog hairs off my legs. I felt full of failure and sexual obsession, but this would dissipate as soon as I left the palace. Marie insisted on making me coffee. While we were in the kitchen alone, she told me there was something she wanted me to know about her, that she'd had a disastrous first marriage to an Egyptian. They'd married here in Paris, but after art school, he'd come to the States with her and disappeared. She'd kept the whole thing secret from her parents and had gotten divorced only to marry Frank.

I said I was touched but didn't know why she was telling me all this.

"Because you think I've never suffered," Marie said flatly.

I was speechless for an instant. *But I see you suffering now,* I could have said. Instead, I hugged her, and while she pressed me she thanked me for being Alexi's godmother, said she and Frank needed me as much as he did.

"Get rid of creepy Nick," she said.

I agreed, and left.

Instead of rejoining Rhino, I took a room in Rome's ancient Jewish quarter and spent the day touring what must be the world's most impressive architectural compost heap. I thought about my mother's ancestors: men sweating in armor, with their bangs cut straight across their foreheads; vague women in white shifts. I liked being in a new city alone: I felt taut, as sensitive as a drumhead. But by nightfall I was lonely and ducked into a cheap, loud tourist restaurant in the Piazza Navona, the kind of place I usually was too snobbish to patronize. It had long communal tables; a sign over the cash register announced that the owner loved life, since life was the best there was. Two women from Minnesota were sitting behind me, having an American conversation that sustained me: "I mean, he's really unaware . . ." "I *know!* I *told* you!"

My food came, a plate of shells with a minimum rinsing of tomato. Giving me the wide, flat bowl, the huge Neapolitan waiter pronounced this baritone aria: "*Guarda, la bella donna, tanto sola, tanto fragile.*" Look at the beautiful woman, so alone, so fragile.

Salvatore, I wanted to call him: my most recent, perfect knight.

RINGWORM

It's been two years since I left Pingyan Monastery, but every time my head itches I still think it's that ringworm. It was the blind cat's fault, or mine for getting distracted and feeding her and having a special feeling about her, as if her eyes full of blank green fire could see something beyond what there was — white stucco walls stained with red mud from the monsoon, beautiful brown people walking slowly up and down, meditating. Dust, mud, garbage, jasmine. Every single thing, different from here.

She first showed up at the end of the hot season, gray and black tiger, like a cat I used to have in California. I couldn't tell where she'd come from; she was obviously from outside the orange-and-white gene pool of the monastery cats. Maybe she'd wandered in from the Muslim slum next door. She was so weak she fell down the steps into the basement that was given to us foreign women as a meditation hall, down under the dorm for Burmese women over fifty. There was a special building for older women, mostly devout widows who came to meditate after their familial duties were accomplished. We six Foreigner Women, all younger than that, had to walk through their quarters to get to the toilet. In the long oven of the hallway, there was mutual inspection. I'd peek sidelong into their rooms and see the grandmothers oiling their long hair or resting after lunch, always lying on their right sides because this was the posture in which the Buddha slept. They lay very still, often with their eyes open. Were they thinking of anything? Maybe not. They frequently offered me bananas or a little dish of fermented tea leaves fried with garlic and peanuts. They felt sorry for the foreigners, I think, because we had no families to come and visit us and bring us nice things to eat.

I was a nun, with a shaven head and four layers of pink, vaguely Grecian robes. I'd gone to Burma on recommendation from travelers I met in India. They said that Burma was a fragment of an older world, that in isolation it had worked out the world's strictest, most effective technique for spiritual enlightenment. I waited a year and a half for a special visa, and when it finally arrived I was ready, primed: I told Pingyan's abbot that I wanted nothing but complete freedom of the heart and mind. Because I'd meditated quite a lot in the past, he offered me the robes, a nun's ten rules of conduct, and the name Sumanā, meaning "Open Mind" or "Open Heart" (Burmese don't make a distinction), and also, "Queen of Jasmine."

The monastery covered forty acres in a suburb near the British consulate, and had enough buildings to accommodate the entire bourgeoisie of Rangoon as well as devotees from places like Mandalay, Sagaing, and the Shan and Karen states. There were usually a thousand people meditating, both ordained and lay; four thousand during the Water Festival. As in any religion, females predominated in number, but there was a good minority of monks who were the authorities, as well as a dozen foreigners. We foreign women lived and meditated by ourselves and saw the men only at meals. After a while my eyes turned Asian, and Western males began to look like the barbarians on a Chinese plate, hairy and coarse, their naked pink skin like boiled shrimp.

Breakfast was at five and lunch at ten-fifteen. There was no solid food, then, until the next breakfast. The monks said eating at night causes lust. We woke at three to the clanking of an iron pipe. Each day there were seven one-hour sittings, interspersed with six or seven hours of formal walking meditation, pacing slowly up and down. At eight P.M. the abbot discoursed to the foreigners; Burmese got sermons only on Saturday. Every other day we had an interview, a completely formalized affair in which we described our meditation and the abbot instructed us about how to proceed. Bed was at eleven.

We didn't talk, nor make eye contact with anyone. We were told to keep the mind protected like a turtle in its shell, but to notice everything occurring in that field. Thus, when not sitting with eyes shut, we moved very slowly, minutely attending to sensations and avoiding complex, rapid movements. If strong thoughts or emotions came, we noticed their presence but discarded their content. This practice was intended to lead to the famous and misunderstood Nirvana, which the Burmese call Nibbāna, Liberation, the end of suffering—*cessation* was the word the Burmese used. I believed I could experience cessation because I was in Burma where, it was said, lots of people had psychic powers and the young girls would attain their first cessation during summer holidays from school.

Possibly my great faith contributed to slackness in my practice. I was fascinated with everything. My notebook was stuffed with observations that I knew the monks would disapprove of. "Toothpaste tube still hot at nine

P.M.," "Burmese girls grow their toenails long and paint them." I was constantly enmeshed in situations with other Westerners, or with Burmese who wanted to get visas to the States, practice English, teach me Burmese, or donate things to me because gifts to a nun would generate good karma. It didn't matter that I intended to disrobe whenever I reached Nibbāna or the government quit extending my visa — I could have been a nun for a single day and still deserved the same respect. The merit gained by paying respect to ordained people is gauged by what they represent, rather than anything personal. Once I comprehended this, it was easier to let the young girls kneel in the dirt and bow, or simply take off their shoes as they handed me a banana or a sack of boiled cane-juice candy. Giving to a male monk would have been precisely ten times better, but my Westernness seemed to give me an extra value not included in traditional calculations. I got lots of presents; I had a fan club of twenty young girls. One medical student told me I must be a very pure being indeed, for having first merited, and then forsaken, the sensual pleasures of the "United State."

At interviews the abbot said I was progressing and that I should keep a relaxed attitude. So I had little incentive to change, except perhaps the example of my senior nun, Sīlānandī, "Bliss of Morality." She was French, and had done PR for a ritzy yacht club before firmly renouncing the world. Her posture, the result of a childhood in Parisian ballet classes, impressed the girls in my fan club as evidence of deep meditative powers.

I was taking a break, standing at the row of sinks in line with the other women, all of us mixing up glucose tea, which we drank in the afternoon to keep from getting dehydrated. My feet were bare and dirty on the hot black boards, the sinks were giving off their intense slime smell, and my four layers of robes were stuck to my skin with the heat, as usual. Now I heard a thin mew, turned, and saw this pathetic creature, all bones, tottering then falling down the steps.

Next to me, Sīlānandī slowly turned her head to look, slowly turned it back again, and resumed her tea-making with glacial care. Do not be diverted, her behavior said. I watched her hand closing around the cup, its conical fingers perfectly familiar to me. In my mind I heard the abbot, our teacher.

One moment of kindness is greater than a hundred years of ordinary life. One moment of perfect attention is greater than a hundred years of kindness.

Slowly Sīlānandī raised the cup and drank.

The perfume of mindfulness rises even to the seat of the gods.

Indeed she was perfect, but I suspected she wanted all of us to notice.

Me, I'd already grabbed a spare jar lid and mixed up in it some glucose and my powdered milk from Bangkok. The cat didn't know what it was at first, but I pushed her nose into it so that she had to lick it off, with a charming little sneeze.

Now the Swiss woman came and crouched next to me, smiling intensely. I understood that she was enraptured by this feeding of the cat and also wanted an excuse to talk. This was one of the dangers of getting involved in events. There was a snowball effect. The most microscopic loophole permitted the world to draw me back into itself.

I smiled a tiny Buddha's smile and moved my hands slowly, as Sīlānandī would, to show that I was meditating diligently in spite of what might appear. In other words, Scram.

But the Swiss woman's need was great. "I am afraid," she muttered. "Office give my money back to me when I go to visa extension. My money was smelling very bad, I think."

"No, no," it was my role to say. Except that she was

fed and taken care of, I thought the Swiss woman shouldn't be here. In the silence her mind created labyrinths of paranoia. "The price of visas was just reduced so we all got fifty kyats back. Everybody's money stinks here. The bills are old. Don't worry."

"Ah."

Suddenly my pretended concentration caught, and I stopped seeing or thinking about the unbalanced Swiss woman. I was just noticing the little cat, the softness of her fur and the pain of her starvation. I felt it through me like a fire.

Her eyes were unusually glowing, like a florist's green glass marbles, but I didn't realize then that she was blind and this was why they were so luminous. She didn't understand the milk; she just stood over it, weakly bobbing her head. Maybe, I think now, she couldn't find it again.

I turned to go back into the meditation hall, but the kitten tried to follow. I took her up the steps and deposited her under a jasmine bush, together with the jar lid. Ten ants already had drowned in white. As I wet the cat's nose one last time, a passing crone cried out her disapproval.

Animals are incapable of refined mental states. A gift to an animal is of little merit.

I scurried back into the meditation hall.

After that I didn't see the kitten for a long time. If I'd thought about it, I'd have guessed she died, but I didn't think of her.

The place was full of cats. The so-called Warden of the older women's dorm had two toms, horrid orange things with heavy heads and balls the size of grapes. They ran around pissing on everything, ate pork pasties and white rice, even slept with their mistress on her hard Burmese cot like a narrow Ping-Pong table. The rest of the cats had to compete for garbage with dogs, rats, crows, and pigeons. Kittens were loose-boweled and scrawny, but nonetheless retained an infant grace. Their mothers were pathetic. Swaybacked, degraded by constant pregnancy, at puberty they lost some core of self-respect essential to a creature. They didn't wash; they couldn't look you in the eye. One calico in particular — I'd come out from lunch and find her making obscene love to the sandals outside the dining hall. Caught, she'd cringe and slink away, as if some faint memory had stirred of a time before base drives had ruined her life. It was enough to make anyone into a feminist, or depending on your turn of mind, you might begin to agree with the pious Burmese, who say celibacy is a virtue and look down on married people.

Yesterday, sir, I sat seven hours and walked seven hours. I slept five. In sitting, the rising and falling of the abdomen was the primary object. At three o'clock, in the rising I noticed movement and tightness, in falling softness and heaviness. Burning arose in the lower back. I focused on the burning, and it became unbearable.

Did you twist and turn to find relief?

Yes.

The sufferings of life should be known. Do not move to conceal the truth from yourself. Grit your teeth. You can keep pain dancing in your hand.

Every Saturday I shaved my head. At a stale hour of the afternoon I would retire from the meditation hall to the green-tiled bathing room with its dark, cool tank of water. My equipment was a mirror, a thermos of hot water, a bar of blue Chinese soap, and a Gillette Trac II cartridge razor I'd brought in from Bangkok. Shaving took an hour, and except for the bliss of leaving behind the hall and my companions, suddenly comical in their diligence, I hated it. The textures put my teeth on edge

— cheap lather like saliva, sandpapery stubble, sticky smoothness of my scalp. Next day, the back of my head always erupted in a thousand tiny pimples. Irritation, I suppose. Eventually I learned that a hot washrag cured this.

One shaving day I found a small, red patch on my right temple. By then I was used to various grossnesses of my flesh and found this one interesting. When I pulled my skin a little, it jumped into a perfect circle. There were few perfectly made things in that environment, and this roundness pleased me. But now it itched.

A few nights later, after the abbot's discourse, I went to ask the monastery nurse about it. She was Warden of the Foreigner Women's Dorm, and so she lived downstairs from us.

Saya-ma Aye Shwe, Nurse Cool Golden, was sitting under her mosquito net. As she was deaf, I had to walk into her room and touch her on the shoulder.

"It 'tis a sunburn," she breathed, in English. "Leave it." Her voice was deceptive, as soft as a baby's sigh.

Though she'd trained as a nurse in East Germany and in Australia, Nurse Aye Shwe ascribed most physical ailments to faulty concentration, heat, or cold. She'd cured herself of stomach cancer by meditating alone in a forest hut, vowing not to come out until she died or attained enlightenment. Now it was her right to despise infirmity; one visited the clinic only in a mood of boldness. Westerners were too soft, always sick, always wanting pills. The body is good only for practice, we must learn that it is full of sufferings! To Sīlānandī, who had severe edema in her arms and legs, Nurse Aye Shwe refused any medicament. "It is very good to die in meditation," she reminded

I retired from her presence that night without a murmur, even though I knew I had no sunburn. It wasn't bothering me much, yet.

A week later the spot was the size of the rubber ring on a Mason jar and itched so much I couldn't sleep. I returned to the nurse's quarters, tilted my head to the light from her barred window.

"Is it ringworm?" I asked, but she didn't have her hearing aid on. "*Ringworm?*"

It was often hard to tell what Nurse Aye Shwe had understood. Where deafness came to an end, there some obscurely motivated willfulness took over. "You are not used to our water," she said sadly. "Try with Go-Min."

"Go-Min!" I laughed, throwing my head back for Nurse Aye Shwe's benefit. In all fairness, it was very difficult to get Western medicines in Burma, especially for one such as a nurse who disapproved of the black market. But Go-Min was made in Burma, and very cheap, a rude little jar of pig fat mixed with aromatic oils. I had heard the nurse prescribe it for swollen gums, varicose veins, abdominal bloating, scabies, and mosquito bites. Weeks ago, she'd given me a jar of it for hemorrhoids; the most I can say is that it burned as if it were having a radical effect.

"Sister Go-Min, they call me," Nurse Aye Shwe said with a smirk. "If your meditation is good, Go-Min will be very effective."

Later that day I was doing walking meditation next to the Hall of the Diamond, where the Burmese women meditated. It looked like a cinema and was fixed up inside like Versailles, with mirror mosaics and a giant aquarium up front, enclosing an enormous white enamel Buddha with a gold-leaf robe and red smiling lips. Foreigner Women were forbidden to meditate there, which was a disappointment to me. Our basement hall smelled of rotting mud and had no Buddha. Often it was invaded by fleas from the Warden's pissing tomcats. More importantly, the Burmese women seemed to have more fun than we did. Every morning they chanted in a haunting minor key. Young girls did their walking meditation arm in arm, and no one was terribly serious about the rule of silence. When sad thoughts or terrifying visions came, the women groaned and wept aloud. "Oiyy! Oiyy!" Sometimes their entire hall would erupt in these lugubrious sounds, like a pack of she-wolves howling, and I'd wish desperately to be there, not cooped up with the grim Calvinists in the Foreigner Women's Basement.

Suddenly I was at the center of a bunch of teenaged nuns who were giggling and rapidly speaking Burmese. They pulled me around the corner, out of sight of the women's supervisor or any passing monk. I nearly fainted with delight. I regularly got crushes on these temporary nuns who came, like me, to ordain for a few months or a year. Physically they were lovely — supple bodies in the narrow elegant pink robes, faces exquisite in concentration. I imagined them uncorrupted creatures, isolated in medieval Burma from the evils of the world.

One tall girl pointed at my ringworm, crying, "Pwe! Pwe!" It was so big now, they must have seen it from afar. A pudgy lay girl explained in English, "She bring med-cine fo' you." As we stood there, an old woman came up, as stout as a gnome and dressed in the brown laywomen's uniform of sash, sarong, and jacket. She had diamonds in her ears, rims of gold around all of her incisors. She pulled a tube out of a ratty vinyl purse.

"My son," she said, showing me the tube. TRIMOX-TRIM, it said, USE ONLY UNDER THE DIRECTION OF A PHYSICIAN. "Put," she said, shaking the tube toward me. When in Rome, I thought. I put on a tiny dab.

"Tomorrow, fie o'clack," the fat girl said, pointing at the ground.

The next day they were waiting, the dry, brown gnome amid gardenias. To meet them I had to cross the Burmese women's walking ground, a no-man's-land of hard, barren dirt. Slowly, slowly, eyes downcast — I was in sight of the elder monks' cottages. My shadow flew over dull rocks, smashed brick, eroded asphalt, struggling weeds. Two monks swished past on important business, as fast as Jaguars on a freeway.

The tall nun's name was Nandāsayee, Expert of Delight. She carried a long, flexible branch in her hand. "Lady gah-din, she *find*," the fat interpreter announced. Nandāsayee pulled off seven leaves, rolled a cylinder, tore off one end. She whispered to it quietly; then, puh, puh, puh, she breathed on it.

"'Life, not life,'" the interpreter offered. "She tell to leaf."

Cradling my head, Nandāsayee now rubbed the leaves onto the ringworm, carefully following its outline counterclockwise. This stung a little. Later I learned that the leaves were from a hot pepper bush. Her finger pads were slightly moist and soft, like frogs' palps. I could smell the green crushed leaf, and her body, scorched where mine was sharp.

This could cure me of anything, I thought. I'd been there six months then, physically touched by no one.

Finished, Nandāsayee walked a few paces off and threw the leaves over her shoulder. She came back grinning.

"Tomorrow three time," the plump girl said. "Aftah brehfass, aftah lunch, fie o'clack." I pointed to the Foreigner Women's Hall, and the nuns giggled mischievously. Not long before, a man had come from the office and pounded a sign into the ground just at our door, three rows of Burmese curlicues. I'd gone to the office to ask what the words meant.

"Foreigner Women Are Practicing Meditation," the monastery vice president importantly said. Before assuming this duty he'd been Minister of Finance for all of Burma. "Do Not Stare, Do Not Go In, Do Not Try to Start a Conversation."

Before we all dispersed, the woman in brown anointed

me again. Methophan was this cream's name. READ CIR-
CULAR DIRECTIONS CAREFULLY.

Nurse Aye Shwe was in a mood of laxity. That night she
beckoned me into her room.

"I have got! Burmese medicine for ringworm. When
you are finish, please return me, unused portion." It
was a whitish, grainy cream in a hot pink plastic tub. I
made the first application right away. It stung fiercely,
satisfactorily. Its job must be simply to kill infested
flesh.

Nurse Aye Shwe offered me hot plum concentrate in
an enamel cup. "I teach meditation now, in Rangoon
Asylum," she remarked. "Soon cure." Her face was a
mask of satisfaction; I was filled with nostalgia for such
certainty as hers, the same feeling as when I wish to have
been born in some past century.

"Today I select my patient," she went on, proudly.
"One man present himself. 'Take me!' he say. But he is
naked! I say, 'You, never.' Another man come. *Ol'* man.
On his head, hat. Under hat, plastic bag. Under plastic
bag, paper bag. Under paper bag, leaf! This one, I say,
'Please come with me.' "

"The Swiss woman has strange thoughts," I suggested.
"Swiss woman, very strange!"

"I know," Nurse Aye Shwe said. "I am so sorry for the
Western people."

That night I couldn't sleep. I lay under the mosquito
net's stifling canopy, too dizzy to sit up and meditate.
Everything was breaking into particles, the itching at
my temple, the passionate sounds of the night. Crickets
sawed away, lizards croaked like colliding billiard balls;
in the Muslim slum, a woman sang endless Arab vowels,
the very voice of unfulfilled desire. I knew I'd miss these
serenades, whenever I went home.

*

Before the dawn mists burned off, Sister Nandāsayee slipped into our basement and closed the door behind her. In the half dark, we Foreigner Women were making our postbreakfast cups of milk tea. Nandāsayee came at me with her leafy branch. I bent my head; she performed the little ritual of treatment. I felt like the birthday girl. Even Sīlānandī was intrigued enough to stand and frankly watch until Nandāsayee receded out the door, a finger to her lips.

The Swiss woman surged toward me, an ocean liner beaming, beaming, beaming sympathetic joy. Her eyes were two blue lamps. "So beautiful this Burmese nun," she breathed.

I tore a leaf from my notebook and posted a general notice. "I am being treated for ringworm with herbal medicine."

Next time Nandāsayee was more forward. She hovered over each of us in turn, frowned, and pointed at Sīlānandī's tea bags and milk powder. Obviously she'd never seen either. All of us stood around while Sīlānandī, with perfect art, showed how she prepared her tea in an old Milo jar. At the end she offered the jar to Nandāsayee, who made a suspicious face. She barely touched the liquid with her tongue's tip and scowled. All of us laughed. Dour Cathy from western Scotland presented her with a chewable vitamin C, which Nandāsayee tucked into her sash before rushing out the door as if chased by demons.

This was the beginning of my friendship with Sīlānandī. That day I found a note under my cushion in her spiky European hand. "Will the pink angel rub my swollen ankles too? Mmm."

Last night, sir, I felt strange. Objects appeared as streams of particles dissolving. When I observed the abdomen, I found no physical sensations. I was disoriented until I discovered a subtle sense of space. Happiness arose, then images of an event during the day.

How long did you dwell on the images?

Ten, fifteen minutes.

Too long.

Yes sir.

When objects are subtle, be aware of their pleasantness or unpleasantness. If no objects appear, do not try to find them. Do not ponder, do not ask yourself, "What is this, how is this, why is this?" If you think a thousand ways, you will find a thousand answers. Only direct awareness will show you the nature of the world.

Thank you, sir.

Good. Try to sleep only four hours.

Bigger now and not so weak, the kitten reappeared in the breezeway next to the Foreigner Women's Quarters. I brought back food for her from lunch in a thick white teacup. Chicken gizzards, hunks of pork fat; I barely had time to get my fingers out of the way of her teeth.

A circle gathered. The older women frowned, the girls seemed delightedly scandalized. "*Wet'tha*, pig meat. *Chet'tha*, chicken meat," they chanted. I realized this was better food than they'd had at lunch. Foreigners and monks ate the best foods — pork, eggs, mango, durian, birthday cake, ice cream — donated by the pious. Burmese nuns and laywomen ate in a separate dining room, directly beneath the monks'.

Tomorrow I'd bring only bones and scraps.

Nurse Aye Shwe flew out, a dark, screeching gryphon. "No yogi must have pet! This cup for monks, not animal! Very bad *kamma* for you."

The watching crowd laughed as it dispersed. For two days, the nurse's face was thunder. I persisted in feeding the cat but soon found occasion to donate my last bar of Thai disinfectant soap to the dispensary.

"Sumanā is capitalist," Nurse Aye Shwe said sourly, tucking the soap into her cabinet. But that afternoon she gave me half a coconut shell to use as the cat's dish. "Pussy very t'in. Blind." I wondered why I hadn't noticed. The way she picked her way across the monsoon gutters, shaking her paw, surprised when she stepped in puddles near the outdoor bathing tank.

Soon Nurse Aye Shwe began to scrape her own rice bowl into the cat's. I still brought food from lunch, even though it was a major complication in the closed and narrow circuit of my life. Choosing the scraps, wrapping the cup, finding the cat, enduring the watching, washing cup and napkin, remembering to return them the next day — it all stood out as tedious labor. Our teachers said there were three kinds of suffering. The suffering of pain itself, the suffering of the alternation of pleasure and pain, and the suffering of the cumbersomeness of life. I reported to my teacher that I understood this now. He laughed and said to be more continuous.

But I was bad, bad. I began doing my walking meditation under the shaded breezeway where the cat liked to sit for hours on end, her paws hidden under her chest. "She is meditating," I told myself. When no one was looking, I would carry her the length of my twenty-pace walking track, cradled in my arms. She was developing a belly, a hard little ball; though it didn't look exactly healthy, it seemed an improvement, a justification for feeding her.

The breezeway fronted on another Burmese dorm, this one for younger girls and several women who were permanent residents. Walking there, I learned many new unnecessary things. I saw the wrist motion with which the women beat their laundry on the flat stone; learned that some of the young girls were lazy and would lock themselves in a room all afternoon, giggling and eating cookies. The woman who lived at the end was some sort of witch. I'd see her on a patch of waste ground at the end of my walking track, making strange passes with a twig broom and singing softly to the air. At first I thought her saintly, but one day it struck me that her face was as hard and primitive as an alcoholic's. I guessed her family had abandoned her, or died. In return for her keep, she swept the leaves from the broad cement walkways on the monks' side of the compound.

One day she gave me a boiled egg, the poorest egg I've ever tasted. The white was blue, translucent; the gray yolk tasted of fish. As I should not have done, I imagined the hen it must have come from.

The Swiss woman was deteriorating. Some days she would not come to the meditation hall at all but stayed inside her room with the door closed. Slowly pacing the breezeway, I watched and worried but didn't intervene. She blocked her transom with a cotton blanket. Ten times a day, with a great rattling of the latch, she raced to the bathroom and flung water over herself. Our tank was always empty. I wondered what she reported in her interviews, whether the monks were capable of understanding her condition. Maybe the heat was getting to her, I thought, or just the isolation.

My ringworm was a pale ghost. Who knows which treatment was responsible? I used the Burmese ointment hourly; at ten, as I waited to join the lunch procession, the gnome in brown accosted me with frightening Western creams, halting tales of her son in L.A. And of course, Nandāsayee, my goddess, came three times each day. We were all in love with her. We gave her mint tea, sugar, and chocolates, and she reciprocated with jasmine and frangipani. Once I brought down my camera and got Scottish Cathy to document the treatment. Nandāsayee demanded formal portraits of herself holding hands with each of the foreigner women yogis. She stood very still, unsmiling, as if her image were a sacrifice she offered to the camera. I had several sets of prints made by the monastery photographer at fabulous expense and gave one to her in return for the treatment.

The next day she didn't come, nor the next. I began to see her in the company of senior nuns.

"Your friend, small nun, very successful meditation," Nurse Aye Shwe said.

Now I was galvanized by spiritual urgency. I felt I had been wasting my time in Burma, socializing and feeding a cat, when I could have been saving myself from endless rebirths in the ocean of suffering, the eighteen vivid Buddhist hells. It was all right for Nandāsayee to giggle and laugh; she was Burmese, a fish in water. Circumstances rearranged themselves conveniently: the hot season was coming to an end, and the young nuns were disrobing one by one to go back to Rangoon University.

Even as her contemporaries vanished, Sister Nandāsayee was to be seen, still in pink, running about the nuns' quarters. Her experience must have been especially profound, I thought. Yet, in my new mood, I was glad she came no more to our hall. The healing leaves withered, and I threw them into the monsoon gutter. In a spirit of divestiture, I gave the Burmese cream back to Nurse Aye Shwe and avoided the brown gnome of the squashed tubes. My ringworm must be dead by now, and if it wasn't, I would keep the pain dancing in my hand.

I even stopped feeding the cat.

The first Rains fell, thundering on the galvanized roofs with a heart-stopping roar. My mind settled along with the dust.

As I notice objects, sir, I feel deep stillness, like a forest early in the morning. I am not looking for any particular object. Sensations are mixed with calmness. Then I find

nothingness as an object, more subtle even than space.
Afterward I try to remember it. I think there was some
kind of knowing, but very subtle. When walking I feel
light, barely existing.

Stay with what is present. If your awareness vanishes,
be with that too.

Am I close to cessation?

Ha, ha, maybe so.

Walking on the breezeway, I feel sun's heat transmitted
through iron roof. Ancient cracked cement. Crows dump
over the garbage basket, riffling through fruit peels, caw-
ing. Left foot, right foot. I am trying to concentrate because, in an hour, I have an interview.

A brown hand appears, waving in my field of vision:
here are Nandāsayee's wide feet in red velvet thongs.

I look into her dancing eyes, this tall, strong, young
woman. "My mother," she says, indicating a vast coarse
hag in brown. I smile and shake hands. Mother grins
back genially. She must have come to celebrate Nandāsayee's finishing her meditation, from their home village a day's ferry ride up the Irrawaddy, that village I had
tried to imagine.

"Potograh," Nandāsayee insists, miming a snapshot. I
go up to my room and load my last roll of fresh film into
the Japanese idiot camera for this occasion in my friend's
life. I expect to take one or two pictures of the family, but
she grabs the camera and I have no heart to refuse her. I
am still trying to keep my mind like a turtle in its shell.
I pretend nothing is happening, stalk up and down in a
fury while Nandāsayee poses her mother with a book,
asks bystanders to photograph the two of them. Girls
come out and learn to push the button, laugh at the
automatic flash. I learn a new thing from the gross, grinning mother, that Burmese women wipe themselves on
their sarongs and hide the wet spot in the front pleat. I see
this while she is rearranging herself for a portrait.

"Sistah!" I sit on the steps with my eyes shut, feigning meditation. Nandāsayee pushes my chin up a little, then stands back and clicks the shutter. When all thirty-six frames are shot, she brings me the camera; I remove the film and hand it to her, wondering how she will find the cash to develop it.

Nandāsayee explains that she will be a nun for life. I am happy for her. Her family is poor and she will now have the chance to go to the Thilashinjaun, nuns' school. Maybe she'll even become fully enlightened and die, when it will be her time, into the unnameable beyond the suffering of name and form; maybe when she is cremated, her bones will reveal the tiny crystals.

"Sister, give me bow-peh," she says angrily, plucking at my notebook. "Bow-peh, bow-peh!" She wants my ballpoint pen. Her soft features gather at the center of her face.

"No," I finally say. "I need this for myself."

Time is moving slowly, sir.

For one who cannot sleep, the night seems long. For a lazy meditator one hour seems long.

I have been trying to make an effort.

Then there should be more activity in your practice.

This little nun came just now and disrupted my walking period.

You find many objects of interest in the body. Then you see that what is in the body is boring, of no interest.

"Pussy has deliver," Nurse Aye Shwe announced.

"What?"

"Your cat, is mother now."

I had given up walking in the breezeway. When in the evenings I didn't see the cat, I restrained myself from asking the nurse where she had gone. Now I was sent to peek under the stairs, where my cat crouched in awkward defensiveness over two orange kittens nearly as big

229

as she was. Aha. Now I understood her belly's sad, hard bulge. One of the orange toms had often visited her on the breezeway. She'd snarled at him and cowered in the rain gutter. No wonder, I thought. But now I had to admit she seemed happy and fulfilled, as she curled herself, purring, round her suckling children.

At once I resumed stealing fat pork and giblets from lunch. I gave her Thai milk powder, full-fat. My effort to be perfect had lasted two weeks. Now, I rationalized, if I couldn't make it to enlightenment acting normally, I didn't want to get there.

Sīlānandī wrote me a note, which I tore up. "I think I'm close! Subtle lights! *Espace!*" Her arms were sticks.

In the middle of the Rains, the Swiss woman set fire to a straw mat and was asked to leave. She said she would go to a great Hindu teacher, Sattya Ma, who took your head in her lap as if you were a two-year-old child. I thought it would be good for her to go where she could talk, touch, and spend all day in rituals of devotion.

"I must remain as nun," she said with Swiss determination. "Nothing in the world is good for me."

The kittens made wobbly appearances in our rooms at night, left runny piles in the hall. Their mother left them mewling to resume her vigils in the breezeway. The ringworm came back in two places on my head and one on my left breast. I asked for more Burmese cream, which was slow in coming. In the end, I had to go to a clap clinic in Bangkok and a doctor in Australia, and even now I believe the fungus may be dormant in my skin.

"You will never attain cessation with all your pets," the nurse grumbled. "I will give them to ol' lady. She will feed them, you can forget about."

"All right," I said. Sīlānandī was writing me notes of triumphant phenomena; I was determined to resume my progress.

The nurse took the kittens away in a box and blocked

the lower half of the Foreigner Women's Dormitory gate with chicken wire. My little cat was confused; she cried heartbreakingly at the barrier day and night. I hardened my heart and remembered the nurse's threat to report me to the abbot. The witchy sweeper was the new mother and would feed the cat only rice scraps. But walking at night in the breezeway, I watched the cat tease and kill a black scorpion and convinced myself that she could catch the food she needed, despite being blind.

One afternoon she dragged her children back and forth in the pouring rain trying to bring them back to the stairwell. The babies died, Nurse Aye Shwe told me days later.

I had known nothing; I was in the meditation hall.

Their mother forgot the kittens long before I did. I saw her meditating under the breezeway, paws tucked under, vacant eyes afire, as enigmatic as an idol of the East.

I was tortured by guilty thoughts: I never should have agreed to the eviction of the little family; my selfish spiritual desire had cost two infant lives. Finally I realized there was nothing to be done anymore and I tried to follow the cat's example, living on calmly with my share of pain. In a way, I thought, it was better for her not to have those mouths to feed.

It didn't matter what I thought.

I tried to remember what time I sat down. I think it was eleven. I felt as if I had been sitting for two minutes, but actually an hour had passed.

How was your posture?

Straight.

Did you have any dreams?

No dreams.

How did you know the time had passed?

Consciousness came back when the gong sounded midnight.

This is all right. Please continue.

Why is this happening?
Maybe later I will tell you.

Puzzled by this interview, I compared "experiences" with Sīlānandī and found that she had undergone the same sudden, extended vanishing of time. I ran to the abbot's cottage and asked whether this was cessation. He smiled with the utmost pride and indulgence and asked me whether I thought it was. "Yes," I hazarded. The experience repeated itself for shorter periods over the following week; the abbot had me and Sīlānandī listen to a tape that described the progress of meditation and various subtleties of cessation. At the end of the tape it said:

You must look in the mirror of the truth and see whether your experiences conform to this description, whether your cessation is genuine.

My teacher wanted me to work with resolves to strengthen the mind, but I was enervated, jumpy — after so much effort, neither able to make further rules for myself nor, much less, follow them. I asked for something new: the meditation on loving-kindness. He agreed and instructed me to repeat four phrases, constantly, in my mind.

May you be free from danger. May you be physically happy. May you be mentally happy. May you have ease of well-being.

Sir, should I listen to the sound of the sentences? Should I think about the meaning? Should I consider the welfare of all beings, the objects of my good wishes?

Just practice and don't worry. Send your loving feeling.

It was absolutely different. My mind was on rails, a locomotive. The body swung free, unconstrained by perpetual attention. But shortly after I began this blissful practice, I realized that the sounds I'd taken for taxis backfiring in the neighborhood were gunshots.

I went to the nurse and asked her to tell me what was going on outside the walls.

"They break the law," she said, both vague and fierce. "Do not disturb your practice."

No one wanted me to disturb my practice; but I went from one person to another, parlaying one tiny piece of information into the right to hear another. The day a machine gun shattered the air — the loudest sound I'd ever heard — I knew that unarmed demonstrators were being mown down. The people of Rangoon had risen against the military government. During the time I'd sat with my eyes shut inside Pingyan's high, thick walls, the prices of rice and oil had risen four hundred percent, so that a single measure of each now cost two weeks' average salary. Yesterday, in the poor suburb of Okkalappa, men had beheaded two police, cut out their hearts and livers, roasted and eaten them.

May you be free from danger. May you be physically happy.

A column of children, placed at the head of a peaceful prodemocracy demonstration, had been mown down.

May you be mentally happy. May you have ease of well-being.

Curfew: we were forbidden to walk in sight of the main gate after five P.M. The food got worse: gray, thin gruel of rice with a few dried shrimp. Like what most Burmese have been eating, I thought. People went home; Nandāsayee, too, vanished like some spirit, without a good-bye. Pingyan was nine-tenths empty, as lonely as the sky without the moon.

A green viper slithered in the bush next to the water tank; I sent it loving-kindness.

After sundown, bullhorns started squawking lies and threats; the nuns retreated into certain rooms, closed the shutters, and listened to the BBC World Service. I heard that Western embassy personnel were being evacuated;

Air Force planes were on alert in Thailand to rescue U.S. citizens in the event of a general emergency.

In the depths of the hot season, I'd taken to waking at two A.M., when the air was cool and I could walk as fast as I liked, wherever I liked, unseen except by the servant who rang the hourly bells. Wrapped in the softness of sleepers, dreamers, my wakefulness was thunderbolt and diamond; I loved to look up at the enormous mango tree near the Western men's quarters, an ink cumulonimbus blocking clots of stars.

Nights were a toxic yellow now, marred by the sound of troop trucks grinding into position for the next day's massacre. Shooting began after lunch, politely at eleven-thirty A.M., and lasted three hours.

The air felt as full of passionate love as of disaster. People were willing to die for better lives. People were dying right next to us, even though we couldn't see them, because of the monastery walls.

Sound is only sound, impermanent, ungovernable, a source of pain. Sound is a material object, a wave that strikes the sensitive consciousness at the ear door. Sound is not a story. It is not your thought, it is not the image you may see in your mind about what produced the sound. For hearing to occur, three elements are needed . . .

Each night, the abbot dryly dissected the process at one of the sense doors: eye, ear, nose, tongue, body, and mind. But his discourse was cut to half an hour; then he disappeared behind the curtain, leaning on his translator's arm. I knew he was going into his bedroom to listen to the BBC.

Then he stopped giving discourses at all. Interviews were left to a handsome twenty-two-year-old monk whose name meant "Uncle Beautiful." He told me he was not qualified to instruct me in loving-kindness practice.

I wanted to go to the abbot, but the jalousies and curtains were closed, and Nurse Aye Shwe was visiting the cottage twice a day, carrying a steel kidney pan covered with a handkerchief.

"Heart," she told me. Flicking up the handkerchief, she let me glimpse bottles of medicine, a blood pressure bulb.

"Has he had a heart attack?"

"No, but his heart is sick."

May you be free from danger. May you be physically happy. May you be mentally happy. May you have ease of well-being.

The phrases ground through my brain unlubricated; I began to wonder whether it was appropriate for me to stay in Rangoon. Who could possibly benefit from my presence? I went to the monastery's vice president, who reassured me. "Don't be afraid. Even besieged, we have rice and dried fish to keep you for a year. All Burmese respect a monastery, even the army."

I wasn't afraid for myself, but I imagined some U.S. Marine wading through a sea of blood to reach me, and dying — or the monastery officials gunned down for harboring me, like the doctors and nurses who'd rushed to the doors of Rangoon Hospital in an effort to protect their patients.

At last I went to the abbot's cottage. First I stood on his porch a long time, wavering. His Chinese clock played the first bar of *Eine Kleine Nachtmusik*. The house was dark, forbidding, thick with the smell of an unwashed body.

When I pushed open the door, I'd forgotten that a bell would jangle. *Come in,* he said in Burmese.

He was alone, staring at the inner side of the monastery's high, thick outer wall. "They kill those children," he said.

He spoke in English; I hadn't known he could.

*

But he'd spoken English to me once before. One morning, early in my stay at Pingyan, he'd come up quietly behind me as I was doing walking meditation.

"Sumanā?" he asked, gently prolonging the syllables. He always said my name so, as if in indulgent reproof.

I turned to look at him, a shaven old man a foot shorter than I was, leaning on his telescoping aluminum alpenstock. It had been a gift from some European student.

"Anything?" he'd said. Meaning, anything you need?
"Anything?"
"Anything?"

How will anyone believe in us now?

No one disbelieves in one person because of another person's unrelated crimes. As for me, my mind cannot be changed. It's settled now, because of the meditation.

Good . . .

But I want to leave.

You want to give back your robes and your precepts of morality?

I don't want anyone getting killed on my account.

That will never happen.

My parents are surely worrying.

I cannot stop the waterfall.

Thank you. I'm sorry.

We have not offered you a proper atmosphere.

No! You've influenced your students deeply — for life. Me, for example. I know there is no happiness to be found in outward things now. It's something deeper than mere belief. I've seen it for myself.

Then it should be easy for you to remain celibate. For life?

I don't know . . . maybe a year.

One year. Okay!

Wily old fisherman.

I held a meeting with the Foreigner Women and explained that I would leave on the first day it was safe to do so. No one wanted to come: they were in deep, practicing without regard for body or life. They didn't want to lose their time. Sīlānandī was making resolves, finding that her mind obeyed her automatically.

As it turned out, the shooting soon stopped: the army had suppressed the uprising, with four thousand dead.

But I'd already ridden to the airport with the British vice-consul's wife and daughter. We were driven in a white Land Rover down a deblockaded road, lined with gray trucks full of terrified fifteen-year-old conscripts. This was the murderous army. Its helmets slid over its eyes, its rifles trembled at the ready. Even if I'd had film, I wouldn't have dared raise my camera into view.

Soon I was fingering the thick, slick paper of the airline magazine, gazing at a color photo of two women leaning across a grand piano in identical, black, backless silken gowns, advertising the state of mind that could be induced by perfume.

I took the long way home, stopping for a rest on the beaches of South Thailand, where the world's most avant-garde sybarites go to play. There I ate well and lay in the sun, my body slowly thickening into concreteness. I didn't know whether I was ahead of the game or behind it. Milanese women played in the surf, the tops of their bathing suits rolled down.

There'd be no kamikaze operation: I'd smuggle no boxes of medicines to Rangoon Hospital.

I could not stop the whirling of this world.

Was removing myself not, truly, the best that I could do? So the Burmese taught.

The Buddha said, *Long have you wandered, and filled the graveyards full. You have shed enough tears on this long way to fill the four great oceans.*

On my last day on Koh Samui, I spotted another woman with hair as short as my ex-nun's fuzz. Blond sparks in the sunrise: she picked her way across the hummocky white sand as delicately as my cat crossing rain gutters, leaning heavily on her boyfriend's arm. She wore a baggy, faded purple dress; she looked wonderful.

I was sitting cross-legged, facing the pale coralline sea from which a cooked red ball was rising. Exquisite light. The world was as delicate as baby skin.

Sister, my mind called out.

Suddenly I realized she was mind-blown, blitzed, so high on acid or the much-advertised local mushrooms that she could hardly walk.

European chocolate. Fresh fish. Green salads. Long before arriving in the "United State," I had confirmed Nurse Aye Shwe's prediction: "Now your virtue will go down. You will eat at night, you will eat whenever you like." Generous, she was. But I kept the promise I gave to the abbot of a year's celibacy, and I dedicated any merit that might arise to the Burmese people.

I also followed his injunction not to describe cessation. There could have been a way to talk about it, but really there was nothing to describe, for there had been no experience, nothing on which to base a statement. Afterward I felt different, but not in any way I could grasp. This bothered me, subtly, pervasively. I might say it was as if I now had a hole at the bottom of my consciousness rather than any solid foundation; but this was difficult to assess.

Difficult to build any sense of achievement, even of event, on no basis. Why had I gone to Burma? What had I done there?

For a year I embodied the qualities the tape had said would reveal themselves as signs of a true cessation. I never lied, I didn't drink a drop, I had no interest in sex or money. I lived in an apartment as small and dark as Nurse Aye Shwe's rooms on the first floor of the Foreigner Women's Quarters. I felt happy to think that I no longer was a candidate for hell or rebirth in the animal realm.

And I wrote letters to my senators, asking them to remember the plight of Burma.

One night my father came to my city and took me out to a very good restaurant. He is a Republican businessman, but he'd found a way to be proud of my exploits in Burma by comparing me to some of the grand Victorian women travelers who "dressed in burnouses and went everywhere on camels." At this dinner he proposed a toast to me and my adventures. I didn't stop him from filling my glass with French wine. After he raised his glass to me, I took an experimental sip, just to see if I was capable. The first drop told me I was capable of anything.

That drop would have brought my kittens back to life; as I drank it, the monastery gates closed behind me. The most rigorous enlightenment system in the world shut me out. Or so I felt that night, not understanding my own rigorousness.

"Here's to you, too, Dad," I said, and drank the rest of the glass. I didn't quite know how I'd go on living, but I knew that I must.